He wanted to drag her
into the woods, rip her clothes off,
and make wild, passionate—

"Do you know how beautiful you are?"

His gaze dropped to her mouth, then back to her eyes.

Her heart melted.

He stretched a hand toward her. She placed her hand in his.

An instant frisson of electricity shot up her arm. She gasped and stepped back. Howard grabbed her by the shoulders to steady her.

She cried out as a flame of heat seared the birthmark on her right shoulder.

"Are you all right?" Howard leaned close to her, his eyes worried.

She scrambled out of his reach, grasping her shoulder. The heat from her birthmark scorched her left hand, and she let go. Good Lord, her palm was red. Burned.

Oh God, no. She clenched her sore hand into a fist. It couldn't be real. Her mother had always warned her this could happen, but she'd never believed it.

She glanced at Howard, who was watching her with a confused look. *Oh God, please! Not him.*

He'd activated the curse.

By Kerrelyn Sparks

KERRELYN
SPARKS

Wild
ABOUT YOU

AVON

An Imprint of HarperCollinsPublishers

AVON BOOKS
An Imprint of HarperCollins*Publishers*
10 East 53rd Street
New York, New York 10022-5299

Copyright © 2012 by Kerrelyn Sparks
ISBN 978-0-06-210771-8
www.avonromance.com

First Avon Books mass market printing: December 2012

Avon Trademark Reg. U.S. Pat. Off. and in Other Countries, Marca Registrada, Hecho en U.S.A.
HarperCollins® is a registered trademark of HarperCollins Publishers.

Printed in the U.S.A.

10 9 8 7 6 5 4 3 2 1

To the best critique partners an author could wish for—
MJ, Sandy, and Vicky.
For thirteen books now, you have watched my back
and helped me do my best.
Many thanks for your friendship, patience, and loyalty.

Acknowledgments

I have to confess—some books are easier to write than others, and Howard's book was a real bear. For those who helped me survive my journey into the were-bear culture, I owe many thanks. First, there were my critique partners: MJ Selle, Sandy Weider, and Vicky Yelton. A special thanks to Sandy's husband, Paul, who came up with the name for the series—Love at Stake—and spent many hours tutoring my daughter in chemistry.

Thanks also to Jimmy Franklin, good friend and super realtor, who helped us move and sell a house while Howard's book was being written and produced. Jimmy, I hope you enjoy having a young were-bear named after you.

As always, I owe a big thank you to my husband, who is always encouraging and supportive, and even makes the best grilled cheese sandwiches when I'm in deadline hell. Thanks also to my son, Jonathan, who reads galleys with an eagle eye and spots typos at the last minute.

And there are so many at HarperCollins who work tirelessly to help my books succeed. To my editor, Erika Tsang, and her assistant, Chelsey:

thank you for your patience and wise advice. To Pam and Jessie and the Publicity Department: thank you for arranging fabulous events and book tours. To Tom and the Art Department: thank you for the beautiful covers! And then there are others in sales and marketing—many thanks to you all!

Finally, my heartfelt gratitude to all my readers around the world. Without you, my Undead friends would have died years ago. Many thanks for your support!

Wild
ABOUT YOU

Chapter One

*I*n the dim light of a cloud-shrouded moon, Shanna Draganesti cast a forlorn look at the flower beds she'd once tended with care. They'd become choked with weeds since her death.

To be honest, gardening had ranked low on her list of priorities for the past three months. She'd had bigger things to fret about, such as adjusting to a steady diet of blood when six years ago she would have fainted at the sight of it, and dealing with an increased amount of psychic power that made it too easy to hear people's thoughts whether she wanted to or not.

Practically overnight, she'd been expected to master all the vampire skills. Levitation? Downright scary to look down and see nothing beneath her feet. With no way to ground herself, she kept tipping over. *Mental note: never wear a skirt to levitation practice.*

And what about teleportation? She was terrified she'd materialize halfway into a tree or a rock. And why the heck couldn't she materialize ten pounds lighter? Her scientific genius of a husband couldn't answer that one. Roman had laughed, under the impression that she was kidding.

Then there were the fangs. They tended to pop out at inopportune times. Thankfully she couldn't see her scary new canine teeth in a mirror. Unfortunately she couldn't see herself, either. She'd nearly dropped her three-year-old daughter on the floor the first time she'd seen Sofia floating in a mirror, held by an invisible mother.

And that was the most difficult part of being a vampire. She was no longer the same mother she'd been before. Every scraped knee or bruised feeling her children experienced in daylight hours would be soothed away by someone else. Because during the day, she was dead.

She'd never fully appreciated what the other Vamps went through each day at sunrise. Death-sleep was easy enough, since you just lay there like a lump, but getting there was the pits. She had to die. Over and over, as the sun broke over the horizon, she experienced a burst of pain and a terrifying moment of panic. Roman assured her it would get easier in time when she learned to relax, but how could she remain calm when she was dying? What if she never woke again? What if she never saw her children or her husband again?

There was no comforting light in the distance, reaching out to her with the promise of a happy afterlife. There was only a black hole of nothingness. According to Roman, that was the way it was for vampires. As a former medieval monk, he had interpreted the darkness as one more indication that he was cursed and his soul forever lost.

He now believed differently. When he'd fallen in love with her, he'd accepted that as a blessing from above and a sign that he wasn't entirely abandoned. And then dear Father Andrew, may he rest in peace, had convinced the rest of the Vamps that they had not been rejected by their Creator. There was a purpose to everything under heaven, Father Andrew claimed, and that included the good Vamps. They were the only ones with the necessary skills for defeating bad vampires and shifters. The good Vamps protected the innocent, so they served an important purpose in the modern world.

Mental note: remind yourself every night that you're one of the good guys. It should make that glass of synthetic blood easier to swallow.

"Come on, Mom!" Constantine ran ahead of her and charged up the steps to the front porch.

Not to be outdone by her older brother, Sofia clambered up the steps, too.

"I don't have to wait for Mom to unlock the door," Tino boasted. "I could teleport inside."

Sofia scowled at him, then turned to Shanna. "Mom, he's bragging again."

She gave Tino a pointed look. How many times had she warned him to be mindful of his little sister's feelings? So far, Sofia had not displayed the ability to teleport, and she was growing increasingly sensitive about it.

"There, now." Shanna's mother, Darlene, gave Sofia a hug. "Everyone has their own special gifts."

Sofia nodded, smiling sweetly at her grandmother. "I can hear things that Tino can't."

"Mom, she's bragging again," Tino said in a high-pitched voice to mimic his little sister.

With a snort, Shanna carried her children's empty suitcases up the steps to the front door. In spite of the recent upheaval in her personal life, her kids continued to behave normally. Like the weeds, they seemed capable of thriving in any environment.

"Nice porch." Darlene looked around. "It needs to be swept, though. And you'll need to get the yard tidied up before you post a For Sale sign."

"I know." Shanna set the small suitcases down so she could unlock the door. This was the first time her mother was seeing their home in White Plains, New York. And maybe the last.

Since Shanna's transformation, they'd all lived at Dragon Nest Academy, the school she'd started for special children, mostly shifters or hybrids like Tino and Sofia. Roman had claimed she'd sleep easier, knowing their children were well supervised during the day.

He was secretly worried that she wasn't happy, that she wasn't adjusting. And deep inside, he was afraid that she blamed him for transforming her and separating her from her children. He never said it, but she could read it in his thoughts. And sense it whenever they made love. There was a desperation in his kisses and an extra tenderness to his touch, as if he hoped to eradicate her fears and heal her sadness with the sheer force of his passion.

She blinked away tears as she opened the front door. Poor Roman. She should reassure him that she was fine, even if it was a lie.

She wheeled the two suitcases into the foyer that was already well lit. The porch light and a few lights in the house switched on each evening thanks to an automatic timer so the house would appear inhabited. "Come on in."

"Oh my, Shanna!" Darlene looked around, her eyes sparkling. "What a lovely home."

Shanna smiled sadly. "Thank you." She'd procrastinated for three months before accepting the inevitable. They had to move. No matter how much she loved this house, it no longer worked, not with her and Roman both dead all day.

Thank goodness her mother was back in her life. Only recently had Darlene broken free from the cruel mind control imposed on her by her husband, Sean Whelan. She spent all of her time now with her children and grandchildren, trying to make up for lost time.

"Come on, Grandma!" Sofia clambered up the stairs. "I want to show you my room."

"Don't forget her suitcase." Shanna handed the pink-and-green Tinkerbell suitcase to her mother. "She can bring whatever toys she can fit in there."

"I want my Pretty Ponies!" Sofia shouted, halfway up the stairs.

"And there's another suitcase in her closet," Shanna said. "She needs more clothes."

"No problem." Darlene started up the stairs. "I'll take care of it."

Shanna handed her son his orange Knicks-decorated suitcase. "Here you go."

Constantine regarded her quietly before responding. "Do we really have to move?"

She nodded. "It's for the best. There are more people at the school who can watch over you during the day."

"I don't need a babysitter."

Shanna sighed. Sofia was delighted with the move, since the school now boasted a stable of horses for equestrian classes. But Tino wasn't so easily swayed. "You'll have other kids there to play with, like Coco and Bethany."

He wrinkled his nose. "They're girls. They just want to do silly stuff."

She tousled the blond curls on his head. "Girls are silly now?"

"Yeah. They just want to dress up and pretend they're movie stars. I want to play basketball or backgammon or Battleship."

"Where did you learn those?" She knew her son played basketball with his dad, but she'd never seen him play board games.

"Howard taught me."

"Oh. That was sweet of him." Howard Barr had been the family's daytime bodyguard for several years now. As a bear shifter, he made a fierce protector, but he had such a gentle nature that Shanna had always considered him more of a honey bear than a grizzly.

"Howard loves games," Tino continued. "People always think he's slow 'cause he's so big and eats so many donuts, but he's really fast."

"I'm sure he is."

"He's smart, too." Tino narrowed his eyes, concentrating. "He says winning is a combination of skill, timing, and . . . stragedy."

"Strategy?"

"Yeah. Howard's real good at stragedy. When is he coming back? He's been gone forever!"

She thought back, recalling that he'd gone to Alaska at the end of May, and it was now the end of June. "It's been about a month."

"Yeah! That's almost forever!"

She supposed it was for a five-year-old. "I'll call your uncle Angus and ask him, but for now, I need you to pack whatever stuff you want to take back to school."

"Okay." Instead of heading for the stairs, he positioned himself underneath the second-floor landing.

"Tino, wait—" She was too late. He'd already experienced lift-off and was quickly levitating beyond her reach. "Be careful."

He peered down at her with the frustrated half smile he always gave her when he thought she was being overly protective. "Come on, Mom. It's not like I can fall." He reached the second-floor balcony and tossed his empty suitcase onto the landing.

She gritted her teeth as he swung a leg over the balustrade and straddled the flimsy railing. He could certainly fall now if he lost his balance or the balustrade collapsed. She tensed, prepared to levitate and catch him, but he landed neatly on his feet on the second floor.

She exhaled the breath she'd been holding. "Are you all right?"

"I'm fine. Don't worry so much." He rolled his suitcase toward his bedroom.

Don't worry so much? She was a mom. How could she not worry?

His words echoed in her mind as she wandered into the family room. She *was* worried. She was afraid he'd try something really dangerous. Like teleport into a moving car. Or levitate to the top of a cell phone tower.

She'd heard him ask Angus MacKay how high a Vamp could levitate. And he was always begging Angus and the other guys at MacKay Security and Investigation to talk about the dangerous adventures they'd managed to survive over the centuries.

In the family room, she rested her handbag on the back of an easy chair to retrieve her cell phone. She'd ask Angus about Howard and remind him that the guys needed to be careful what they said around an impressionable five-year-old boy.

Her gaze drifted to the space between the sofa and coffee table where Tino had taken his first baby steps. Why was he in such a hurry to grow up? If he attempted something dangerous during the day, she wouldn't be there to stop him. How could she live with herself if something happened to her children while she was unable to protect them?

The solution was obvious. Howard needed to come back. He could guard her children better than anyone. Tino wouldn't dare disobey when a Kodiak were-bear told him no.

With a twinge of shame, she realized she'd been too fixated lately on her own problems. She should have realized something serious was happening with Howard. It wasn't like him to be gone for so long. In the six years that she'd known him, he'd only taken a day or two off each month so he could go to his cabin in the Adirondacks and shift. Was he having some sort of personal problem? Was he ill again?

She recalled the way he had looked when she'd first met him—a balding, middle-aged man with a broken nose. He'd had a ready smile and a cheerful sense of humor, so she had never guessed that he was ill.

Roman had explained that right after high school, Howard's were-bear clan had banned him from Alaska. He'd spent four years at the University of Alabama on a football scholarship, and then three more years as a linebacker for the Chicago Bears. Separated from his kind, he had no safe place to shift.

In fact, the first time he shifted in Tuscaloosa, news of a grizzly on the loose had quickly spread, and he'd spent a terrifying night dodging bullets and shotgun shells. After that, he was reluctant to risk shifting. He was even forced to play football on nights when his body had desperately needed to shift. It had taken an enormous amount of control and strength to suppress his inner nature, but he'd managed it, knowing he would lose his career and endanger his species if the truth was revealed.

Refusing to shift had caused a chemical imbalance in his system whereby he was slowly poisoning himself. He aged. His hair fell out. The injuries he incurred on the football field wouldn't heal.

It was a chance occurrence that had saved Howard's life. Gregori had dragged Roman and Laszlo to a play-off game at the old Giants stadium, where they'd sensed an ailing shifter on the field. Even in pain, Howard had managed to sack the opposing quarterback three times. Impressed, they sought him out and convinced him he would die if he continued on his current path.

Relieved to find a job where he no longer had to hide his true identity, Howard began working for Angus at MacKay Security and Investigations. He built a cabin in the Adirondacks where he could shift, and slowly, his bones mended, his hair grew back, and he regained the younger, more virile appearance that shifters normally enjoyed for centuries. But he never returned to Alaska where he had been banned. Until now.

Shanna wondered what had changed. She leaned against the back of the easy chair as she scrolled through the list of contacts on her cell phone to call Angus.

"Did you call yet?"

She nearly dropped her phone. Her son had suddenly materialized by the coffee table. "Tino, you startled me. I thought you were upstairs packing."

"I was." He climbed onto the easy chair, kneeling so he was facing her. "Did you call Uncle Angus? Is Howard coming back? Will he live with us at the school?"

"I suppose he will."

"Then why don't we pack some of his stuff?" Tino asked. "We could get a room ready for him."

Shanna glanced toward the hallway that led to

Howard's rooms. Since she and Roman shared a large, windowless suite in the basement, they had let Howard use the master bedroom and office on the ground floor. As a were-bear, Howard was very territorial, so they had allowed him to treat that part of the house as his private domain. She'd seen his office a few times, but she'd never ventured into his bedroom.

She shook her head. "He wouldn't like us rummaging around in his room. Besides, he's been on vacation for over a month. He must have plenty of clothes with him."

"But he won't have his games." Tino bounced on the seat cushion. "We can't play without his games."

Shanna bit her lip. Howard might not mind her going into his room to fetch a few games.

"And he'll want his secret DVDs."

She turned toward Tino. "His what?"

"His DVDs. He has a box of them hidden under his bed. He watches them when he's not working."

"They don't sound very secret if you know where they are."

Tino shrugged. "I just call them secret 'cause he won't let me watch them. He said they're for older people."

Adult only? Shanna swallowed hard. Was there a side to Howard no one knew about? No, she couldn't believe it. Sweet Howard, who always had a smile on his face and a donut in hand? Surely he wasn't . . . "Did he say anything else about these DVDs?"

Tino tilted his head, considering. "There's a girl and two guys. The guys are called Big Al and The Hammer—"

"Okay." Shanna tried to keep any alarm from showing on her face. Good Lord, she'd trusted her children with Howard. Forget privacy issues. As a responsible parent, she had to investigate. "I . . . think I could look in his room for a few board games."

"Cool! Can I come with you?"

"No!" Shanna softened her voice to continue. "Why don't you be a sweetie and help Grandma bring your sister's suitcases down?"

Tino frowned. "All right. But remember to get the chess set, too. Howard promised he would teach me."

"I will." She waited for her son to teleport upstairs, then hurried down the hallway.

She glanced inside the office Howard used as his security headquarters. One wall was covered with monitors. A few screens normally showed the outside perimeter of the house in White Plains, while others were linked to surveillance cameras in Roman's townhouse on the Upper East Side. The monitors were all dark now, since no one was living at either place.

Her gaze wandered across the room. A file cabinet topped with a few trophies and awards Howard had earned during his football career, a plain wooden chair, a pair of hand weights on the floor. Fifty pounds each? Good Lord. Howard would be formidable if ever crossed. It was a good thing he was so sweet-natured. Or was he? How

well did she really know him? She eyed the handcuffs on his desk.

Howard loves games. Tino's words slipped back
into her mind with a new and disturbing mean-
ing. No, this was easily explainable. Howard was
their security guard. He needed silver handcuffs
to prevent bad vampires from teleporting away.
But what about the adult-only DVDs under his
bed?

The door to his bedroom was locked, but that
didn't present a problem with her new vampire
strength. *Mental note: repair the splintered doorframe
and broken doorknob before the house goes on sale.*

She flipped on the light as she entered the bedroom, then stopped with a small jolt of surprise.
This was how Howard had furnished his room?
She'd visited his hunting cabin on several occasions when Connor had hidden the Draganesti
family there in dangerous times. The cabin was
exactly what you would expect from an Alaskan
were-bear. Lots of wood, leather, Indian blan-
kets in shades of earth and sky, and a few animal
heads mounted on the walls.

There was nothing rustic about this bedroom.
Sleek, sophisticated, and modern, it didn't seem to
match Howard. Was there a secret side to him that
no one knew about?

The king-sized bed was covered with a black-
and-white striped comforter and bright red pil-
lows. The bedside tables were chrome and glass.
Across from the bed, a shiny black dresser was
topped with a wide-screen TV. A black leather
recliner rested in the corner next to a glass and

chrome bookcase. She spotted the games Tino wanted on the bottom shelf.

But what about the secret DVDs? As she approached the bed, the unusual headboard drew her attention. Tin ceiling tiles?

She ran her fingers over the embossed tin. How interesting. The tiles were mounted on a piece of plywood to make a headboard. Had Howard made this himself? Apparently, there was a lot about Howard that she didn't know. With an uneasy feeling, she dropped to her knees and peered underneath the bed.

There it was. A black alligator-skin box. She pulled it out, then took a deep breath and opened it.

Homemade DVDs. She rummaged through the stack, reading the labels Howard had written and attached to the plastic cases. *Elsa in London. Elsa in Amsterdam. Elsa in Berlin.* This Elsa certainly got around. *Elsa in Pittsburgh. Elsa in Cincinnati.* Was this like *Debbie Does Dallas*?

Shanna inserted the first disc in the DVD player on Howard's television, then lowered the volume in case she happened across a scene with loud moaning.

A collage of stately old homes rolled across the screen, then the title of the show appeared. *International Home Wreckers.* A map of the U.K. and the Union Jack flashed by, followed by the photo of a well-dressed man. Alastair Whitfield aka Big Al. The outline of Germany and its flag, followed by another photo. Oskar Mannheim aka The Hammer. And finally, the map and flag of Sweden, followed by the photo of a beautiful blond woman, dressed in cut-off jeans, a plaid shirt tied beneath her breasts, a pair of work boots, and a utility belt resting on her hips. Elsa Bjornberg aka Amazon Ellie. A commercial began for the network, HGRS. Home and Garden Renovation Station.

"Oh my gosh," Shanna breathed. "I love this channel." She glanced back at the tin-tiled headboard. Howard was into home décor?

As the show began, the two male stars were gutting a Victorian townhouse in London that had fallen into disrepair. Alastair, dressed in an expensive designer suit, was selecting new wallpaper for the parlor. Oskar, wearing jeans and a T-shirt, was ripping up a hideous orange shag carpet to expose a wooden floor underneath.

"It's extremely important to preserve a site's proper heritage," Alastair explained in a crisp British accent. "But at the same time, we must be sensitive to the needs of the family who will be calling this home. They have their hearts set on a more modern, open concept, so we have agreed to take down part of the wall separating this parlor from the room behind it. Fortunately, we have the perfect person for busting down a wall. Elsa!"

Shanna sucked in a breath as Elsa Bjornberg strode into the room. Good Lord, she had to be over six feet tall. Either that or her costars were a little short. She wore a pair of white overalls splotched with paint and a short-sleeved T-shirt, also white, that contrasted nicely with her golden, tanned skin. Her long blond hair was pulled back into a ponytail, and the upper part of her face was covered with an enormous pair of safety goggles. In her gloved hands she carried a large sledge-hammer.

She wasted no time, just hauled off and slammed her hammer right through the wall.

Shanna watched, amazed. No wonder they called her Amazon Ellie. She was a big woman. Big bones, big muscles, and a big smile she flashed at the camera as the last of the wall crumbled to dust.

Returning to the black box, Shanna inspected the contents more thoroughly. A TV guide listed the show as coming on in the afternoon. That explained why she'd never seen it. But why was Howard being so secretive about his interest in house renovation?

Underneath the DVDs she discovered a maga-zine article with an interview of Oskar, Elsa, and Alastair. And underneath that she spotted a stack of photos that looked like they'd been printed off the Internet. Every one of them showed Elsa. Elsa in her cut-off jeans, which highlighted her long, tanned legs. Elsa in an evening gown showing off her generous curves. A close-up of Elsa's face and her pretty green eyes.

"Oh my gosh," Shanna whispered. This was why Howard was watching the show. He had a crush on Amazon Ellie.

She glanced up at the television just in time to see Elsa rip a bathroom sink off a wall. "Wow."

Her heart pounding, Shanna rose to her feet. Howard had found the perfect woman for a were-bear!

She turned off the television, and with trembling hands, she returned the DVD to the black alligator-skin box. The perfect woman for Howard! She had to make sure he met her. But he was watching the show in secret. At this rate, he'd never meet his dream girl. He needed some help.

Her heart lurched. The old gate house! Just the other night, she and Roman had discussed the possibility of making the old house their new home. Only a few miles from the school, it was part of the estate, so they already owned it. Unfortunately, it was in sad shape. A money pit, her mother called it.

But that made it the perfect project for the International Home Wreckers! It was exactly the sort of historic gem that they specialized in renovating.

She shoved the box back under the bed and jumped to her feet. Did she dare do this? Play matchmaker to a were-bear? Her heart raced, and for the first time in three months, she realized she was grinning.

She grabbed the games off Howard's bookcase and rushed back to the family room. In a few seconds, she had Angus's number ringing on her cell phone.

"Hi, Angus. Can you bring Howard back right away?"

"Is there something wrong, lass?" he asked.

"I'm worried about my children's safety during the day, especially Tino. I'm afraid he'll try something dangerous, and Howard is the only one who can keep him safe for me. I need him back."

There was a moment of silence before Angus replied. "His vacation time ran out over a week ago. There was a mission I wanted to send him on, but he refused to go."

"What?" Her nerves tensed. "He's not quitting, is he?"

"He dinna say he was, but the bugger stopped answering my calls. I sent Dougal and Phil to hunt him down."

Shanna winced. "He's not in any danger, is he?"

"We doona know," Angus said. "That's why we're looking for him. I would have sent more lads, but we have three missions going on right now. We're short on manpower."

"I see." She took a deep breath. Finding a baby-sitter for her children probably seemed trivial compared to the other issues Angus had to deal with. But that didn't make her worry any less. "If you find Howard, can you tell him that we need him? Tino is asking for him."

"Aye, we'll tell him."

"Thank you." Shanna dropped her cell phone back into her handbag.

It wasn't like Howard to take more vacation days than he was allotted. Or to ignore phone calls from his boss. Angus had sounded annoyed that he'd been forced to track him down.

What on earth was Howard up to?

Chapter Two

*H*oward peered over the edge of the cliff. Even in the dim light of a cloud-covered moon, his sharp eyesight could make out the jagged rocks where Carly had been discovered all those years ago, her body broken, her long brown hair matted with blood. His first love, the girl he'd hoped to marry. Murdered on the night of their senior prom.

His gaze drifted to the small collection of lights that marked the nearby town of Port Mishenka on the eastern coast of the Alaska Peninsula. Twenty years had passed since he'd last been here, but not much had changed. The most noticeable lights were still those that illuminated the high school football field. He'd been a hero there at one time, but none of the residents would welcome him back now. Not when they believed him guilty of Carly's murder. Her family still claimed he had thrown her off the cliff along with a few guys.

It was impossible to deny all the charges. He had tossed three guys off the cliff. Werewolves. He'd believed them all dead until two months ago. Now he knew the truth. The worst of the three had survived.

He didn't blame Carly's family for turning against him. They were heartbroken over her death. He'd felt the same way for years. Heartbroken and guilty, for there was a kernel of truth to the family's claim. Their daughter had died because of him. She'd become an unwitting pawn in Rhett Bleddyn's game of revenge.

He had found little solace in believing he'd killed Rhett. The bastard had found the perfect way to torture him by making him feel responsible for Carly's death.

But now the truth was out. Rhett Bleddyn was still alive.

And the game was back on. Unfortunately Rhett had the hometown advantage. Recently acknowledged as the Pack Master of all of Alaska, he had hundreds of werewolves on his team. Howard could only call on a few were-bears from their dwindling island community. What he lacked in manpower, he had to make up for with superior timing and strategy.

Speaking of timing, it was about time for the two men climbing up the mountainside to finally reach him. The scent of werewolf wafted toward him, and Howard instinctively squeezed his fist around the carved wooden hiking stick he'd borrowed from his grandfather. The staff was thick enough to use as a weapon and about six foot four inches long, ending right at his eye level.

He relaxed his grip. This werewolf was one of the few Lycans he called friend. Werewolves always assumed they had the most advanced sense of smell, but that was one area where a were-bear had them beat. He could distinguish Phil's scent over two miles away. Not that Phil normally smelled differently from other werewolves. It was the influence of his wife, Vanda, that made him unique. She had him using some kind of fancy shampoo and conditioner.

Phil had obviously caught Howard's scent and was tracking him down. What the werewolf might not realize was that Howard wanted to be found tonight. It was all part of the strategy.

Phil's companion was a little harder to figure out. The lack of any strong scent indicated a vampire. The smell of damp sheep suggested a kilt-wearing Scotsman who'd been caught in a light rain. But which Scottish vampire? Was Angus so pissed that he'd come in person?

They were moving quietly up the mountain path, as if they could sneak up on a were-bear. The thought made Howard smile. There was no mistaking the soft swish of a kilt or the grinding of Phil's boots.

Not Angus, he decided. Phil was taking the lead, and he wouldn't do that if the boss was with him. Ian or Robby? Or maybe it was Connor, resuming his work after a long honeymoon.

Howard's smile faded. All of the guys were getting married, having children. That sort of domestic bliss was unlikely to happen for him. There were a few female were-bears on the island, but they were either taken or related to him.

His gaze drifted back to the rocks where Carly had died twenty years ago. She had trusted him completely, even after he'd confessed to her that he was a were-bear. Since her, he hadn't met another mortal female he had felt he could trust with his secret.

There had been a time when the pain and guilt of Carly's death had nearly crippled him. All through college and his football career he'd allowed himself to suffer as a way to punish himself. But as the years went by, his burden of guilt slowly changed. Instead of feeling guilty for wanting to forget, he now felt guilty that he could barely recall her face. How cruel life was that she had paid the price for Rhett Bleddyn's rage.

Death was too good for Rhett. Howard wanted to watch the sick bastard squirm. He'd have to go about it secretly and stealthily in order to keep his people safe, but with the proper strategy, he felt confident about pulling it off. And if he avenged Carly, then maybe he could finally lay his guilt to rest. He'd been banished for long enough.

A cool breeze swept up from Mishenka Bay, and he closed his eyes to focus fully on the scent—a glorious mixture of salty sea and lush forest. *Home.* He took a deep breath to let the comforting fragrance seep into his soul, and a new face formed in his mind. Elsa. Beautiful Elsa. She was invading his thoughts more and more each day. Unfortunately that only proved that no matter how clever a strategist he tried to be, he was still a fool.

Elsa Bjornberg was a celebrity, a breathtaking, gut-wrenching beauty, who traveled the world for her successful career. Why would she want to meet some guy from an obscure island in Mishenka Bay, Alaska? Especially a guy who was over-sized and turned into a real bear on occasion. The cold reality was that they would never meet. He'd known months ago that his obsession with her was ridiculous. Pathetic. Juvenile. It was embarrassing, so he kept it secret.

And yet, whenever he saw her on television, he felt drawn to her. Not just mildly attracted but somehow irrevocably attached to her. It didn't make sense, but knowing that didn't make the strange feeling go away.

The soft scuffle of a footstep behind him made him stiffen. Holy crap, he'd allowed himself to get distracted. He masked his reaction by swinging the staff up and across his shoulders, gripping each end with his hands.

With his back to them, he listened carefully as he gazed up at the moon, a dull silver disc shrouded in clouds. It would be full tomorrow night. If everything went according to plan, he'd score a touchdown. "Hello, Phil."

There was a moment of silence, then a whoosh of air as Phil Jones exhaled. "How did you know it was me? Alaska is overrun with werewolves."

"They don't use that fancy, girly shampoo." Howard smiled when he heard a low growl in response.

A slight mechanical click emanated from the vampire behind him. Could it be Dougal Kincaid? The Vamp had lost his right hand in combat a few years ago, and Roman had recently fitted him with a mechanical one.

"Dougal?" Howard turned, widening his smile

when he saw he'd been correct. "It's good to see you again. You arrived last night?"

The Scotsman tilted his head, studying him. "Someone told you?"

"No. It rained last night, and your kilt smells like wet sheep."

Dougal's mouth curled with amusement. "Ye're in trouble with Angus, ye ken."

"Not enough trouble, if he only sent two of you."

"Believe me, he's pissed," Phil grumbled, then shoved his long, shaggy hair back over his shoulders. "It's cheaper to use the same shampoo that my wife buys."

"I understand." Howard gave him a sympathetic smile. "I won't mention it again since you're so . . . sensitive about it."

Phil's eyes narrowed.

Dougal chuckled. "We have orders to take you back to Romatech immediately."

Howard nodded, still smiling. "Good luck with that."

Phil snorted. "What the hell are you up to, Howard?"

"I thought you'd never ask. I need more players on my team."

"Team?" Dougal asked. "Ye're playing a game?"

"Yes. It's called Payback. It'll be easier to score if I have a few more hands." Howard slanted a wry look at the Vamp's fake right hand. "No offense."

"None taken." Dougal wiggled the fingers on his mechanical hand. "Ye'd be surprised what I can do."

"Tell it to the ladies." Howard motioned to Phil. "Are you in?"

"If you're getting back at Rhett Bleddyn, then yeah, I'm in. Angus can wait."

Dougal scoffed. "Now there are two of you no' following orders. Angus will be royally pissed."

"Maybe not," Phil argued. "He knows what an asshole Rhett is. The guy tried to force my sister into marriage. He was going to kill off my entire family and steal all our land and followers. He's a power-hungry, ruthless bastard."

Dougal nodded, then turned to Howard. "I can see why Phil wants revenge, but what do ye have against him?"

Howard remained silent, then swung his staff off his shoulders and planted one end in the gravelly dirt next to his feet. "I have my reasons. Are you in?"

Dougal's hand produced a series of clicks as he curled the fingers into a fist, then stretched them back out. "What is the purpose of yer game? Are ye wanting to kill Bleddyn?"

"Do I look like a murderer?" Howard frowned when the two guys exchanged glances. "Okay. You've seen me kill, but only in battle."

"You're ferocious," Phil muttered. "You rip heads off with a single swipe."

"So I'm efficient," Howard grumbled, then smiled. "No one has ever complained about my efficiency before."

Phil snorted. "We're just relieved you're on our side."

Howard's mouth twitched. "Are you sure about that?"

Phil stiffened. "You big lummox, why don't you—"

"Enough." Dougal lifted a hand, then shot an annoyed look at Howard. "I need to know more before I decide. Do ye plan to lure Rhett into battle?"

"No." Howard pointed his staff toward a few lights twinkling far out in Mishenka Bay. "You see that group of islands out there? They're called the Bear Claw Islands 'cause there's a big round one and four narrow ones extending north."

Dougal moved closer to the cliff edge. "That's where ye grew up?"

"Yes. On the big round one called The Paw."

"We saw on your bio that you went to high school down there." Phil motioned at the town below and snickered. "A were-bear playing football for the Port Mishenka Marmots? That had to be embarrassing."

Howard arched a brow at him. "I kicked ass on that field. Would you care for a demonstration?"

"Enough, you two." Dougal gestured to the Bear Claw Islands. "Does yer family still live there?"

"Yes. That group of islands and Kodiak Island to the north are where most were-bears live. We're down to about a hundred now."

"Shit." Phil frowned at the islands. "You're in danger of extinction."

Howard sighed. "There was a time, a few hundred years ago, when were-bears flourished and covered the mainland. There were over a thousand of us. But then settlers began moving in, searching for gold, and werewolves moved in, wanting the land. The Alpha wolves tended to bite any guy who found gold, so he would become their minion."

"And then they would have his gold," Phil muttered.

Howard nodded. "The werewolves quickly amassed land and wealth. If someone had something they wanted, they simply bit him to bring him in line."

"The were-bears dinna bite people?" Dougal asked.

"Not usually. It's not in our nature to live in packs. Especially the male bears. We're loners. Unfortunately, that always worked against us. We were spread out thin, each male bear taking a huge territory, and it made us vulnerable. A single were-bear might be able to defeat a small group of wolves, but they started attacking us in packs of thirty and forty."

Dougal muttered a curse. "Ye wouldna stand a chance."

"No. Eventually, in order to keep the cubs safe, most of the were-bears moved to these islands. To make a living, many of the men turned to fishing, but whenever a storm capsized a boat, we would lose five or six of them. With our numbers depleted, a loss like that was devastating."

Phil winced. "The werewolves know which islands your people are living on?"

"Yes. Rhett has over five hundred followers, so we can't afford to draw him into battle." Howard gritted his teeth. "I just want to play with him, make him wish he was dead."

"What did he do to you?" Dougal asked.

Howard stabbed at the ground with his staff. No way was he going to discuss lost love with two guys. "He deserves far worse than what I have planned. Are you in the game?"

Dougal gave him an apologetic look. "I may no' be much help to you. I'm lucky if I'm able to stay awake for more than a few hours at night. The blasted sun here is always up."

Howard smiled. "You could use that as an excuse for not reporting in. Then maybe Angus would send more men."

Dougal tilted his head, his eyes narrowed. "Is that why ye stopped returning his calls? So he would be forced to send us?"

Phil scoffed. "You jerk, you had us worried about you. Why didn't you just ask for help?"

"If I asked, Angus could refuse." Howard leaned on his staff. "Any chance of getting more guys here?"

Dougal gave him an irritated look. "Angus will have smoke coming out his ears."

"Then he should come and help," Howard suggested.

"He's busy coordinating three other missions right now," Phil grumbled. "A lot has happened since you left for vacation."

Howard frowned. After the skirmish with Rhett in Montana, everything had seemed to calm down. "What's going on?"

"We're still trying to find Russell," Phil began. "J.L. and Rajiv went to China to hunt for him."

"That's good." Howard had often wondered how Russell was doing. The former Marine and newly turned vampire had gone AWOL in China after their last mission there. As Russell's sire, Angus probably felt some responsibility for him. Everyone assumed Russell was hunting for Master Han, the evil vampire who had left him in a vampire coma for forty years.

"There was an outbreak of murderous Malcontents in Albania," Phil continued. "Angus sent some guys there to help Zoltan track them down."

"I see." Howard knew that as Coven Master of Eastern Europe, Zoltan was charged with the task of protecting mortals in his jurisdiction. It wasn't a job he could always do alone, so he often requested help from Angus.

"And then we got an urgent request from President Tucker," Phil muttered. "And when the government asks for our help, we have to comply."

Howard nodded. Now that the president knew about vampires and shifters, he and the CIA were likely to make many such requests in the future. "What is it this time?"

"Seven American tourists taken hostage by a drug cartel in Mexico," Phil explained. "The president asked us to locate them and teleport them out. The only safe way to do it is to have a vampire for each hostage. So that's seven more Vamps. Carlos went with them as their day guard and translator."

"Now ye ken why Angus wasna pleased with yer antics," Dougal said. "He's short on manpower. He had to call me away from my station in Texas."

"I understand." Howard had hoped for a bigger team, but he could manage with only two more. "If you both join us, then we'll have a team of six. The three of us. A journalist and good friend, Harry Yutu, in Anchorage. And two young were-bears from the island, my twin cousins, Jimmy and Jesse."

"What's the plan?" Phil asked.

"We call it Operation Three Little Pigs," Howard replied. "We're attacking three of Rhett's houses. Our first target was one of his fishing cabins. We removed everything from inside, stashed it in our trucks, then huffed and puffed and knocked the walls down. It wasn't too hard, since it was just a shack."

"That was yer house of straw?" Dougal asked.

Howard nodded. "Some hungry cubs on The Paw are enjoying the food, and an old woman got a new wood-burning stove she was needing. My grandfather is very happy with his new rod and reel."

Phil crossed his arms. "You probably left your scent behind. Rhett will know it was you."

"My cousins left behind some deer and squirrel carcasses. The place will be a magnet for hungry animals. There'll be a lot of scents there by the time Rhett discovers it." Howard took a deep breath, then continued, "Last week, we tackled the house of sticks, Rhett's vacation home on the coast of the Kenai Peninsula. We emptied it so we could give all the stuff to some needy were-bears, then took a few axes to the stilts and watched the house slide down the bluff and break apart on the rocks. Most of it floated out to sea."

"I like it." Phil grinned. "And the house of bricks?"

"It's log and stone, actually. One of Rhett's main residences." Howard glanced up at the sky. "We'll hit tomorrow night when the moon is full, and Rhett and his minions are away from the house on their monthly hunt."

"He'll leave behind a few guards," Phil warned.

"That's why I wanted more men. If they discover us invading his home, there could be trouble. I was hoping to get a few Vamps on our team so we could use your mind control or at least teleport away if we need to. We could really use your help." Howard extended a hand, palm down. "What do you say? Are you in?"

Phil gave them a wolfish grin. "Yeah, I'm in." He slapped a hand on top of Howard's.

Dougal snorted, then rested his mechanical hand on top of theirs. "Aye, I'm in as well."

Chapter Three

The following night, Howard drove a black SUV toward Rhett's house. After turning off the headlights, he eased down the narrow road for the last few miles. When he spotted the sharp curve ahead, he pulled over and stopped. A quick glance in the rearview mirror assured him they hadn't been followed. In the backseat, his seventeen-year-old cousins, Jimmy and Jesse, snored away. Phil was dozing, too, in the passenger seat.

It had been a long trip from Paw Island. They'd left early in the morning, with Dougal safely doing his death-sleep in the dark basement of his grandfather's house. After a short ferry trip from the island to Port Mishenka, they'd caught the bigger ferry to Anchorage. At a local diner, they met his old high school buddy, Harry Yutu, who worked as a reporter for the popular local tabloid, *Northern Lights Sound Bites*. His cousins and Phil wolfed down a dozen hamburgers while Howard and Harry discussed the finer points of the game they called Payback. They couldn't afford to let Rhett know who was playing with him, so Harry had arranged for them to secretly borrow an SUV through a rental agency that owed him a favor.

After dropping Harry off at the newspaper office, Howard had driven north toward Fairbanks. It was just after 11:00 p.m. now. The full moon had risen, but the sun still lingered on the horizon. He turned off the engine.

Phil woke with a jerk and quickly looked around. "Are we there?"

Howard pointed at the two-lane road that curved to the right then disappeared from view. "Rhett's estate is a mile down there. I reconnoitered it about a week ago. He had one guard at the gatehouse and four more watching the exterior of the house. All mortals, so they're probably working tonight while the werewolves are forced to shift."

Phil nodded. "They'll be off in the woods, hunting. Unless they're Alpha like me, but I doubt Rhett allows any of his minions to gain that much power."

"I'm hoping they stay in the woods. We'll be in deep shit if they discover us." That was the main reason Howard had wanted more Vamps on his team. If they were attacked, the Vamps could have teleported them away. Without that emergency exit strategy, they had to count on the plan working without a hitch.

Phil gave him a curious look. "You and your cousins don't need to shift tonight?"

"Different species, different rules." Howard dropped the car keys in his jacket pocket. "To stay healthy, we need to shift at least once a month, but it doesn't depend on the moon. We can shift at will."

"Oh." Phil was quiet for a moment as he scanned the woods. "I knew you could shift whenever you wanted, but I figured you were an Alpha."

"No such thing in our culture. Or I suppose you could say we're all Alphas." Howard slanted an amused look at the werewolf. "I guess that makes us superior—"

"Ha. We're not the ones on the verge of extinct—" Phil stopped himself. "Sorry." Frowning, he turned to Howard. "If Rhett does like my father, he'll have a bunch of pack members here for the monthly hunt. If they catch the scent of were-bear, they'll come after you and your cousins."

"Worried about the three little bears? How kind of you."

"Will you be serious? There could be a hundred werewolves out there."

"I know. We came prepared." Howard checked his watch. It was a quarter after eleven. "After the sun sets, we can call Dougal and get down to business. We've got about a ten-minute wait."

"Okay." Phil settled back in the passenger seat. "So how does your friend Harry fit into the plan? He's a were-bear, right?"

"Yeah. Harry Yutu. His last name is Eskimo for 'The Claw.' " Howard smiled, remembering how they'd been best friends all through school. "He was always reminding me that he's bigger. He shifts into a polar bear."

Phil's eyebrows lifted. "Are you kidding me?"

"Didn't know about them, huh?" Howard's smile widened. "His dad and my dad were best friends. They owned a lumber company together up north off the Yukon River."

"Past tense?"

Howard nodded, his smile fading. "They died in a fire when I was four. I think Harry was three."

"I'm sorry."

Howard waved a dismissive hand. "It's okay. Our mothers took us to the Bear Claw Islands, and we grew up there. My grandfather was always more like a father to me."

"He kept you in line?"

"Bearly." Howard smiled when Phil groaned at his pun, then reached back to shove at his cousins. "Wake up, guys."

Jimmy jerked awake and looked out the window. "Are we there yet? Is it time to play secret agent man?"

Jesse stretched. "This is going to be so cool!"

"I know, right?" Jimmy agreed.

Jesse smiled at Howard. "We're so glad you came home. The summer was totally boring till you showed up."

"The summer?" Jimmy scoffed. "How about our entire lives?" He glanced at Phil. "We were born after Howard was banished."

"Yeah. We didn't even know him till a month ago," Jesse explained. "But we grew up hearing about him. He's a legend, you know. He tossed Rhett and two other werewolves off a cliff."

Phil glanced at Howard. "That's why you were banished? You killed werewolves?"

Jesse winced. "No offense, wolfman. I guess I shouldn't have mentioned it."

"That's right." Howard scowled at his cousin.

"Was it the same cliff where we met last night?" Phil asked. "Is that why you thought you'd killed Rhett?"

Howard shrugged. "He looked at me funny."

"Really?" Jesse scratched his head. "I thought he killed your girl—"

"Enough," Howard interrupted. "Listen, you two. You've got to be careful tonight. Your mom will have my hide if anything happens to you."

"Your hide." Jimmy snickered.

"Get your disguises on," Howard continued. "And your gloves. Don't leave any fingerprints."

Jesse saluted. "Aye, aye, Captain!"

Jimmy elbowed him. "Come on, bro. Let's get stinky."

They turned toward the back of the SUV, kneeling on the backseat while they pried the top off a plastic bin they'd stashed in the trunk.

"Stinky?" Phil twisted around to watch.

"Our new coats," Howard explained. "We've got them triple-wrapped in plastic and stuffed in that container to keep the aroma fresh."

"I was wondering why you guys were hauling around that bin—" Phil stiffened when Jimmy ripped the Saran Wrap off the first coat and a strong odor escaped. "Wolves?" His jaw clenched. "Dead wolves?"

"Sorry about that, wolfman." Jimmy shook out a huge coat covered with wolf skins. "We gotta blend in, you know." He handed the coat to Howard. "This one is yours."

Phil glowered at him. "You killed wolves?"

Howard shrugged. "We have to cover our scent. It was either this or have you piss all over us."

"That could be arranged," Phil muttered.

Jesse snorted. "Yeah, like we'd go for that." He took the plastic wrap off a second coat. "Don't worry, wolfman. No werewolves were harmed or killed during the production of this movie."

"You killed wolves," Phil growled.

"Just a few." Jimmy unwrapped the last coat and put it on. "Isn't that like doing you guys a favor? I mean, don't you have to compete with real wolves when you're hunting?"

Phil groaned. "Some werewolves might agree with that, but I've always considered them noble creatures."

"Well, now they're being noble enough to protect us from your werewolf buddies." Jimmy pulled on a pair of leather gloves.

Phil glanced toward the woods. "Those aren't my buddies."

"Wow, you're like some kind of movie hero." Jesse raised a gloved hand as he imagined. "The Lone Wolf."

Phil snorted.

"Are you really married to a vampire?" Jimmy asked. "I heard she was hot."

Phil shot Howard an annoyed look.

"They wanted to know why you smelled like girly shampoo." With a grin, Howard ignored Phil's glare and climbed out of the SUV.

As he slipped on the smelly wolf-skin coat, his thoughts returned to Elsa. The image of her beautiful face had crossed his mind often on the long drive. Her wild blond hair, her sparkling green eyes, her bright smile that always made his heart pound. He'd studied her photos, so he knew how she looked, but he was becoming increasingly curious about her scent. As a were-bear, scent was important, and it bothered him that he was clueless about such an essential part of her. And even though he teased Phil, he had to admit to an unfortunate amount of envy. He'd jump at the chance to use the same shampoo as Elsa.

He shook his head. What an impossible dream. He pushed away all thoughts of Elsa and called Dougal on his satellite phone.

A few seconds later, Dougal materialized beside him, dressed entirely in black with pants, turtle-neck sweater, and trench coat. His claymore was strapped on his back in a black leather scabbard.

"Whoa, dude." Jimmy clambered out of the SUV, followed by his brother. "What happened to your skirt?"

"Yeah, you went like all Matrix on us," Jesse added.

Dougal waved his mechanical hand in front of his face, grimacing at the strong scent of their wolf-skin coats. "This is a covert operation," he whispered. "We should keep the talking to a minimum."

"Really?" Jesse peered around the vampire. "Hey. Did you bring your humongous sword?"

Jimmy nodded. "That sword is freakin' awe-some."

Jesse grinned. "I know, right?"

Howard arched a brow at them. "What part of minimum talking did you not get?"

"Huh?" Jesse gave them a blank look.

"Bro." Jimmy nudged him. "They're telling us to shut up."

"Oh. Right. Covert." Jesse nodded, then whispered with a grin, "This is so cool!"

"Give us three minutes, then meet us at the gatehouse," Howard said quietly. "Got it?"

"Aye, Captain." Jesse studied his wristwatch. "Three minutes on my mark. Five, four, three—"

"Why are you counting?" Jimmy whispered.

"That's what they do in the movies," Jesse replied. "Shoot, now I have to start over."

Phil groaned. "You're leaving me alone with these two?"

Howard grinned, then motioned for Dougal to follow him. "Let's go." They moved quickly through the woods, staying close to the road, till the gatehouse came into view.

"I'll draw the guard out," Howard whispered. "You know what to do?"

"Aye." Dougal slipped a black leather glove onto his left hand.

Howard eased into the road, and a few seconds later, the guard stepped out. A big mortal in a khaki uniform.

"Hold it right there." The guard rested a hand on his sidearm.

Dougal teleported behind him, and his eyes glowed as he turned his Vamp power on high. The guard's face went blank, his eyelids closed, and then he slumped onto the road. Dougal picked him up and carried him into the gatehouse, while Howard jogged toward them.

Inside, Howard studied the two monitors. There appeared to be only two security cameras, one showing the front of the house, and the other, the back. Rhett probably wasn't too concerned about security. His family had amassed a lot of power over the past fifty years, and they were known to be ruthless. Who was going to mess with Rhett when he had five hundred minions at his beck and call?

The monitor displaying the huge backyard showed Rhett and some companions in the process of stripping and shifting. In the front, two guards stood by double doors of leaded glass.

Dougal settled the guard in a chair. "He'll have no memory of this, and he'll sleep for about ten minutes. Is that long enough?"

"Yes." Howard snapped on some latex gloves and eyed Dougal's mechanical hand. "No fingerprints?"

"Nay." Dougal gave his right hand a wry look. "No feeling, either, but it's better than wearing a bloody hook like a pirate."

Howard smiled and went to work. He recorded thirty seconds of the guards standing by the front door, then programmed the recording to loop for the next ten minutes. That way, if anyone checked the surveillance tape, they'd never see him and his team invading the house. Meanwhile, all the werewolves in the backyard completed their shifting and slipped into the woods.

When he and Dougal left the gatehouse, Phil and the boys slipped out of the woods and joined them.

"Let's go." Howard motioned for them to follow him down the long winding driveway. "Stay away from the back of the house. There's a surveillance camera there still working and a bunch of werewolves in the woods."

As soon as the front of the house became visible, Dougal teleported to the guards, and they slumped onto the ground.

"Whoa," Jimmy whispered. "What was that?"

"Some kind of vampire voodoo?" Jesse asked.

"Mind control," Howard answered. "The guards will have no memory of this. You guys watch the front. I'll be back soon."

He jogged toward the double front doors and entered the sprawling stone-and-log house. A quick glance back reassured him that Phil had the situation under control. Thank God he and Dougal had come. His cousins were enthusiastic and well-intentioned, but they were totally inexperienced in this kind of work.

It took less than a minute for him and Dougal to locate Rhett's home office. Howard retrieved a sixty-four-gig flash drive from his pocket and plugged it into the USB port on Rhett's computer.

Dougal stood guard at the office door. "I doona hear any other heartbeats. The house is empty." He approached slowly. "What are ye doing?"

"Downloading. Bank accounts, passwords, you name it. I designed this program to be super quick. It should take less than four minutes."

"Impressive."

Howard nodded, watching the monitor. "I didn't

just play football in college. I majored in computer science."

"Och, I dinna know that."

Howard slanted an amused look at the vampire. "How do you think all the computers at MacKay S and I and Romatech manage to stay secure? That's what I do during the day while you guys are sleeping." He grinned. "And you thought I was just eating donuts."

Dougal chuckled. "Aye." He looked around the room, then, with a wince, he motioned toward the stone fireplace. "No' someone ye know, I hope."

Howard's eyes narrowed on the white bearskin rug resting on top of the polished hardwood floor. A polar bear. He gritted his teeth.

" 'Tis no' a were-bear, right?" Dougal asked. "I thought shifters turn back to human form when they die."

"That's right." Howard sighed. "I wish we could take the bear with us, but we have to leave everything exactly as it is."

"Ye doona want to rob this house and destroy it like ye did the others? We could set it on fire."

"An old friend of mine named Smoky told me to never start a forest fire."

Dougal snorted. "This is all fun and games to you."

Howard shook his head. "When it comes to strategy, I'm dead serious. We have to get in and out of here without anyone knowing. We would be vastly outnumbered if they caught us. And we have to keep everything the same, because if Rhett suspected we were here, he would change his passwords and secure his accounts." He leaned over to check the progress of his software. Almost done.

"Is it worth it?" Dougal asked. "Playing yer game of revenge when ye canna let him know ye're the one toying with him?"

Howard straightened slowly. "I don't have a choice. I have to protect my family and friends."

Dougal stepped closer. "But if ye had a choice—"

"I don't." Howard removed the flash drive. "We're done here. Let's go."

Dougal followed him. "If ye had a choice, would ye play the game differently?"

"There would be no game." Howard glanced back. "I'd kill him."

Chapter Four

The following afternoon, Howard and his team arrived at his grandfather's house on Paw Island. His cousins were sent home, two houses down the street, so their parents would know the boys were all right. A quick check in the basement assured him that Dougal had safely teleported back the night before and was now in his death-sleep.

Phil settled in the small family room with Howard's grandfather, Walter, and they found a baseball game to watch on TV. Howard greeted his mother, who was busy in the kitchen, then hurried down the narrow hallway to his old bedroom.

While his laptop booted up, he looked around. The twin bed still sported an NFL comforter in red, white, and blue, and the small window had matching curtains, although faded to the point that the names of football teams were barely legible. His old trophies were still lined up on the dresser.

He sighed, remembering how much his mother had cried when he'd left for college. He'd kept in touch with her over the years, and she'd always pretended like he was coming home to visit soon.

He hadn't reminded her that he could never return. He knew if he mentioned his banishment, she would burst into tears.

He dragged a hand through his hair. His mother had suffered too much because of him. She acted like everything was rosy now that he was home, but when he gazed around his old room, he cringed at the thought of his mother keeping it exactly the same for twenty years. The poor woman had lost her husband, and then years later, when Howard was eighteen, she'd lost him, too.

After he'd tossed Rhett Bleddyn off the cliff, Rhett's father had threatened to annihilate the were-bear community if Howard wasn't punished, so the Council of Elders, which included his grandfather, had banished him for life. But Howard no longer felt obligated to honor the old decree, not when he obviously hadn't managed to kill Rhett. Rhett's father had passed away a year ago, and Rhett had emerged from hiding to become the new Pack Master. As far as Howard was concerned, he could now go home whenever he wanted. And he'd make sure that Rhett finally paid for his crimes.

He sat at his small desk where he used to do homework and downloaded the flash drive onto his laptop. He'd managed to steal a ton of information. Bank accounts, financial records, files on all of Rhett's minions. Just as Howard suspected, Rhett wielded a huge amount of political power. One Alaskan senator and several congressmen were actually werewolves who had sworn allegiance to the Bleddyn family. Rhett also controlled numerous Lycan politicians at the state and local levels.

Rhett's financial records revealed a tangled web of businesses and organizations from all over the world. His net worth was easily over two hundred million, with bank accounts not just in Alaska but in Canada, New York, Switzerland, Hong Kong, Australia, and Singapore, as well. The tangled design appeared purposeful, so that money could be shifted around, even hidden, and it would be difficult for Rhett's business partners and shareholders to know what he was up to.

No doubt, if Howard had broken into one of Rhett's numerous business offices in Alaska, the records for that business would appear clean. But he'd hacked into Rhett's personal computer, hoping it would pay off. And it did. After an hour of digging around, he discovered Rhett's dirty little secret.

Rhett had a hidden bank account in the Cayman Islands under the name of a bogus business. And there, he had been paying himself a salary of five million a year. The account now had fifty million in it, so he'd been embezzling from his other businesses for ten years.

Fifty million. Howard smiled. If he spent some money from the secret account, what could Rhett do? A police investigation would reveal the company as bogus, and he'd be in big trouble. Hoisted by his own petard.

"Thanks for the play money, Rhett."

Howard compiled a list of all candidates who were running against Rhett's political puppets, and then, using an untraceable Internet card, he made hefty donations to their campaigns. He chuckled, imagining how Rhett's puppets would react when they discovered their master was suddenly supporting their opponents.

His friend Harry had been investigating Rhett's activities, and he'd learned that the bastard had been harassing small towns that were in debt, trying to buy them out so he could turn them into exclusive werewolf communities. The mortals would be given a cruel choice: leave their land or be forced to become werewolves. Howard donated ten million to the towns so they could fight back.

"What else?" he murmured to himself as he tapped his fingers on the desk. A vision of the polar bear rug drifted into his mind and he smiled.

"That's going to be one expensive rug, Rhett." He donated five million dollars to a polar bear conservation program.

When he was done, he'd spent over half the money in the secret account. Howard sat back, staring at the computer screen. He needed to muddy the water, make it difficult to trace his movements.

"How about a shell game, Rhett?" For the next thirty minutes, he transferred chunks of money from one account to another, from one country to another. Before it had been a tangled web, but now it was a multiple train wreck. It would take Rhett months to figure out what the hell had happened.

To finish up, Howard e-mailed some incriminating evidence to Harry so the reporter could leak the news to the *Northern Lights Sound Bites* over the next few days. Harry was a talented enough journalist that he could write for a more prestigious paper, but he enjoyed writing for a tabloid, where he had the freedom to poke fun at Rhett and his minions without fear of being sued or reported for violation of journalistic ethics. No one questioned his claim that werewolves were real, not when his articles were in the same paper with stories about Bigfoot and alien abductions.

Smiling to himself, Howard sauntered into the family room. His grandfather, Walter, was resting in his worn-out recliner, half asleep but with the remote control still clutched in his hand, while Phil sprawled on the nearby couch. An ice chest filled with bottles of beer rested on the floor beside them.

Phil sat up. "Are you done?"

Howard nodded. "I just spent thirty-five million dollars."

"*What?*" Walter blinked awake and yanked his recliner into a sitting position. "Where the hell did you get that much money?"

"It was a gift from Rhett Bleddyn."

Walter snorted and turned off the television. "The only gift he'd give you is a bullet between the eyes."

Howard's smile widened. "The feeling is mutual."

"You spent thirty-five million of Rhett's money?" Phil asked.

Howard nodded and explained the details.

Phil laughed. "I'd like to see how his political puppets react. It's going to be a bloody dog fight."

Walter's mouth twitched, but he aimed a glare at Howard. "You shouldn't be stealing, boy. I taught you better than that."

Boy? Howard groaned inwardly. His grandfather and mom acted like he was still eighteen and had been away only twenty days instead of twenty years. But since a were-bear could easily live for five hundred years, twenty years might not seem that long to his elders. "I only used the money that Rhett had stolen. He started it. Besides, I want to make him suffer."

Walter nodded with a resigned look. "I can't blame you for that. The bastard deserves to suffer."

Phil leaned forward, his elbows on his knees. "So Rhett killed your girlfriend?"

"It was a long time ago," Howard replied quickly to stop Phil's fishing for more information. "Hand me one of those beers. We should be celebrating. Two of Rhett's houses have been destroyed, and now we've done serious damage to his finances and political power."

"Congratulations." Phil passed him a cold bottle. "What's your next move?"

Howard twisted off the top. "Rhett's planning to run for governor, so we'll ruin his reputation." He took a sip. "It won't be that hard, actually. We'll just tell the truth about his shady financial deals. I e-mailed the proof to Harry, so he can leak it anonymously to the newspaper."

With a sigh, Walter opened another bottle of beer. "This is a dangerous game you're playing."

"We're covering our tracks," Howard assured him. "Rhett won't be able to prove that we've done anything."

"He doesn't need proof, son. His family has always been ruthless. They hurt innocent people all the time."

Howard's heart stilled in his chest for a few seconds. Had he made an error in his strategy? He'd assumed Rhett would react logically, searching for proof before he retaliated. But what if he flew into a rage and attacked the were-bear community? "Rhett has so many enemies. I thought you would be safe as long as he had no proof."

Walter regarded him sadly. "All he has to do is think about who hates him the most, and he'll know it was you."

Howard closed his eyes briefly. *Damn*. He'd let his hunger for revenge consume him to the point that he'd blindly assumed he could protect his people.

"You think Rhett will attack these islands?" Phil asked.

"It's possible." Howard slumped into the easy chair next to his grandfather. "I'm sorry, Grandpa."

Walter shrugged. "I thought about stopping you, but I'm tired of catering to those bastards." He drank some beer. "What the hell, Rhett can come here if he wants. I've got a shotgun with his name on it."

Howard frowned. "They outnumber us."

"Let them try something," Walter growled. "We're on a damned island. If they try to land a boat here, we'll blast them out of the water."

Howard nodded. "You're in a good defensive position. Post guards around the island, and make sure no one lands without your approval." He groaned, thinking about all the innocent were-bears in the community. "I shouldn't have done this."

Walter grunted and drank more beer. "We should have done this twenty years ago when Rhett's father threatened to annihilate us."

"What exactly happened twenty years ago?" Phil asked.

"Nothing," Howard said quickly.

"Nothing? We thought you'd killed Rhett." Walter turned to Phil. "The only way I could stop Rhett's father from attacking us was to banish my own grandson." He shook his head, frowning. "I shouldn't have agreed to it. It wasn't fair to you."

"You did the right thing." Howard patted his grandfather's arm. "You had the whole community here to protect. You couldn't put them at risk because of something I had done."

"Rhett deserved to die," Walter grumbled. "When I think about what he did to that poor girl—"

"It's over and done with," Howard interrupted, letting his grandfather know he didn't want to discuss Carly.

Walter finished his beer, then clunked the empty bottle on the side table. "It's not your fault, Howard. It's that damned curse."

Howard groaned. Not that again. Whenever his grandfather had too much to drink, he blathered on and on about a stupid curse.

"There's a curse?" Phil asked.

"Don't get him started," Howard warned him. "It's a load of crap."

"It's our history!" Walter gave him an indignant look. "Are you calling our history crap?"

"The curse is crap," Howard muttered. "It's a cowardly way to dodge accountability. If the were-wolves attack us because of the game I'm playing, then I take full responsibility."

Walter shook his head. "Our race has been dying out for generations. And we roamed the earth, suffering, for a thousand years. All because of the curse."

"It sounds interesting," Phil said.

"Oh, it is," Walter agreed, his eyes lighting up. "It starts with the legend of how we came to be. Pass me another beer, and I'll tell you all about it."

With a groan, Howard leaned his head back on the seat cushion and stared at the ceiling. He'd heard this story four times in the last month and about a thousand times in his youth. "It's a stupid fairy tale."

Walter huffed as he opened another beer bottle. "There aren't any damned fairies in our legend. We're descended from fierce warriors."

"Fine," Howard grumbled. "But do us a favor and tell us the abridged version."

"There is no abridged version—"

"Oh yeah?" Howard interrupted, sitting up. "We had a magical guardian who created us with some weird hocus-pocus, and then the jerk be-trayed us. End of story."

"It's not the end until we find our guardian and get her to lift the curse," Walter insisted.

"Her?" Phil asked. "Your guardian is female?"

Howard snorted. "She's nonexistent."

"They were real. The guardians are real." Walter gulped down some beer and wiped his mouth with the sleeve of his flannel shirt. "All right. Once upon a time—"

"Told you it was a fairy tale," Howard mumbled.

Walter glared at him. "Once upon a damned time, there were three magical sisters. Guardians, we called them, for they guarded our village in Norway. The oldest was the Guardian of the Sea, 'cause she could talk to the creatures of the sea. The middle one was the Guardian of the Forest, and she talked to the woodland creatures. The youngest, the Guardian of the Sky, spoke to birds."

Phil nodded. "Cool."

"Eagles would warn the youngest sister if an enemy was coming over the mountain," Walter continued. "And the birds of prey would attack them, scaring them away. If the enemy came by sea, the seals would warn the oldest sister. Then she would ask the whales to capsize the boats. Over the years, the village flourished, the three sisters had daughters who inherited their powers, and all was well for many generations."

"Till they all died of boredom," Howard grumbled.

"That's not how it goes, and you know it." Walter scowled at him.

Howard stood and ambled toward his bedroom. "I'm going to see if Harry got my e-mail."

"You'll miss the best part," Walter called after him.

With a snort, Howard shut his bedroom door. The last thing he wanted to hear was how some magical Guardian of the Forest had created a bunch of berserkers. He wasn't sure how his ancestors had come into being, but it had happened over a thousand years ago, so as far as he was concerned, it no longer mattered. He called Harry, and they discussed their strategy for ruining Rhett's reputation.

Thirty minutes later, he returned to the family room.

Phil looked up from the couch, his eyes twinkling with amusement. "You never told me you're a berserker."

Howard arched an eyebrow at him. "Do I look crazy to you?" When Phil grinned, he muttered, "Don't answer that."

Walter motioned toward the werewolf. "Phil agrees with me that if we find our guardian, we could convince her to lift the curse."

Howard scoffed. "There is no curse. And there's no guardian."

Walter scowled at him. "How can you deny your own heritage?"

"I don't deny being a were-bear. Or the descendant of a berserker," Howard replied. "But the curse is crap. We're responsible for our own decisions in life. And I seriously doubt the guardians ever existed. If we did have one, she betrayed us, so good riddance."

"There could still be guardians out there," Walter insisted. "There were three sisters, and they had daughters."

Phil nodded. "It makes sense. If your line survived, then their line could have survived, too."

Howard gave him an incredulous look. "Are you actually buying into this nonsense?"

Phil shrugged. "I know it's bizarre, but my ancestors have a weird history, too. We were created by some Celtic wizards in ancient Wales. If my story is true, why wouldn't there be some truth to your grandfather's story?"

"Exactly." Walter finished his beer and set the bottle down with a clunk. "So all we have to do is find our guardian."

Howard snorted. "Fine. I'll put an ad on Craigslist. Wanted: single female willing to be guardian to a pack of grizzly were-bears. Warning: former guardian murdered on the job. Yeah, that'll work."

Phil chuckled. "Even if some lady was crazy enough to respond, how would you know if she was an actual guardian?"

Howard shrugged. "Who knows? It's a load of crap."

"You would know," Walter said quietly.

"How?" Howard asked.

Walter paused for a moment, considering. "I'm not sure. But somehow, you would know."

Howard gave him a wry look. "I'm not looking for an imaginary woman."

"How about a real one?" his mother said from the doorway, her eyes sparkling with humor. "But first, come and eat your supper."

After their late supper, Howard went back to his room to check his e-mail. Angus had sent a message, demanding that he and Phil return to New

York immediately. The mission in Mexico wasn't faring well, so Angus and Emma needed to go there and help out. That would leave Romatech and the school without security. Howard and Phil were supposed to report to the school by tomorrow night no later than ten o'clock.

Howard paced about his room, considering his options. The guys in Mexico were his friends. He couldn't remain here if it jeopardized their mission. He also harbored strong protective instincts toward Tino and Sofia. He couldn't leave them and the other children at the academy unguarded. And then there was the Payback game he was playing. The shit was about to hit Rhett's fan, and it might be better if he was far away when it happened. That way, Rhett might think one of his other enemies was responsible.

A few hours later, Dougal came up from the basement, a bottle of synthetic blood clutched in his mechanical hand.

"Angus left an urgent message on my phone." He looked at Howard and Phil. "I have to teleport ye back tonight."

Howard nodded. He'd already said his goodbyes to his mother and grandfather. As long as he had his laptop with him, he could continue the game against Rhett.

"I understand." He swung his packed duffel bag over his shoulder. "Let's go."

Chapter Five

Dark and creepy. Elsa Bjornberg eyed the forest that hugged the winding two-lane road. For the last hour that she'd been driving, the forest had been getting thicker. Darker. Creepier.

A shiver crept down her spine. "This house is in the middle of nowhere."

Alastair's only response was a light snore. Jet lag had caught up with him, and he'd fallen asleep two hours ago. Still, she was glad he was there in the passenger seat and she wasn't alone. In a dark, creepy forest.

For the hundredth time, she glanced at the GPS that came with the rental car. It claimed she was right on target. Then why was she feeling so uneasy?

Another shiver skittered across her skin, raising the tiny hairs on the back of her neck. She turned on the heat. Ever since they'd entered the forest, she'd become increasingly on edge. Her nerves tingled, as if she expected something to happen around the next bend.

She glanced in the rearview mirror and gasped when a shadowy form moved across the road. Her heart lurched, then settled back down as she realized it was just a deer. Thank God it had jumped onto the road behind the car and not in front.

With a tightened grip on the steering wheel, she glanced again at the rearview mirror. What the hell? There was a whole herd of deer in the road. Looking at her.

Her heart thudded in her chest. Too much caffeine. That had to be it. She glanced at the huge cup of coffee in the cup holder. She'd gulped it down to make sure she stayed awake.

It had been a horribly long day, starting with their flight from London to New York City, a train ride to White Plains, and then a rental car for the trip to the foothills of the Adirondacks. They should have spent the night in Albany. They were both exhausted, but for some strange reason, the owner of the house had insisted on meeting them at ten o'clock tonight, so they had pressed on to make the appointment.

She'd felt fine for the first part of the drive. She loved to travel and see new places, and the Hudson Valley had been lovely. But then the sun had set, and they'd left the main road to enter a forest that seemed endless. She hadn't passed another car in over an hour.

The road curved back and forth around the foothills, like a dark ribbon that had caught her and was pulling her deeper and deeper into the forest. Definitely dark and creepy, but oddly enough, she felt more excited than afraid. She felt . . . compelled.

She drove up a steep hill, cresting it just as the

nearly full moon emerged from clouds. Moon-beams shot out, illuminating the forest before her as if an artist had painted the treetops with luminous silver. Her breath caught, and her foot lifted off the accelerator. For just a second, it felt as if time stretched out, as endless and ancient as the woods.

It was beautiful. More than beautiful. It was . . . *home.*

She shook her head. Sleep deprivation was making her imagine things. She'd never lived in a dark and creepy forest. She'd always been a city girl.

Alastair stirred in the passenger seat. "Sorry, luv. Didn't mean to conk out on you." He rubbed a hand over his face. "It's bloody hot in here."

"Sorry." She turned off the heat. "The forest was giving me the willies."

He peered out the side window. "Blimey. Where the hell are we?"

Elsa smiled to herself. Whenever Alastair was half asleep his Cockney accent slipped through. But as he became more awake, he sounded increasingly like Mr. Darcy. "The town of Cranville should be coming up soon. Then it's another ten miles to the house."

"Excellent." Alastair stretched. "Perhaps the town will have an inn."

"You know, it might be hard to get supplies out here in the middle of nowhere."

"It could prove difficult, I give you that. But so far, all of our shows have taken place in metropolitan areas. I believe it would behoove us to try a different locale."

Elsa's mouth twitched. He was now in full Darcy mode. He'd probably want to stop in Cranville for tea and crumpets. "Well, if it would behoove us, then we'd better do it. I haven't been behooved in years."

He snorted. "Naughty wench. Ah, I see lights ahead."

She slowed the car as they entered the town of Cranville. Most of the businesses were closed for the night.

"Aha!" Alastair peered out his window. "An inn. Of sorts. And it has vacancies. A bit rustic looking, but I've seen worse." He turned to face front and blinked. "Where did the town go?"

"That was it."

"Blimey." He cleared his throat. "I daresay this location will be a challenge."

With a smile, she nodded. She was used to challenges. It had been a challenge to work with Alastair at first. He was slim and fine-boned and, to be honest, prettier than her. The wardrobe department loved him because he looked so dapper and elegant in a designer suit. With her, they highlighted her size and shape, usually with shorts that displayed her long legs and tight T-shirts that hugged her chest. Short-sleeved T-shirts, since they always made sure that the strange red birthmark on her shoulder was covered.

Alastair's sandy hair was always perfectly cut and groomed, while her long hair was so wild that the makeup artists had surrendered in despair and pulled it back into a ponytail. The end result: Alastair looked like he traveled in a chauffeur-driven Rolls Royce, and she looked like she'd arrived in an old pickup truck.

Even Alastair's movements were graceful, while she felt huge and cumbersome. At six foot two, she was three inches taller than Alastair. Four inches taller than Oskar. In the very first episode of *International Home Wreckers*, the writers gave her the nickname Amazon Ellie.

It had hurt. But she had smiled and done her job. After all, where on earth could she get a better job than this? Traveling around the world, transforming ruined old houses into masterpieces— it was a dream come true.

The show's producers loved the irony that the big, tough guy on the show was the girl. That's why they had hired her. For the first time in her life, her size had worked to her advantage. She was a lucky girl. A very large and lucky girl.

She sighed. Would there ever be a time in her life when she didn't feel large? Didn't feel like her entire identity centered on her size? Even the fan mail she received came from other large women who praised her, not for her building skills or talented woodwork but for being bold enough to show off her size. As if she had any choice? No diet on earth could make her shorter.

After another five minutes of driving, the GPS system guided her to take the next left. She turned onto an even narrower road. The forest crowded in, thicker than ever. Darker. Creepier.

Three minutes later, she turned right onto a gravel road. Tiny pebbles pinged against the underside of the car, and she slowed to a crawl.

"I think we'll have to surface this driveway." Alastair leaned forward as they came around a bend and the forest stopped. "There it is!"

Elsa's breath caught. It was larger than she'd expected. And even more beautiful than the photo the owner had e-mailed them. "It's magnificent."

The two-story gatehouse sat at the end of a circular drive. The forest had been cleared around it, but the yard was overgrown and wild.

"Look at the cupola on top." Alastair grinned. "I love it! It reminds me of Monticello."

"Yes." Elsa nodded, smiling. "It's very . . . stately. And elegant." She pulled to a stop parallel to the house and pointed at the floodlights on each end. "They have a generator. That's good."

Alastair peered out his window. "Redbrick, colonial Federalist style. We've done just about every architectural style but that one."

"And it would behoove us to do something different," she added with a wry smile.

"Precisely. We need variety." He unbuckled his seat belt. "I can't wait to see the interior. When is the owner supposed to arrive?"

Elsa glanced at the clock before turning the car off. "We have ten minutes."

He opened his car door. "I need to make a pit stop in the woods, if you catch my drift, and then I'll take a look around." He grabbed a flashlight, then stepped out, his feet crunching in the gravel. "Text me when the owner arrives. What was her name again?"

"Shanna Draganesti. Doesn't it seem odd that she wanted to meet us at night?"

Alastair leaned over to look at Elsa. "I don't care, as long as she lets us do this house. I love it!" He shut the car door, then jogged toward the side of the house and disappeared around the corner.

Elsa surveyed the house, noting the simple, but elegant, symmetry. It was definitely a gem, a hidden treasure out here in the middle of nowhere.

She took a deep breath and rotated her tired shoulders. What an endless day. And an endless forest. Her gaze drifted to the woods. Who would live way out here? Were the owners antisocial? Or hiding something?

A movement caught her eye. A deer had slipped from the forest and was enjoying the thick grass in the overgrown yard. Another deer joined him. And another. And another till there was easily a dozen.

They lifted their heads in unison and looked at her.

"Sheesh." With a shudder, she turned her attention back to the house. It was bigger than she'd expected for a gatehouse. A basement, two floors, and an attic. Red brick with white shutters. Four white columns outlined the semicircular porch in front, and a round white cupola crowned the roof. The floodlights didn't quite reach the center of the house, leaving the area around the front door in shadow.

Even if the interior was a disaster area, it wouldn't deter her and the guys. The house had beautiful bones. Once it was fleshed out, it would be absolutely stunning.

Headlights flashed as a car entered the circular driveway. The owner was right on time.

She watched in the rearview mirror as the car pulled to a stop behind her. With the glare from the headlights, she couldn't make out the driver inside. The car engine and lights turned off. The driver side door opened.

No one came out. Some movement nearby caught her attention. The small herd of deer was scattering into the woods.

When she heard the car door slam shut, she glanced once again at the rearview mirror. Still no one there. Strange.

She grabbed her cell phone from where she'd left it on the console. Alastair needed to get back here quick.

A knock on her window made her jump, and the cell phone tumbled into her lap.

"Sorry!" A blond woman stood by her car window. "Didn't mean to startle you."

Elsa caught her breath. Where had this lady come from so quickly?

"I'm Shanna Draganesti, but please call me Shanna." She grinned. "I'm so glad you're here! I'm a big fan!"

"Thank you." Elsa grabbed her handbag from the backseat floor, slipped her cell phone inside, then opened the door slowly while Shanna moved out of the way. "It's a pleasure to meet you. I'm Elsa Bjornberg."

"Oh, I know." Shanna's eyes widened as Elsa climbed out of the car. "Wow. You must be over six foot."

Elsa gritted her teeth and shut the door. *Yes, I'm freakishly large. I'm so tall I occasionally suffer from altitude sickness.* "I'm six foot two."

Shanna's eyes lit up. "You're perfect!"

Huh? That wasn't the usual response. Elsa hitched her handbag onto her shoulder. "Thanks. By the way, Alastair is here, too. He's taking a look around. He's very excited about renovating your house. I am, too. We think it has enormous potential."

"Oh." Shanna's smile looked strained. "That's nice."

Another odd reaction. Owners were usually bouncing with joy at this point. Elsa motioned toward the house. "Can we take a look inside?"

"Of course." Shanna glanced at her watch, then down the driveway.

"Hello," Alastair called out as he approached. "You must be Mrs. Draganesti?"

Shanna spun around to greet him. "Oh, my. It's Big Al." She shook his hand. "I'm a big fan of your show. Please call me Shanna."

"Delighted to meet you, Shanna." Alastair turned off his flashlight. "I just finished a quick exterior inspection, and I must say I absolutely adore this house. I can't wait to start work on it!"

Shanna gave him a weak smile. "Well, you might change your mind once you see the inside." She dug in her handbag and removed a set of old keys.

Alastair gave Elsa a questioning look, and she shrugged. The owner seemed to be having second thoughts about them working on her house.

Shanna climbed the steps to the front porch. "I'm afraid the inside is a disaster. The electricity and plumbing don't work, and I think there are some birds living in the attic."

"Those are fairly common problems with an old house," Elsa assured her. "We're accustomed to completely redoing the wiring and plumbing."

"And Oskar loves trapping birds," Alastair added with a smile.

"I see." Shanna unlocked the door, and it creaked open. "I have some extra flashlights here." She reached inside a basket by the door and handed one to Elsa, then took another for herself.

Alastair clicked his on and gasped. "Good Lord, Ellie, look at the staircase! It's magnificent."

"Wow." She moved forward, running her flashlight beam up the elegant curve of the staircase.

"Look at that!" Alastair aimed his flashlight straight up at the cupola. "Stunning, absolutely stunning."

"And this is a gatehouse?" Elsa turned to Shanna. "There must be a really spectacular main house somewhere near by."

Shanna winced. "Well, yes. There's a mansion about three miles down the road. But it's a very private school, and under no circumstances can its existence be made public."

That amount of secrecy seemed a bit odd. Elsa exchanged a look with Alastair. "There would be no need to ever mention the school on our show."

"But it would be interesting to see the mansion," Alastair murmured.

"No!" Shanna shook her head. "No one can be

allowed anywhere near it. It has . . . troubled children. Juvenile delinquents. It wouldn't be safe for you to go there."

Very strange. Elsa exchanged another look with Alastair.

"We'll be fine, Shanna," he insisted. "We can post security guards here at night to watch over the supplies. We always do that when we work in metropolitan areas."

Shanna glanced at her watch and bit her lip. "I hope you didn't have any trouble finding the place. This is such a remote location. I'm afraid it could be terribly hard for you to get your supplies here."

Was the owner just nervous, or was she trying to back out? Elsa took a deep breath and smiled. "Please don't let that concern you. We don't think the location will be a problem. It will be a nice change for our show."

"I see." Instead of looking relieved, the owner looked more agitated.

"I sense you're having second thoughts," Elsa said gently. "That's a fairly common reaction once people realize that their house will actually be featured on our show. There are privacy and financial concerns."

Shanna sighed. "There is a problem. I didn't think about it when I first contacted you. I was just so excited about you coming here. But when I discussed it with my husband and his . . . colleagues, they pointed out some serious security and privacy issues I'd forgotten to consider."

"We would do our best to comply with your needs," Elsa assured her.

"I appreciate that," Shanna said. "My husband and I work far away during the day, and we would never be able to do any interviews for your show. Our names would have to remain private, and we would have to use someone else to represent us."

"We've done that before," Alastair said. "To be perfectly honest, the focus of the show is the house, not the owner. As long as your representative can meet with us during the day and doesn't mind doing an occasional interview, then we're fine with that."

"Well, I'm not sure if he'll agree to it." Shanna glanced at her watch once again. "He was supposed to be here by now."

"If he agrees to represent you, will you let us do the house?" Alastair asked. "We can cover the cost of the renovation up to the amount of fifty thousand, and we won't go over that without consulting you."

"And we stand by all our work," Elsa added. "We have to. Everything we do is thoroughly documented on the show."

"And we'll put it all in writing, of course," Alastair said. "We'll turn this house back into the masterpiece it deserves to be."

Shanna heaved a sigh. "It's so tempting. Believe me, I really want you to do it. I just haven't convinced—" Her eyes widened. "I hear a car coming."

She must have awfully good hearing, for Elsa didn't hear anything.

Shanna smiled at her. "Howard's coming. He doesn't know you're here, so he's going to be totally taken by surprise. He's a huge fan!" She dropped her flashlight in the basket by the door and hurried outside.

Alastair sidled up close to Elsa. "Are you getting strange vibes?"

She snorted. "Tell me about it." She'd been getting them since they'd entered the forest.

"Something odd about the owner," Alastair whispered. "But I really want to do this house. If the rep seems like a decent chap, I say we go for it."

Elsa nodded. "I agree." The house was very tempting, but the strange vibes were tempting, too. It was as if she'd caught a glimpse of a puzzle she was anxious to solve.

She finally heard the sound of a car engine. "Let's go." She returned her flashlight to the basket and peered outside.

Alastair turned his flashlight off and joined Elsa by the front door.

"Howard!" Shanna called out. "Thank you for coming."

"Is there a problem?" a masculine voice responded. "Toni told me to come here right away."

Elsa swallowed hard. Whoever this Howard was, he had a sexy voice. Deep and powerful enough to make her insides quiver. She inched out onto the dark porch.

Shanna ran forward to meet the newcomer, who had parked an SUV down the driveway in a dark area beneath the trees. "We're thinking of renovating this house. You won't believe who's here!"

Howard emerged from the shadows, partially lit by a floodlight.

Elsa gasped.

"Blimey," Alastair whispered. "He's bloody huge."

Elsa pressed a hand to her chest as her heart thundered. He was tall, taller than her. And big, bigger than her. Solid as a boulder, yet he moved with a stealthy, fluid grace. She eased forward, waiting for him to enter fully into the light. Any second now.

There.

Her heart lurched up her throat. He was gorgeous. Strong, masculine face, beautiful blue eyes, and thick brown hair. His black T-shirt molded to a wide, muscular chest, and the sleeves stretched across biceps that made her mouth water.

Her skin tingled with goose bumps. Was this what she had anticipated ever since she'd entered the forest? Somehow, she had known something was waiting for her just around the bend. Something big.

He was definitely big. And having a big effect on her. She felt breathless, weak at the knees, and dazed, as if she were in a dream.

He halted suddenly at something Shanna had whispered to him. "*What?*"

"It's true," Shanna said. "She's here."

His eyes widened as he turned to stare at the house. His gaze found her on the dark porch, and his mouth fell open. Her heart leaped in response.

He closed his eyes, and his chest expanded as he took a deep breath. Was he trying to smell her? When his eyes opened, they gleamed a richer blue. He looked at her, and his gorgeous mouth curled slowly into a smile.

Alastair snorted. "I don't think he'll mind working with you."

She'd certainly like to work with him. She ventured out of the shadow and into the light.

Howard sprinted toward her, then skidded to a halt in the gravel in front of the porch. He gazed at her, an amazed expression on his face.

"Elsa," he whispered.

His voice went through her like a delicious shiver. "Hi," she breathed.

He continued to stare at her. "Hi."

"How do you do?" Alastair stepped forward, extending a hand. "I'm Alastair Whitfield."

"Howard Barr." He glanced at Alastair, then focused once again on Elsa, forgetting to shake hands. "It's really you."

"Yes." She licked her lips, suddenly as nervous as a schoolgirl.

His gaze dropped to her mouth, then back to her eyes. "Do you know how beautiful you are?"

Her heart melted.

"Too bad we don't have a camera rolling," Alastair muttered.

"I knew it," Shanna whispered, her eyes glistening with tears.

"So do we have a deal?" Alastair asked. "We can renovate this house?"

"Perhaps," Shanna answered. "If I can convince my husband. And if Howard will agree to oversee the project—"

"I will," he said, never taking his eyes off Elsa. He stretched a hand toward her. "I'm very happy to meet you."

Her heart fluttered. "Howard." She placed her hand in his.

An instant frisson of electricity shot up her arm. She gasped and stepped back, stumbling on the porch steps. Howard grabbed her by the upper arms to steady her.

She cried out as a flame of heat seared the birthmark on her right shoulder.

"Are you all right?" Howard leaned close to her, his eyes worried.

She scrambled out of his reach, grasping her shoulder. The heat from her birthmark scorched her left hand, forcing her to let go. "Agh." Her palm was red. Burned.

Oh God, no. She curled her injured hand into a fist. It couldn't be real. Her aunt had always warned her this could happen, but she'd never believed it.

She glanced at Howard, who was watching her with a confused look. *Oh God, no! Not him.*

He'd activated the curse.

Chapter Six

*W*hat the hell had happened? He could have sworn she liked him, but now she was recoiling in horror.

"Elsa?" Howard reached out to her, and she jumped back.

Her handbag slipped off her shoulder and she grabbed it, wincing as if in pain.

"Are you hurt?" He could still feel the heat stinging his left hand from when he'd touched her.

"I . . . excuse me." She gave Shanna and Alastair an apologetic look. "I need to make a personal call." She rushed down the steps, giving Howard a wide berth, then dashed to her car and climbed into the driver's seat.

Alastair plastered a wide grin on his face. "The poor girl is exhausted. We started the day in London, don't you know. It's been a dreadfully long day."

Shanna nodded with a sympathetic smile, then glanced toward the car. "I hope she'll be all right."

Howard eased a little closer to the car. With his superior senses, he might be able to hear her phone conversation. It was wrong to invade her privacy, but dammit, he had to know what had happened. He couldn't strategize his next move without more information.

"Shanna, I do hope you'll allow us to renovate this house," Alastair said. "It would be perfect for our show."

Howard turned his head toward Alastair and Shanna so it would look like he was focused on their conversation.

"Aunt Greta," Elsa whispered urgently into her phone. "I—I think it happened. You told me to call you immediately if my birthmark ever—"

Howard strained but couldn't catch what the aunt was saying. If only Elsa wasn't closed up in a car.

"Yes, it's burning," Elsa said. "Something terrible."

He flexed his left hand. It was still sore from touching her. Apparently, the mysteriously hot birthmark was on her right shoulder.

"I'll discuss it with my husband," Shanna distracted him as she continued her conversation with Alastair. "We'll give you an answer tomorrow night."

"Excellent," Alastair replied.

"Our biggest concern is the school down the road," Shanna added. "We can't allow any mention of it, and none of your employees can go anywhere near it."

Alastair nodded. "Understood."

Howard knew Roman and Angus wouldn't be pleased to have a production crew so close to the academy. It was a definite security risk, but the prospect of having Elsa so close was too tempting to resist. He refocused his attention on her.

"Yes," she whispered in the car. "I did touch someone. We shook hands."

He tensed, waiting for more.

"No, he was a perfect gentleman." Elsa gasped. "Greta! I don't believe it. There was nothing wild or crazy about him."

He winced.

"I can't go home," Elsa insisted. "I'm working here." A pause. "No. You don't need to come here. Really, Greta, I'm a big girl. I can take care of myself."

"We'll be staying at the inn in Cranville," Alastair told Shanna. "I'll have a contract ready tomorrow night and hope for the best."

Shanna nodded and gave Howard a questioning look. "You're all right with representing Roman and me?"

"Sure. No problem." He caught the end of Elsa's line.

"I told you I don't believe in that nonsense!"

He gritted his teeth. What nonsense?

"Do we really have to make such a big deal out of this?" Elsa asked. "He seemed perfectly safe to me. And normal."

Howard groaned inwardly. The truth was he wasn't normal. And if he pursued Elsa, he'd eventually have to tell her he was a were-bear. Would she be able to handle it? Maybe, if she liked him enough. He could have sworn she had felt an attraction before his touch had caused her to burn. What the hell was that about?

Elsa sighed. "Okay. I'll try to avoid him. Yes, I'll be careful. I'll call you later. Bye." She lowered the phone to her lap, frowning.

"I don't believe in it," she muttered to herself, then shook her head. "Why should I avoid him?"

Howard agreed. There was no way he'd let her avoid him. He strode to the driver's side window and tapped on it.

She jumped and gave him a wary look.

"Are you all right?"

She paused, then cracked the door open a few inches. "I'm fine, thank you. We should be going now. If you could tell Alastair—"

"How is your shoulder?"

A fleeting look of shock crossed her face. "I'm fine."

"I have a first-aid kit in my truck." He motioned toward his SUV.

"I don't need anything." She dropped her phone into her handbag, refusing to look at him. "We've put in a really long day, so Alastair and I should go."

He glanced at Alastair, who was describing some of his plans to Shanna, in no apparent hurry to leave.

"I'll be right back." He jogged to his SUV to retrieve the burn ointment from the first-aid kit.

"Here." He handed her the tube through the narrow crack in the door. "You need to treat the burn on your shoulder as soon as possible."

"Thank you." She accepted the ointment, carefully avoiding any contact with his hand. "How did you know?"

"I touched you." He showed her his palm, still pink from heat. "I felt it."

She winced. "I'm sorry. I didn't mean to hurt you. I—I don't know why it happened."

Fate. That was why. From the moment he'd first spied her on television, he'd felt a bond to her, a strong and irrevocable attachment. He leaned close to the narrow opening. "Did you have dinner? I could meet you and Alastair at the diner in town."

"Well, I—I am hungry, but . . ."

"Good. I'll see you there."

She turned to him with an alarmed expression. "I don't really know you."

Howard straightened, dragging a hand through his hair. Maybe he was pushing too fast. "I'm sorry. I've been watching your show every week for months, so I feel like I already know you." But did he know the real Elsa? She might be different than the persona she portrayed on television.

"You . . . watch the show?"

He smiled. "You seem surprised."

Her cheeks flushed a light pink. "You don't seem like the type to be into home decorating."

He was more into watching her, but that admission would probably scare her off. "I love the show. I think you guys do amazing work."

Her blush deepened. "Thank you."

"So how about a quick hamburger in town? It would give you and Alastair a chance to know me better, since we'll be working together."

She gave him a wry look. "You're persistent, aren't you?"

"I don't give up easily." *Not when I want something as badly as I want you.*

Her eyes met his, and a fierce longing hit him in the gut. He clenched his fists to keep from wrenching the door off her car and pulling her into his arms.

Her words came back to him: *There was nothing wild or crazy about him.* He'd have to control the animal inside him or end up scaring her away.

A multitude of emotions danced in her eyes— desire, fear, frustration, regret. Whatever had caused the burn was making her afraid. But the desire was there—he could hear it in her heartbeat, smell it in her blood, feel it radiating just beneath her skin.

His choice for strategy was obvious. Make her desire greater than her fear. Give her so much joy and pleasure that she had no room for regret. Channel her frustration into more desire until she was burning for him.

The bear inside him growled in anticipation. He smiled slowly. "I'll see you in about fifteen minutes at the diner."

She nodded, her cheeks still flushed, then she turned away and tapped on the horn to get Alastair's attention. He shook Shanna's hand, then climbed into the car.

Howard stepped back as Elsa drove away. Why did her birthmark burn when he touched her? Dammit, he'd better be able to touch her again without hurting her.

"Well?" Shanna ran toward him, her eyes glittering with excitement. "What do you think?"

"I think you're one hell of a matchmaker."

She grinned. "She's perfect for you."

"I'm grateful." He tilted his head. "But curious. How did you know . . ."

Shanna's smile faded, and she ducked her head. "Well, it's sorta a long story. Tino was missing you so much that he suggested I move some of your belongings to the school so you could live there with us, and then he mentioned some secret DVDs under your bed—"

Howard stiffened. "You looked through my stuff?"

"Tino said you were watching adult DVDs with a girl and two guys named Big Al and The Hammer—"

He snorted.

"As a responsible parent, I had to check it out." She flashed a smile at him. "But it all worked out for the best, right?"

"You should have trusted me."

"I know. But it occurred to me that we don't really know you very well."

"I'm a loner. It goes with being a bear."

She patted his arm. "You don't have to be alone anymore."

"Thank you." He returned her smile. "I appreciate your help, but from now on, I'll be handling the matter myself without any outside interference. You understand?"

She gave him a wry look. "Is that your polite way of telling me to butt out?"

"Does a bear piss in the woods?"

Fifteen minutes later, Howard walked into the diner in Cranville. This late at night, it was almost empty. A few people sat at the counter, enjoying a late snack of homemade pie. Elsa and Alastair sat at a table for four.

"We've already ordered," Alastair informed him. "We're exhausted from traveling all day."

"I understand." Howard sat next to Elsa, and she gave him a nervous look. "I just arrived myself. I was in Alaska yesterday."

"Alaska?" Elsa asked, her eyes wide. "I've never been there."

He smiled at her. "You'd love it."

She smiled back, her cheeks blushing.

"Business or pleasure?" Alastair asked as he unrolled the paper napkin holding his silverware.

"A bit of both," Howard replied. "I have family there."

"Children?" Alastair asked while Elsa winced.

"No children. I'm not married."

"And what kind of business do you do?" Alastair asked.

Howard's mouth twitched. Was Alastair interrogating him to make sure he was suitable for Elsa? She was sitting there, looking highly embarrassed with her pink cheeks. "I work for MacKay Security and Investigations. I'm into keeping people safe."

"Ah." Alastair nodded. "Elsa tells me you're a fan of the show."

"I am." He waved at the waitress and ordered a hamburger.

"Which show did you enjoy the most?" Alastair asked.

Was this a test to see if he actually watched? "I thought the house in Berlin was the biggest challenge, especially since the owner was so uncooperative."

"He was an ass," Alastair muttered.

Howard grinned. "I thought so, too. But the house in London is probably my favorite. Elsa did a fantastic job on the woodwork."

She smiled shyly. "Thank you."

"What does the show mean to you?" Howard asked, wondering if she loved all the attention of being an international celebrity.

"For me, it's about our heritage." Alastair arranged his silverware neatly on the Formica-topped table. "It's important to preserve our history, to honor it. Otherwise, we have no idea who we are and where we're going."

Howard nodded. His grandfather would agree with this. He was always droning on and on about their history as berserkers. "And you, Elsa?"

She sipped some water as she considered. "For me it's all about family. Creating a home where a family can make their own history, where year after year holidays are celebrated and birthday candles are blown out."

Howard smiled. "Do you come from a big family?"

She shook her head. "No. I was an only child. I lost my mom when I was young, so my aunt and uncle raised me."

"Then you place a high value on family because it's always been scarce."

She tilted her head, considering. "I never thought about it that way, but it's true. Nothing makes me happier than seeing a family settled into one of the houses we renovate. If we can give them a good solid home, then it seems like we're doing something really special."

"You are."

Her gaze met his, and instantly he felt the connection, the pull. Would he be able to touch her again without hurting her?

Alastair cleared his throat, and Howard wondered how long he and Elsa had stared at each other. The waitress brought their food, and they busied themselves eating.

"How did you learn to do woodwork?" Howard asked.

Elsa swallowed her bite of hamburger. "I learned from my uncle Peder. It was his hobby." She sipped some more water. "He passed away about a year ago."

"I'm sorry."

She shrugged. "I miss him, but I'm forever grateful to him. He was a builder by profession and taught me so much. My aunt is an interior designer, so I grew up surrounded by sawdust, paint and carpet samples, and swatches of fabric."

Alastair wiped his mouth with the paper napkin. "My family was into construction, too. It gets into your blood."

Elsa nodded. "I became fascinated with the whole process of turning a few boards and brick into an actual home, a place where children could play and couples grow old together."

Howard smiled. This was the Elsa he'd fallen for on television. She was genuine. Real. And he was going to pursue her in earnest. If he could touch her without hurting her.

After paying for dinner, he followed them outside.

"I'll go get us some rooms." Alastair headed across the street to the motel office.

"He's leaving me alone with you?" Howard smiled at Elsa. "I must have passed inspection."

She snorted. "Alastair considers me his little sister. A rather big little sister."

"Not too big to me."

She gave him a puzzled look.

He stepped closer. "Can I see you again?"

"I'm sure we'll see each other often at the house."

"That's not what I meant." He reached out to touch her arm, but she moved back. "Does your shoulder still hurt?"

"A little. I should go to my room and put some of that ointment on it. Thank you for dinner." She stepped off the sidewalk to cross the road.

"Elsa."

She glanced back.

"Aren't you curious? Don't you want to know what will happen?" He extended a hand toward her.

Frowning, she turned to face him. "Why would I ask for more pain?"

"Maybe it won't hurt this time."

"It hurt before. It's too big a risk."

"It's too big a loss if we give up on our future."

She scoffed. "What future?"

"You're the most beautiful woman I've ever met. I really want to see you again." He was tempted to tell her they were somehow connected, but he didn't want to frighten her.

She groaned with frustration. "I'm not sure I can trust you."

He turned his hand palm up. "Try me and see."

After a moment of hesitation, she extended her hand and gently tapped his fingers with her own. Her gaze lifted to his. "It didn't burn."

With a grin, he took her hand in his. "Then I'll see you tomorrow?"

She nodded, her cheeks blushing. "Good night, Howard." She let go and dashed across the street.

Chapter Seven

Elsa wiped a circle of steam off the bathroom mirror so she could get a better look at herself. After a hot shower, she felt more capable of dealing with her life.

She gathered her long, damp hair into a towel turban on top of her head, then peered at her shoulder in the mirror. It was an odd birthmark—an ugly splotch on her upper arm with four clawlike marks extending over the curve of her shoulder, as if some sort of wild beast had grasped her and refused to let go. It had returned to its usual dull maroon color, but earlier, when she'd examined it in the restroom at the diner, it had glowed a brighter red.

The mark had always embarrassed her, especially in her teenage years, making her reluctant to wear tank tops or swimsuits, but it had never caused her physical pain before. Not until she'd touched Howard.

What was so special about him? She snorted. What wasn't special about him? He was big and gorgeous. He seemed intelligent, polite, and genuinely concerned about her.

From her handbag, she retrieved the tube of ointment he'd given her. He'd said she was beautiful. And not too big. He'd looked at her with desire simmering in his gorgeous blue eyes. With a sigh, she smeared some ointment over the birthmark. She'd finally met a man like Howard, and she was supposed to avoid him?

Why? Because of some vague curse Greta and Ula talked about? Why would she let that nonsense stop her from seeing him? He'd touched her again, and it hadn't hurt. The first time must have been a fluke.

She slipped on her favorite green pajamas, brushed out her hair, then collapsed on the bed. As exhausted as she was, sleep should come easily.

Thirty minutes later, she sat up and turned on the bedside lamp. Too many questions were bouncing around in her mind. The whole interview with Shanna Draganesti had seemed odd. Why did Shanna and her husband insist on having a rep? Most people relished the idea of appearing on television. And why could she never visit the site during the day? Most people with day jobs could arrange to have an hour or so free. Where did they work? Where did they live? What was the deal with the secret school down the road?

Where did Howard live? And why did his first touch make her birthmark burn?

She didn't know how to answer her questions about Shanna or Howard, but she could at least get some answers about her birthmark. She called Aunt Greta in Minneapolis.

"Ellie!" Greta answered the phone on the first

ring. "Are you all right? You haven't been attacked, have you?"

"What?" Elsa gave her phone an incredulous look. "What are you talking about?"

"Where are you?"

"In my hotel room. Cranville, New York."

"Make sure the door and windows are locked. Don't let anyone in. Do you have any weapons?"

"What? Aunt Greta, what's going on?"

"I just got off the phone with Aunt Ula. I'm sorry to say this, but the situation is much more dire than I had realized."

Elsa groaned. Her great-aunt Ula was wacky. The old woman lived on an island in Sweden and claimed she could talk to seals. "Look. You shouldn't take anything Ula says seriously."

"We have to," Greta insisted. "You're in grave danger. You must stay away from the man who activated the curse. Ula is taking the first flight out of Stockholm—"

"She's leaving her island?" Elsa had never heard of Ula stepping foot off her beloved island.

"Yes. She's flying to New York, and then Albany. I'm packing up to leave now. I'll meet her in Albany, and then we'll come see you."

Elsa winced. "You have to stop her. You don't need to come here. The whole thing was a mistake. I touched the guy again, and it didn't burn at all."

Greta gasped. "You touched him again?"

"We shook hands after dinner."

"You had dinner with him when I told you to avoid him?" Greta let out a long groan. "Why didn't you listen to me?"

"I told you before. I don't believe in this non-sense."

"Well, it believes in you!" Greta muttered a curse. "I'm leaving as soon as I finish packing. I'm going to drive so I can bring Peder's hunting rifle and shotgun—"

"*What?*"

"Thank God I kept them after he passed away. We're going to need them. You're in grave danger."

Elsa jumped to her feet and paced across the small hotel room. Uncle Peder had been an avid hunter, but Greta and Ula were a couple of hopeless amateurs. "The entire state of New York will be in danger if you're roaming around with weapons. Not to mention the fact that you could be breaking some laws."

"I'll keep them unloaded and in their case in the trunk. Don't worry about us. You're the one in danger."

"I'm fine! You're overreacting. The second touch didn't hurt at all."

"It's the first one that counts. I know you don't believe in the curse, but it's real."

Elsa gritted her teeth. The stupid imaginary curse was real enough to have caused her pain over and over again. Her mother had been so afraid of it, she'd accidentally killed herself. Her great-aunt Ula was so afraid of it that she'd packed Elsa up at the age of seven and shipped her to the States to live with Aunt Greta in Minneapolis. Elsa had lost her home, her country, her mother—all because of the curse.

Hot tears stung her eyes. "I'm sick and tired of

this stupid curse! It only has power over you because you believe in it!"

"Of course I believe in it!" Greta cried. "I lost my mother because of it. And my only sister, your mother."

Elsa's vision blurred as more tears gathered. It was fear that had killed her mother, nothing but stupid fear. But what had happened to her grandmother, Greta's mother? This was the first time she'd heard anything bad about her.

"No." She didn't want to get sucked into this make-believe fantasy world. "There's no curse."

Greta heaved a long sigh. "I know it's hard to believe. That's why we're coming to see you. So we can explain it to you in person. And then we can watch over you and keep you safe. You . . . you're like a daughter to us."

A tear tumbled down Elsa's cheek. She shouldn't have yelled at her aunt for her crazy beliefs. Greta and Ula were the only family she had. "You know I love you both. I'm just so frustrated. I don't know what's going on, and I need some answers."

There was a pause, then Greta continued, "We never told you very much because we didn't want to burden you. Or frighten you. It was already hard enough on you, having to adjust to a new country and new language. Especially with those vicious children being so cruel to you."

Elsa rolled her eyes. *Gee, thanks for reminding me.* She'd been a full foot taller than the other kids in elementary school and too shy and uncomfortable with English to defend herself. That was when she'd acquired her first disparaging nickname—

Ellie the Elephant. Her schoolmates came up with a new one in junior high they were especially proud of—Elsie the Cow. She wondered if those same people now enjoyed her new name, Amazon Ellie.

"We thought if we moved you to the States, you would be safe," Greta continued. "The curse would be broken, and you would never have to know."

"Know what?"

Greta sighed. "All right, I'll try to explain a little. You know how I have a birthmark on my shoulder that looks like a bird? And Ula has one shaped like a fish?"

Elsa rubbed her eyes. "Yes."

"Your grandmother had the mark of an animal paw on her shoulder. The three different marks have always been passed down the women in our family."

"Lucky us," Elsa muttered. So she had inherited her ugly birthmark from a grandmother she'd never known.

"As long as each birthmark has a living host, the other women in the family are left unmarked. Your mother was the youngest, so she didn't have a birthmark. And she was so happy when she was pregnant with you, knowing that you would be free from the marks and never burdened with the curse."

Elsa swallowed hard. "But I do have a mark."

"Yes. Unfortunately, your grandmother died before you were born, and the animal paw mark passed on to you. Your mother . . . well, she didn't handle it well. Our mother's death, and then your birth with the same mark on your shoulder . . ."

"So she started drinking." And accidentally drove her car off a bridge in the middle of the night. Elsa closed her eyes briefly. She'd only been three years old at the time, so she didn't remember much. "Didn't I have a father?"

"I—I'm sure you did, but your mother never told us who he was. Someone she met in college, I guess."

Elsa sighed. At the age of twenty-seven, she'd already lived longer than her mother had. "So why are you and Ula freaking out now?"

There was another pause. "I'm afraid some bad things have happened to the women in our family with the animal paw birthmark. We can't seem to stop it."

"What sort of bad things?"

"We're not going to let it happen to you," Greta insisted. "We'll protect you."

"From what?" Elsa asked. "What happened to my grandmother?"

"She was murdered."

Elsa stiffened with a gasp.

"But don't worry! We'll come as soon as we can. I should go now so I can finish packing."

The room swirled around Elsa, and she sat on the bed.

"Are you there? Elsa?"

"Yes."

"Stay locked up in your room as much as possible. We'll be there soon. Love you." Greta hung up.

Elsa collapsed onto her back and stared at the

ceiling. Her grandmother had been murdered? Was that the bad thing that happened to the women with the animal paw birthmark?

She touched her shoulder. Was she marked for death?

A chill ran down her body, and she shuddered. Was she destined, like her grandmother, to be murdered? Was this why her mother had turned to alcohol? She'd been too afraid that her baby daughter was doomed?

No. Elsa shook her head. She would think about this rationally. People were murdered every day. Her grandmother was an unfortunate statistic. As terrible as that was, it had to be true, because the curse didn't make any sense. Who would kill someone over a birthmark? They would have to be crazy.

Greta had asked earlier if Howard seemed wild and crazy.

Elsa sat up. No, she wasn't going to believe it. The curse was nothing more than a self-fulfilling prophecy. You believed you would be murdered, so you confronted a guy with a weapon, and then he was forced to kill you in self-defense. That was probably what had happened to her grandmother. It was her belief in the curse that had killed her.

"I'm not going to believe it," Elsa told herself. "No matter what they say, I won't believe it."

The curse was a sick game that played with your head. It had played with her mother, and she'd lost.

Elsa stood and paced across the room. The walls closed in, making the room seem smaller and smaller.

Stay locked up in your room, Greta had said.

"No!" Elsa cried, anger welling up inside her. She would not cower in her room like a frightened animal. She would not succumb to fear. Fear had killed her mother.

"How could you do that?" Tears filled her eyes, and she tossed a pillow across the room. Her mother had died for no good reason. She'd abandoned a three-year-old child because she couldn't handle her fear.

"How could you be so damned *weak*?" she yelled, then froze with a sudden realization. She'd never admitted it to herself before, but she was angry at her mother. Furious.

Her heart pounded, and her hands trembled as she raked them through her hair.

"I'm not repeating your mistake," she whispered. "I'm going to be strong. I'm going to go on with my life and my job, and nothing is going to stop me."

She turned to look at herself in the mirror above the vanity. "There is no curse."

Chapter Eight

*H*oward was having trouble concentrating on his report at the Dragon Nest Academy. He'd risen early to familiarize himself with the grounds, stable, gymnasium, and huge mansion that housed the school and dormitories. He and Phil were the only security guards at the school now, and Howard had taken the day shift. Phil preferred staying up at night, since he was married to a vampire. Angus and Emma were already gone, having teleported to Mexico the night before to assist with the mission there.

Dougal had teleported Phil straight to the school, but Howard had asked to be teleported to the Draganesti house in White Plains, where he'd left his SUV. He'd packed up the rest of his belongings, including his stash of DVDs under the bed, and made arrangements for his furniture to be shipped to the school. Then he'd driven to the school, arriving later than expected. He'd been immediately instructed to go to the gatehouse.

And there he'd met Elsa.

Now he couldn't think of anything else. Her image kept filling his mind, her wild mane of hair, her forest green eyes, her scent so sweet and fresh like a spring rain.

Get a grip. You're acting like a silly young cub. He had a job to do. He glanced around the office, then started a list of supplies he would need. A file cabinet. The main office had files on every student and teacher, but he wanted his own copies. He also needed a secure place to store rifles and handguns. Every student over the age of fifteen should be trained in firearms so they could be called into action in case the school ever came under attack.

Ian had been in charge of security before this, and he and Angus had always assumed the school was safe as long as it was secret. In Howard's experience, the Vamps tended to be too lax in their security measures, probably because if things got too dicey, they could simply teleport away. But he was a firm believer in always being prepared for the worst-case scenario.

He made a note to check the kitchen and make sure they had a supply of water and food that would last six months if necessary. And dammit, they needed donuts. He wrote that down and underlined it three times. He'd had a rude surprise this morning when he'd discovered there were no bear claws in the kitchen.

How could a man work without donuts? He'd been forced to drive into Cranville at the crack of dawn to pick up four dozen. The donut shop had been across the street from the motel, and he'd spotted Elsa's rental car parked in front of one of the motel's sixteen rooms. Even from across the street, he could catch a hint of her scent, fresh as a forest in springtime.

It had been awfully tempting to knock on the door. He'd almost left a box of donuts on her doorstep, but a deer was close by, munching on the flowers in the pot beneath her window. The donuts might not survive.

And he might appear too desperate. He'd practically begged her last night to see him again.

With a muttered curse, he loaded the donuts into the passenger seat of his SUV, then ate two dozen of them on the drive back to the school.

It was now ten thirty in the morning—time for a coffee break. He settled at the desk, a box of donuts nearby and a cup of coffee in his hand as he checked his e-mail on his laptop. A message from Harry.

Howard, the news is hitting today. See the link.

He clicked on the link, and it took him to the online version of *Northern Lights Sound Bites*. The headline—"Rhett Bleddyn Donates Millions to Unlikely Candidates."

"Sweet." Howard bit into a donut and read the article. Rhett had to be livid. By now, he'd probably checked the disaster area that had once been his bank accounts. He'd probably also discovered more than half of the money gone from his embezzling account in the Cayman Islands.

Howard chuckled and finished his donut.

The office door cracked open and a little face peered inside.

With a smile, he stood. "Tino."

"Howard!" The little boy jumped inside, a wide grin on his face. "You're back!"

He strode over to the boy and wrapped his arms around him. "You're up early."

"I couldn't stay in bed, not when I knew you would be here in the office."

He tousled the boy's blond curls. "Want a donut?"

"Yes! I haven't had one in weeks, not since you left."

Howard feigned an appalled look. "That should be against the law." He strode over to the console and glanced back to find Tino mimicking his long-legged stride.

With a grin, he grabbed a bottle of water and some napkins and set them on the desk. "I missed you, munchkin."

"I missed you, too." Tino climbed into the chair in front of the desk, but his chin barely reached above the surface.

"Hop down a second." When Tino did, Howard stacked a few reams of paper on the chair, then deposited the boy on top of them. He grabbed a donut from the box on the desk, then placed it on a napkin.

Tino grinned. "Thanks!" He stuffed the donut in his mouth.

Howard sat behind his desk and closed his laptop. "So how have you been?"

"Bored." Tino licked his fingers. "Can I have another one?"

"One more." Howard placed another donut in front of the little boy, then helped himself to one.

"My mom was so excited last night." Tino struggled with the top to his water bottle, so Howard unscrewed it for him. "She said you got to meet your dream girl."

"Really?"

Tino nodded and drank some water. "She said it was magical."

"Really."

"It wasn't?" Tino bit into his donut.

"How did your mother know about Elsa?"

"I told her."

Howard sipped some coffee. "You told her about my secret tapes?"

"Yes."

"Do you know what secret means?"

"Yes." Tino stuffed more donut into his mouth. "It means you don't tell anybody." His eyes widened. "Oh."

"Indeed."

Tino gulped down his donut. "Are you mad at me?"

Howard smiled. "Just remember that a man should always respect another man's privacy."

Tino nodded. "Okay." He licked his fingers. "When are you going to teach me chess? You said you would."

Howard finished his donut. There wasn't much going on at the school in the morning. Most classes didn't begin until late afternoon, and then they ran into the night to accommodate the teachers who were Undead or the children who could only attend class after their Undead parents teleported them to school.

"We could play a little now," he suggested.

Tino grinned. "Great!"

Howard returned the donuts to the console and brought back the wooden box that contained his chess set. "First you need to learn how to set it up. You want to be white or black?"

"White. They're the good guys, right?"

Howard smiled as he set the board down on the desk. "When you're at war, the side you're on is always the good guys."

"Even if you're wrong?"

"Afraid so. Even the bad guys can believe they're the good guys."

"Huh?" Tino shook his head in disbelief, then reached for a white chess piece. "Sofia would like this one. It has a horse."

"That's a knight." Howard set up the black pieces on his end of the board. "The small ones are called pawns. They're your front line. They're . . . expendable."

Tino wrinkled his nose. "You mean they're not important?"

A vision of Carly's dead body flashed through Howard's mind. To Rhett, she'd only been a pawn. "They're important. All the pieces are. You don't want to lose any of them."

"Oh." Tino looked over the pieces, frowning. "But can you win without losing any of them?"

"No." He shoved Carly's image from his mind. "You take your losses like a man and press on."

"I don't think I like this," Tino mumbled, then picked up the king. "He's the most important one, right?"

"Even the king is expendable." Howard picked up his queen and ran his thumb over the top. "It's all about protecting the queen." The image of Elsa settled in his mind. Why had his touch caused her birthmark to burn? Why had it frightened her so much that she'd immediately called her aunt? "You'll do anything to keep her safe. If you lose her, then all hope is lost."

"You're worried about your dream girl."

Howard looked up, surprised. There were times when he wondered if Tino had inherited some of his mother's psychic abilities. He could be incredibly perceptive for a five-year-old.

"You should go see her," Tino suggested.

Howard finished setting up the board. "I don't think so."

"Why not?"

He shrugged. "I don't want to seem too pushy. Or desperate. I might scare her away."

Tino laughed. "You're not scary."

Howard smiled. "She doesn't know me like you do."

Tino nodded and fiddled with his chess pieces. "Oh!" He sat up suddenly. "I forgot. I have homework. For math class. It's due this afternoon."

Did he really? Howard suspected the boy was making excuses to get out of playing a game that hadn't lived up to his expectations. "Well, then you'd better get to it." He lifted Tino off the chair.

"Bye, Howard!" Tino grinned at him, then skipped out of the office.

Howard returned to his desk to finish reading the news article on his laptop.

He called Harry. "Great job."

"Thanks." Harry sounded excited. "Everything's going just as we planned. The mainstream news has latched on to the story."

"Really? That's good."

"Yeah. Rhett's in town today, and the reporters are all over him like vultures. He's denying he made the campaign contributions, but the candidates are saying he did and they can prove it. He's got a deer-in-the-headlights look, which is really funny on a wolf." Harry laughed. "I'll send you a photo."

"Good." Howard wished he could personally see Rhett having an anxiety attack, but it was better if he was far away. Out of sight, out of mind, hopefully.

"I'm running an article tomorrow on how he's harassing those bankrupt towns," Harry continued. "And I've got three more exposés after that. He'll never be able to run for office once I'm through with him."

"Great. But be careful, bro. Keep it anonymous."

"Don't worry. My editor agreed to leave off the byline." Harry paused, then his tone turned serious. "I started investigating what happened to our dads."

Howard blinked. "Why? It was a fire. A lightning storm."

"That's what we were told, but we were so young at the time, we never questioned it." Harry sighed. "I checked the records, and there was no storm that night."

Howard stiffened. If the fire had been man-made, then their fathers were murdered.

"I'll see what I can find out," Harry said. "Okay?"

Howard gritted his teeth. "Do it."

"Are you sure?" Alastair hesitated on the front porch of the gatehouse.

"I'll be fine here," Elsa insisted. "There's no point in both of us going."

"All right, luv. I shall return with a sandwich forthwith. Or whatever sustenance I can find." He headed to the rental car. "Cheerio."

"Mustard, no mayo," Elsa called out, then waved as he drove off toward Cranville.

He'd been wily enough last night to wheedle an extra key from Shanna, and they had spent the morning taking photos and documenting problems they found in each room. It was all part of their plan to show Shanna how excited and dedicated they were over the proposed renovation.

Elsa returned to her notepad in the old house's kitchen. There would be a ton of work needed there. New plumbing, new appliances, new countertops, new floor. The old cabinets were solid wood and salvageable, but she doubted there were enough of them to suit a modern owner. This was her area of expertise—woodwork. And it was the sort of challenge she loved. She could fashion new cabinets that were an exact match to the old ones.

Last night, she'd told Howard it was all about family. And it was. She could feel it most strongly here in the kitchen. How many meals had been prepared in this room? How many families had gathered around this old wooden table? Quite a few, since the gatehouse had been built in 1892. She ran a hand over the scarred table. If it was up to her, she'd make sure this old house continued to be a home for another hundred years.

She ventured into a small room next to the kitchen and halted with a wince. The boards were giving too much under her weight. She knelt for a closer look. Wood rot. The window was missing a few panes, so rain and snow had probably come inside. She noted a few huge washtubs leaning against the wall. The room may have been used as a primitive laundry room or bathroom, so there could be a history of spilled water. She exited and stuck a Post-it note on the door. *Danger. Floor about to collapse.*

She headed back toward the foyer and gasped. There was a little boy standing just inside the front door, gazing up at the cupola.

He spotted her and waved. "Hi!"

"Hello." She strode toward him. "You shouldn't come in any further. It's not entirely safe."

"Okay." He smiled. "I'm Tino."

"Pleased to meet you." He was an angelic-looking little boy with blond curls and big blue eyes. "I'm Elsa."

"I know. I came to see you."

That's odd. "That's nice." She peered out the front door but didn't see a car or anyone else. "Do you live close by?" When he nodded, she asked, "And you came here all alone?"

He lifted his chin. "I don't need a babysitter. I'm five years old."

She winced inwardly. That was much too young to be wandering about the countryside. "Where are your parents?"

"They're asleep."

She swallowed down a gulp of indignation that parents could leave such an innocent child on his own. Twinges of her own abandonment at the age of three needled her. She would take this boy home and have a few words in private with his parents. "Do you mind if I walk you home?"

Tino grinned. "That would be great."

"Just a sec." She wrote a quick note to Alastair on her notepad and left it by the front door where he would see it. Then she grabbed her handbag and ushered the boy outside.

She closed the door. "Do you know the way home?"

"That way." Tino pointed at the woods.

She winced. "You live in the forest?" *The dark, creepy forest?*

"That's just a shortcut. Come on." Tino took her hand and led her down the steps and across the driveway.

Sure enough, there was a path through the woods. She held onto the little boy's hand and gazed around. It was a bit darker, but not all that creepy. Very pretty, actually. The dimmer light seemed to make the colors brighter, not so washed out by the sun. It was cooler here, and quite pleasant to be surrounded by her favorite color, green. She took a deep breath. It even smelled good.

A noise behind her made her jump.

Tino giggled. "It's just a squirrel."

"Right." She smiled at him. There was nothing to be afraid of. She'd seen plenty of squirrels around their house in the suburbs of Minneapolis.

She glanced back. There were three squirrels now. Were they following them?

She exhaled in relief when they stepped out onto the main road. "Okay, which way?"

"Down there." Tino let go of her hand to point.

She started walking beside him. Wasn't the school Shanna had warned them about down this road? And she'd promised to never go near it. Maybe the little boy lived somewhere on the way. "How far do we go?"

Tino shrugged. "A few miles, I think."

She halted. "You walked *miles*?"

"No."

"Then how did you get here?"

He wrinkled his nose as if searching for an answer. "I'm special."

She smiled. "I'm sure you are, but that doesn't really explain how you got here."

"I'm not supposed to talk about it."

Huh? Maybe she should wait till Alastair returned with the car. She glanced back and gasped.

A small herd of deer was on the road, along with half a dozen squirrels and rabbits. They were all looking at her.

Tino laughed. "I think they like you."

Her skin prickled with gooseflesh. "I wouldn't know why."

"Maybe they want you to sing to them," he suggested. "Like Sleeping Beauty."

She snorted. "I'm more like Fiona, I'm afraid."

"But you have blond hair like Sleeping Beauty. And you're not green."

She smiled. No one had ever compared her to a willowy princess before. "I'm a bit on the large size."

"You're smaller than Howard."

Her smile faded. "You know Howard?"

"Sure. He's a really nice guy. He feeds me donuts and plays games with me. I like him a lot. You would, too, if you got to know him."

She narrowed her eyes. "Did he send you here?"

"No!" Tino hung his head. "He'll probably get mad at me for coming."

"Where is he?"

"At the school. He's head of se-secoowaty."

"Security?" Was this the school Shanna had warned her to stay away from? Was it such a dangerous place that it needed a huge man like Howard to keep the inmates in line?

"Come on." Tino motioned for her to follow. "I'll take you to the school so you can see Howard."

She followed reluctantly. "I'm not supposed to go near the school. I promised Mrs. Draganesti that—"

"My mom?"

Elsa halted. "Shanna Draganesti is your mother?"

"Sure." He kept walking.

She hurried to catch up. "Where is your mother?"

"At the school. My dad's there, too. We live there." Tino smiled at her. "Howard's there, too. He'll be really happy to see you again."

The little boy was matchmaking. Elsa shook her head. Why had Shanna said the school was full of juvenile delinquents? "I—I thought the school was for troubled children."

Tino's eyes widened. "Troubled?"

"Yes."

"We're not troubled. We're special."

"Special how?"

He frowned. "I'm not supposed to talk about it."

This was getting more and more strange, but it was all part of the puzzle she'd sensed the night before, a puzzle she wanted the answers to. She glanced back. The animals were still there, following them at a distance. "I thought your mother said she worked during the day. Your father, too."

"Oh." Tino nodded. "Yeah, that's right."

Earlier he'd said they were sleeping. "What do your parents do?"

"Mom is a dentist, and my dad is a scientist." Tino smiled proudly. "Mom says he's a genius. He invented syn-syn . . . fake blood."

"Synthetic blood?"

"That's it." He nodded, smiling. "He cloned it from real blood. And he made me and Sofia, too."

"Sofia?"

"My little sister. She's special, too."

"And you all live at this school?" That Shanna wanted to keep secret? A secret school in the middle of nowhere with a brilliant scientist who made *special* children? It sounded like something out of a sci-fi movie. "Are there any other special children?"

Tino nodded. "My aunt Caitlyn just had two. Twins. And Toni and Olivia will have their babies soon."

Elsa's skin chilled. "And do all these women live at the school?"

"Yes. Marielle's going to have a baby, too, but she didn't need a turkey baster like the other ladies."

"*What*?" Elsa stumbled, then kept walking.

"That's what Connor said. He said he was able to do it the old-fashioned way, but that made Toni and Olivia mad." Tino shrugged. "I don't know why. I like turkey."

"Where is this Connor?"

"He's on a secret mission."

Elsa took a deep breath. Good Lord, this was starting to sound like an X-Men school for children. "And when you say that you're special, do you mean you have special talents or skills that normal children don't have?"

Tino wrinkled his nose, then nodded.

She gulped and came to a stop. What on earth was she getting into? "I don't think I should go to the school. Your mother told me not to." And her aunt had warned her to stay away from the man who'd made her birthmark burn. She turned but found the road blocked with animals. All looking at her.

She dragged a hand through her hair. *Damn*.

"Oh, look! Raccoons." Tino moved toward them.

She grabbed him. "Don't. They might carry disease. Rabies or something."

Tino looked up at her, his eyes wide. "You're trying to protect me?"

"Yes, of course."

He smiled. "I know why Howard likes you so much. You're just like him. He keeps me safe, too."

"Does he?" He'd mentioned last night that he kept people safe, but could he really be trusted, when he was the one who'd made her birthmark burn?

"Howard's been keeping me safe all my life," Tino said. "He's a really nice guy."

"Is he . . . special like you?"

Tino scratched his head. "Well, sorta."

The animals suddenly scattered.

"What happened?" Elsa's blood ran cold when a half dozen feral pigs ran onto the road, their hooves clattering, their eyes glued on her.

She gulped and pulled Tino behind her.

"They look mean," he whispered.

They sure did, with their sharp tusks pointed right at her. She clenched her fists to keep from trembling. What to do? She could call on her cell phone, but it could take a long time for help to come. Visions of the little boy getting gored with a tusk flitted through her mind.

"I'll distract them," she whispered. "You run for home as fast as you can."

"No." Tino wrapped his little arms around her. "They'll hurt you. I won't let them hurt you."

"There's nothing you can do—" She gasped when everything went black.

Chapter Nine

*H*oward was in the security office wondering if he should drive into Cranville and accidentally bump into Elsa. Would she suspect it wasn't accidental? Did it really matter, as long as he saw her again?

Somehow he needed to gain her trust. Once her fear was gone, her desire could take over. And then she would be his.

He grabbed another donut, when something on one of the four surveillance monitors caught his eye. Tino, materializing in front of the school with . . . Elsa?

"Holy crap!" He dropped the donut on the desk and ran for the front door.

Dammit, he should have checked to make sure Tino had returned to his room. What was the boy thinking, showing off his skills like that? And Tino had no way of knowing he could successfully teleport another person. It was something the adult Vamps did, but they had years of experience. Centuries of experience. Tino had not only committed a serious security breach but he'd also put Elsa's life in danger.

Howard wrenched open the front door and spotted her collapsed on the ground. "Elsa!" He charged down the steps and skidded to a stop beside her. "Are you all right?"

She blinked up at him, a dazed look on her face.

He scowled at Tino, who knelt on the other side of her. "What have you done? You know you're not—" He stopped when he noticed the tears in Tino's eyes and the trembling of his little chin. "Are you all right? What happened?"

"I don't know," Elsa whispered, "but I think he saved our lives."

Alarmed, Howard looked at her pale face and then the tear rolling down Tino's cheek. "Don't worry. You're safe now." He patted the boy on the shoulder. "Can you walk, big guy?"

"Yes." Tino rose to his feet, wiping his face.

"Good man." Howard slipped his arms under Elsa and straightened, cradling her against his chest.

She gasped.

He froze. "Are you hurt?"

"No. I—I'm too heavy to carry."

He scoffed. She'd scared him for nothing. "Do you weigh over five hundred pounds?"

She huffed. "Of course not!"

"Then you're not heavy." He jogged up the steps to the front door, then glanced at Tino. "Can you get the door, big guy?"

Tino smiled, apparently liking his new nickname. "Sure." He pulled open the door and followed them inside.

Elsa gave Howard a sour look as he carried her

down the hall. "I weigh less than *two* hundred," she grumbled.

His mouth twitched. She felt solid and strong, but soft and womanly at the same time. And her scent was driving him wild. "I think you're perfect."

Her face flushed a pretty pink. "Where are you taking me?"

"To the clinic to check for injuries."

"I'm fine, really. I was just a little dizzy when—" She gave Tino a worried look. "I need to know what happened."

"So do I." Howard stopped in front of the clinic. According to the hours posted on the door, the nurse was on lunch break now. That was lucky. Tino was guilty of a serious security breach, and Howard wanted to keep the matter as private as possible.

The door was unlocked, so Tino was able to open it. Howard looked around as he carried Elsa inside. There was a row of five beds, then an office in the back with a window. He peered through the window and spotted medical equipment and a locked medicine cabinet.

"Are you going to put me down?" Elsa asked softly.

"Do I have to?" His gaze locked with hers. Her eyes searched his, reflecting the confusion she had to be feeling. He leaned closer, studying her. Yes, he smiled. The desire was still there.

She looked away, her cheeks pink.

He set her carefully on a bed. "Do I need to check you for injuries?"

"No." She glanced at him, then mumbled, "Unfortunately."

Stifling a grin, he sat on the bed next to hers. "So tell me what happened."

"I think you should tell me. How did I magically appear in front of the school?"

"Start at the beginning," Howard said. "What were you doing with Tino?"

She sat up with an impatient huff. "I was walking him home from the gatehouse."

He turned to Tino, who was standing between the two beds, looking guilty. "You went to the gatehouse? Alone?"

He ducked his head. "You wouldn't go see her, so I thought I should bring her here."

Howard sighed. More matchmaking. "You are definitely your mother's son, aren't you?"

Tino considered that solemnly, then nodded. "Yes." He shifted his weight. "I wanted to do like you and come up with a stragedy."

"Strategy?"

Tino nodded. "And everything was going just like I planned. Except for the animals. There was a bunch of them following us."

"On the road?" Howard asked. Woodland creatures might cross a road, but they rarely traveled down it en masse. He turned to Elsa. "What kind of animals? How many?"

She shrugged with an exasperated look. "Deer, rabbits, squirrels, a few raccoons. Maybe thirty in all."

"But then they all ran into the woods." Tino

waved his arms dramatically. "And these huge pigs came out with big tusks like elephants!"

"Feral pigs?" Howard sat up. "How many?"

"About a hundred!" Tino exclaimed.

"About half a dozen," Elsa said quietly.

Howard jumped to his feet and strode to the door. Ever since his trip to Alaska, he and his inner bear had been eager to let loose a can of whoop-ass. "I'll take care of them."

"What?" Elsa stumbled out of bed. "But I need some answers. How did I get here?"

"Hmm." He paused at the door. "The age-old question: how did we get here? There are several theories—"

"I'm serious!" She swatted his arm, but he only smiled in return.

"We'll talk when I get back." He stepped into the hallway.

She grabbed his arm. "You're not going after the pigs, are you? They're dangerous!"

"I don't want them close to the school. We have some young children here." He glanced at Tino. "Why don't you take Elsa to the cafeteria for lunch?"

Tino nodded, smiling. "Okay."

Howard smiled back. The little boy had probably saved their lives. Amazing that at his young age, he'd managed to teleport another person. He tousled Tino's curls. "You did great, big guy."

Tino beamed with a wide grin.

He turned to Elsa, who was watching him with worry in her eyes. "Will you wait for me?"

She gave him an exasperated look. "I need some answers."

"I understand." Although he had no idea how he was going to explain. It would be difficult for sure. Taking care of the feral pigs seemed easy in comparison.

"Wait for me." He ran toward the front door.

Elsa barely tasted her grilled cheese sandwich. She'd called Alastair to let him know she'd be late returning. He'd wanted to know what was going on, and she hadn't known what to tell him. It was all too bizarre.

Tino sat beside her, obviously enjoying his meal. He looked like such a normal little boy, but . . . he wasn't. He'd grabbed her around the waist, and a second later, they'd appeared in front of the school.

She should be completely freaked out over Tino, but she wasn't. Not when she was so worried about Howard's safety. He'd run outside without any weapons. How could he handle a bunch of feral pigs without a weapon?

She dropped her paper napkin onto her plate, giving up on the pretense of eating. "When do you think Howard will be back?"

"I don't know." Tino offered her a chocolate chip cookie. "You want one?"

She shook her head, and he wolfed it down. "I want to thank you for rescuing me from the pigs."

He nodded and reached for another cookie. "They were big and scary!"

"Yes. What you did to get us here, it was one of your special skills?"

He dunked a cookie into his glass of milk. "I guess so."

"You're not supposed to talk about it?"

He shook his head. "And I'm not supposed to do it in front of strangers." He stuffed a dripping cookie into his mouth.

"Tino." She rubbed him on the back. "I won't tell anyone. Ever. You saved my life."

He smiled, and a drizzle of milk ran down his chin. "I had to. You're Howard's dream girl."

"Really?" Was that what he called her? She rose to her feet, struggling against a growing sense of panic. What was he doing outside with those pigs? "I—I think I'll wait for him by the door."

"I'll go with you." Tino grabbed another cookie off the plate and followed her into the hallway. "You like Howard, don't you?"

Was it so obvious a child could see it? "I'm just worried about him." She headed toward the large foyer. It was spectacular with its marble floor, large staircase, and ceiling three floors high. Alastair would be jealous that she'd seen it without him.

"Hello?" a woman called as she slowly descended the staircase with another woman.

"Hi, Toni! Hi, Olivia!" Tino called out to them. "This is Elsa. She's Howard's dream girl."

Elsa winced. "That's a bit of an exaggeration. I hardly know him. I just met him last night."

The women exchanged looks, smiling.

"I'm Toni," the blond woman said.

"And I'm Olivia," the brunette said. "We're so happy to meet you."

They were both absolutely beautiful and very

pregnant. Elsa's gaze drifted to their swollen bellies. Were they having *special* children like Tino? Children who could travel a distance in the blink of an eye?

"Howard's outside beating up a bunch of giant pigs!" Tino announced. "And they have huge tusks like this!" He swept his hands forward as far as he could.

"Feral pigs?" Toni asked as she reached the ground floor.

"A half dozen of them." Frowning, Elsa glanced out the narrow window beside the front door. "Howard went out alone about thirty minutes ago."

"I'm sure he'll be all right," Olivia assured her. "He's very capable."

What did that mean? Did he have special skills like Tino? He was certainly having a special effect on her. His smile, his voice, his beautiful blue eyes—they all made her heart stutter and her knees threaten to give out.

She opened the front door and stepped onto the porch, her gaze searching the woods.

"Don't worry." Tino joined her and bit into his cookie. "Howard is really big and tough."

"He'll be fine." Toni waddled onto the porch with Olivia.

Elsa glanced at them. "I don't mean to pry, but are you teachers here?"

Toni shook her head. "I'm the director. And Olivia's the counselor. Our husbands are away right now on business."

Or a secret mission, Elsa thought.

Olivia looked up at the sky, shielding her eyes with her hand. "It's a beautiful day."

A loud roar filled the air, and Elsa jumped. "What was that?"

The pregnant ladies exchanged a look and smiled.

"I think that was the sound of victory," Olivia said.

"I think we'll be having ham for supper," Toni added, and they both chuckled.

A chill ran down Elsa's back. "You . . . you think Howard killed them?"

Toni gave her a wry look. "I don't think they sat around a campfire singing 'Kumbaya.' "

"Shh." Olivia nudged the other pregnant woman.

"But he didn't have any weapons on him," Elsa insisted. "He went out bare-handed."

Toni slapped a hand over her mouth to stifle a laugh. "Bear-handed."

Olivia's mouth twitched. "Behave." She pulled Toni back into the house. "We have work to do. Don't worry. Howard will be back soon." She closed the door.

"Oh, I get it." Tino grinned.

Elsa frowned at him. "Get what?"

His eyes widened. "Nothing." He stuffed the rest of his cookie in his mouth.

With a huff, she crossed her arms. She hated feeling like everyone was in on a joke but her. And what could possibly be funny about Howard facing down a herd of feral pigs? It was downright dangerous.

She studied the woods. What was that roar she'd heard? Why was everyone so bloody sure that Howard would be all right? Her heart lurched when she spotted him running toward them.

She hurried down the steps. "Are you okay?"

"I'm fine." He stopped beside her and smiled.

Her heart fluttered, and she drank in the sight of him. His thick brown hair was messy, and some strands clung to his damp forehead. His face and arms glistened with sweat, but his clothes were still clean and crisp. Shouldn't they be dirty? Ripped or bloody?

Dammit, the more stuff happened, the more she was confused.

"I need to shower." He sprinted up the stairs. "I'll be right back."

She ran after him. "But we need to talk."

He glanced over his shoulder and grinned. She halted. Damn him. With just a smile, he made her heart pound.

"You can have me for the rest of the day." He jogged down the hallway.

She watched him go. So large, so strong, yet so light and quick on his feet. Had he really killed some feral pigs with his bare hands? Tino seemed to think he had. But wouldn't his clothes be ripped and bloody? Besides, who did something that crazy? That violent? And then smiled afterward?

Did he seem wild or crazy to you? Aunt Greta's words came back to haunt her.

She swallowed hard. Maybe it shouldn't matter that he was incredibly handsome. Or that she was wildly attracted to him. The real question was: could she trust him? A man who worked at a mysterious, secret school of special children? The man who had made her birthmark burn?

Chapter Ten

*H*oward opened the passenger door of his SUV for Elsa. "Hop in."

She regarded his vehicle and then him with a wary look. "You're not going to magically zap me back, like Tino? Or fly me there like Superman?"

He smiled. "I usually drive."

She hesitated.

His smile faded. He was doing a lousy job of earning her trust. "Are you afraid to hang out with me?"

"Of course not." She climbed into the passenger seat.

Liar. He closed the door and circled to the driver's side. He couldn't blame her for being cautious, but he hated the thought that she would fear him.

Luckily, she hadn't seen the blood on him after battling the pigs. He'd undressed in the woods before shifting, and even though he'd incurred a few cuts and scrapes, those had healed when he'd shifted back to human form. He'd put his clothes back on before leaving the woods and finding Elsa on the front porch.

She seemed suspicious now. And annoyed. He'd

showered and dressed as quickly as possible, but she'd been forced to wait on him. And wait on the answers she wanted so badly.

He shoved his damp hair off his forehead. The truth was the pigs could have waited. He had deliberately delayed his talk with her. Killing a few pigs was easy, but answering her questions would be damned hard. It was his job to protect the Vamps and their secrets. If he did his job well, he'd tell her nothing. But then he would never gain her trust. He would lose her.

What a mess. He'd desperately tried to come up with a strategy while in the shower. His decision: play offense instead of defense.

He climbed into the driver's seat and started the engine. "Where to? The gatehouse or Cranville?"

She buckled her seat belt. "The gatehouse. I called Alastair, and he's waiting for me there."

"All right." Howard headed down the driveway to the main road.

She shifted in her seat to face him. "Are you going to answer my questions now?"

"Will you answer mine?"

Her eyes widened with surprise. "What do you mean? I'm not involved in anything weird."

"No? Why did your shoulder burn when I touched you?"

"I—I don't know."

"It was your birthmark that burned, right?"

She stiffened. "How did you know that?"

"I heard you talking on the phone."

"I was inside a car. How did you hear me?"

He turned onto the main road. "I have super good hearing."

"Do you have other superpowers? Is that how you . . . vanquished the pigs?"

Vanquished? His mouth twitched. "Yes, my lady. I vanquished the mighty foe in yonder forest."

She glowered at him. "Don't mock me. I'm having trouble dealing with the fact that you apparently *killed* some poor defenseless animals with your bare hands. I have no idea how—"

"Defenseless?" He shot her an incredulous look. "They had huge tusks! And they outnumbered me." Damn, he had thought she would be impressed. "It wasn't easy, you know."

"Then you admit it? You actually killed them?"

He shrugged. "It's part of my job."

She shuddered. "I hate violence."

"Well, if it helps—I asked them politely to leave, but they declined."

"Then you killed them with sarcasm?"

He laughed, then stopped midlaugh when she continued to glare at him. "It had to be done, Elsa. I couldn't let them roam about the school, not when little ones like Tino like to play outdoors."

"I understand, but . . . how could you go out there without any weapons? That was crazy!"

"I—I had a knife strapped to my leg." He winced. Damn, he hated to lie to her. But she'd probably freak if he told her the truth. *I ripped them to shreds and bloody well enjoyed it.*

He'd been frustrated the entire time he'd been in Alaska. For over a month, he'd had to score points against Rhett in secret, when he'd really wanted to confront him in person and bash his face in. But he couldn't afford an open war with the werewolves, not when his family and friends could end up massacred. The result had left him and his inner bear both itching for a fight.

Battling pigs was a lot easier than dealing with one fussy, beautiful woman.

"You should have taken a rifle, at least." She rubbed her brow, frowning. "Or a bazooka. A missile launcher would have been good. I can't believe you would do something so dangerous. I was worried sick."

His heart lifted. "You were worried about me?"

"I . . . of course." She lowered her hand to her lap. "I would worry about anyone in a situation like that."

His heart sank. "Of course." He glanced in the rearview mirror and did a double take. There were a dozen deer following them.

She eyed him suspiciously. "If you killed them with just a knife, you must be super strong and fast."

"You could say that." Damn, she'd taken over the offense. He was playing defense again.

"And you have super hearing." Her eyes narrowed. "What other superpowers do you have?"

"Super smell and vision."

She gasped and crossed her arms over her chest. "X-ray vision?"

He turned to ogle her breasts with great enthusiasm. "I wish."

"Watch where you're driving," she grumbled. "Can you do that thing that Tino did?"

Howard groaned inwardly. How could he avoid telling her the truth? "I have to beg you not to tell anyone about him. He's a sweet kid, and he deserves a normal life—"

"Don't worry. I already told him I wouldn't say anything. As far as I can tell, he saved my life. And besides that, I really like him."

With a smile, Howard nodded. "He's a great kid, isn't he?"

"He certainly likes you. He kept telling me what a wonderful guy you are."

"He's absolutely correct."

She scoffed. "So are you going to tell me what happened?"

Howard took a deep breath. "All right. I'll stop procrastinating."

"Thank you."

He glanced at her, wondering how she was going to handle the truth. "Tino teleported you."

Her mouth dropped open. "You mean like 'Beam me up, Scottie' teleportation? He can do that?"

"I doubt he can do it into outer space, but yeah, he can teleport."

"He's a child who can teleport?"

"That's what I said. He started doing it when he was a toddler. Really freaked his mom out the first time."

Elsa grimaced. "How can he do it?"

"His DNA is a little different."

Her eyes widened. "Because of his father, the mad scientist?"

"Roman isn't mad." Howard winced. "How did you hear about him?"

"Tino told me. He said Shanna was his mom, and his father was a scientific genius."

"They're good people—"

"Who experimented on their children?" Elsa asked with an appalled look.

"It's not like that. They love their children. And you talked to Tino. You saw how normal he is."

"There's nothing normal about teleportation." She shook her head. "It's hard to believe. If it hadn't happened to me, I don't think I could believe it."

"He saved your life."

"I know. It's amazing."

"What's really amazing is that he managed to teleport a hundred and seventy pounds with him. Usually only an adult can—" He stopped when he realized she was glaring at him.

"A hundred and sixty," she ground out.

His mouth twitched. "Are you sure about that?"

She swatted his shoulder.

"I was kidding. You couldn't be an ounce over a hundred and sixty." *My ass.* He turned into the driveway for the gatehouse.

She crossed her arms. "So why didn't you just teleport me back here?"

He glanced at the rearview mirror. Damn, the deer were still following them. "I don't teleport."

She sat back, regarding him with a shocked expression. "You can't do something a five-year-old can do?"

His eyes narrowed. Time to take the offense again. "I have a different set of skills."

"Such as?"

He pulled the SUV over, shifted into park, then leaned toward her. "I can touch beautiful women and make them burn."

Her mouth fell open.

He leaned closer. "Does any other man make you burn?"

Her mouth snapped shut, and she looked away, her face flushing.

"I'm the only one, aren't I? Your face is burning now, and I haven't even touched you. Yet."

She gulped. "I don't know why it happened."

"We could speculate." He touched her cheek and felt the heat of her blush, the soft pliancy of her skin. He traced the line of her jaw, then gently cupped her chin. "It could be instant attraction."

Her mouth parted slightly.

"Or desire." He ran his thumb over her lower lip.

She drew in a shaky breath.

He lifted his gaze to her forest-green eyes. "Or it could be something even stronger, a feeling that we were destined to meet, destined to be together."

Her eyes searched his. "Do you really believe that?"

"From the first moment I saw you on television, I was drawn to you. I felt attached to you." When her eyes widened, a sudden thought popped into his mind. What if he sounded like a crazed fan? She'd already accused him before of being crazy.

He lowered his hand and sat back. "You probably get fan mail like that all the time."

"Not really." Still blushing, she fumbled to open the passenger door. "I should get back to work."

Howard climbed out. "I'll walk you back."

"It's not necessary." She hurried toward the house and waved as Alastair peered out the front door.

"Have dinner with me tonight," Howard blurted out. When she glanced back with a wary look, he quickly added, "Alastair, too. We can celebrate you guys signing the contract."

Alastair rushed down the stairs. "Did Shanna agree?"

"I don't know for sure," Howard confessed. "But the Shanna I know has always been able to convince her husband to do what she wants."

"Excellent!" Alastair grinned at Elsa. "We shall be delighted to dine with you tonight. Right, luv?"

She shot Howard an annoyed look.

Damn. His offensive play may have been too . . . offensive. He'd have to try a different strategy tonight. "See you later."

Elsa was relieved when Alastair launched into another of his long, amusing anecdotes. Howard seemed to be enjoying the stories, but she hadn't said two words over dinner, and that was the way she wanted it.

She was going to remain calm and aloof. Even though she wasn't. She wouldn't let Howard suspect she was attracted to him. Even though she was. Because it was ridiculous to be this attracted to a man she'd just met the night before. The man who had activated the curse. Even though she didn't believe in such nonsense.

Of course, after this afternoon, she might have to adjust her definition of nonsense. Last night, she would have considered a five-year-old boy who could teleport a bunch of nonsense. What was going on at that secret school? What other secrets was Howard hiding? He had admitted he couldn't teleport, but she had no doubt he possessed other powers.

I can touch beautiful women and make them burn.

Just thinking about the way he'd stroked her cheek made her face flame with heat. For a second, she'd thought he was going to kiss her, and God help her, she wouldn't have resisted.

But she was resisting now. She'd made a point of not dressing up for dinner. She was still wearing her jeans and T-shirt. Her hair was pinned to the back of her head with a plastic claw.

She forced her gaze to wander around the small restaurant, anything to keep from looking at him. He had dressed nicely. Khaki trousers and a crisp dress shirt. No tie. Not that she was noticing. He was sitting across from her, politely paying attention to Alastair's stories.

Why did the words that described him the best start with *H*? Handsome Howard. Humongous Howard. Hunky Howard. She stole a glance at him. *Hungry Howard*. He was eating the biggest steak she'd ever seen.

She'd ordered a salad with grilled chicken, since the scales had started inching up toward one seventy. She glanced at him again. *Horrible Howard*. How had he guessed her weight so well?

She stabbed some lettuce onto her fork while Alastair described the problem of getting rid of bats in an attic.

"That was the house in Amsterdam?" Howard asked.

"Yes!" Alastair grinned. "You saw that episode?"

Howard nodded, glancing at Elsa. "I've seen them all."

"Brilliant," Alastair continued. "Of course, I couldn't decide which had more bats in the belfry: the house or the owner." He chuckled at his own joke.

She smiled along. Alastair was so wrapped up in his storytelling that he didn't seem to notice that Howard kept sneaking glances at her with his beautiful blue eyes. Unfortunately, she knew that because she was sneaking glances at him, and sometimes their glances would collide.

And then heat would rush to her face and she'd find her salad completely engrossing for about five minutes. *He-Man Howard.* Even when she avoided looking at him, she could feel his presence as if he were the only one in the room. His deep voice rumbled right through her, as if her ears were especially attuned to him.

She could smell him, too, and that seemed odd. He wasn't wearing cologne, like Alastair. And yet his scent filled her senses. A totally He-Man scent that made her feel warm and tingly all over. She wanted to drown herself in him, wrap him around her like a cocoon.

There was only one explanation for this. She was losing her mind.

That had to be it, for there was no way she was going to lose her heart.

Come to think of it, there was adequate proof
that she was losing her mind. Just that afternoon,
a young boy had teleported her. And somehow,
she was taking that in stride. It was the man
across the table who had her on edge.

She was definitely losing her mind.

His cell phone jangled, and he retrieved it from
his pocket. "It's Shanna."

Alastair sat up. "Good news, I hope."

"Hello?" Howard listened, then grinned.

Happy Howard. Elsa's heart fluttered. The man
had the most adorable smile, and he used it often.
Like a weapon.

"Hang on a sec." He lowered the phone to his
chest. "She's agreed to let you do the house."

"Excellent!" With a grin, Alastair turned to Elsa
and gave her a high five.

Her heart pounded. This meant she would see
Howard often over the next few months. She stole
another glance at him. *Handsome, hunky Howard.*

"She would like to sign the contracts tonight,"
he continued.

"Not a problem." Alastair tapped his fingers
on the brown envelope on the table. "I have them
right here. How soon can she get here?"

"In a minute or so." Howard stood, still holding
the phone.

"She's driving here now?" Alastair asked.

"I'll meet her outside and bring her in." Howard
strode toward the entrance and brought the phone
back up to his face. "Hang on a minute."

Elsa watched him exit, then looked at the windows along the front of the restaurant. It was dark outside, the nearest streetlamp a block down the town's main street.

"I'm so excited about this project!" Alastair exclaimed.

"Me, too." She smiled at him, then stiffened when Howard walked back into the restaurant with Shanna by his side. "She's here."

"Blimey, that was fast." Alastair jumped to his feet to greet her.

Really fast. Elsa glanced out the window. She hadn't seen any headlights from a car parking out front. Her breath caught with a sudden thought. Had Shanna teleported to the restaurant? If her son could teleport, maybe she could, too.

Elsa's heart raced as Shanna greeted them. The woman seemed normal, although she was a bit pale, and her handshake a bit cold.

Alastair motioned to the table. "Would you like to join us for some wine or dessert to celebrate?"

"That's very kind." Shanna smiled at him. "But I already ate with my family."

At the secret school? Elsa wondered. She refrained from mentioning Tino. "We're very excited about renovating your house. And we'll be very mindful about protecting your privacy."

"Thank you. My husband is still concerned about that, but I convinced him that you'll respect our privacy." Shanna grinned. "I'm so excited about this!"

What pointy teeth she had. Elsa glanced at Howard. What other secrets were these people hiding? Or was she just becoming paranoid? After Tino's teleportation stunt, she might be looking for weird stuff where none existed.

Alastair removed the contract from the envelope. "It will take about ten minutes to go through this. And then, if you don't mind, I'd like to ask you some questions regarding the house. How open do you want the floor plan? Should we put in more bathrooms and closet space? Things of that nature. It will be our goal to match our work to your expectations."

"I understand." Shanna turned to Howard. "There's no need for you to sit through all this. Why don't you take Elsa for—"

"I disagree," he interrupted. "If I'm going to represent you, I need to know what you want."

"I'll send you a memo." She gave him a pointed look. "You should take Elsa for a walk around town. The park is lovely." She smiled at Elsa. "There's a creek running through it and some falls. You'll love it."

"Shanna," Howard muttered, giving her an annoyed look.

"I'm just trying to be friendly," she whispered, her eyes wide and innocent.

He shifted his weight and dragged a hand through his thick hair.

Hesitant Howard. Elsa smiled to herself. *Helpless Howard.* The huge guy could annihilate a half dozen feral pigs, but he couldn't handle one matchmaking woman. It was too cute. "I'd be happy to take a walk with you."

He blinked. "You would?"

"Sure. Why not?" She hitched her handbag over her shoulder.

"Wonderful!" Shanna beamed at them both. "Off you go."

Elsa glanced at him as he moved toward her, and her heart stilled. The hesitant look on his face was gone, replaced by an intense, determined glint in his blue eyes.

She swallowed hard. Howard wasn't helpless. He was . . . hungry. Hungry for her.

"Let's go." He touched her elbow.

Her chest filled with warmth, but instead of rushing to her face like it usually did, it slipped into her belly, intensifying into a ball of fire that sizzled between her legs.

She dragged in a shaky breath. Oh God, she shouldn't have agreed to be alone with him. Howard was so much more than handsome and hunky and huge.

Howard was *hot*.

Chapter Eleven

*H*oward was struggling with his new strategy. To keep from frightening Elsa, he had decided to act calm and aloof. And to gain her trust, he'd decided to be honest and sincere. He'd managed fairly well in the restaurant, even though it had been difficult every time he'd caught her looking at him. The bear inside him interpreted all her glances as an invitation to mate.

Real subtle, he thought wryly, but what could he expect from a beast? That was the problem with this new strategy. He could only be honest and sincere about his human half. The bear would frighten any sensible woman away. But was it fair to hide the beast from a woman he was interested in?

He glanced at Elsa, who walked beside him on the sidewalk. She was the first woman since Carly who tempted him to reveal his secret. And that could only mean one thing: she was the one he wanted. Not for a short term, but for the long haul.

The bear inside him growled in anticipation. He took a deep breath to calm himself, but her scent filled his nostrils. Holy crap. He wanted to drag her into the woods, rip her clothes off, and make wild, passionate—

"Tell me the truth." She leaned close to him. "Shanna teleported, didn't she?"

He blinked. Damn, he was ravishing her in his mind, and she wasn't even thinking about him. "We shouldn't discuss that in public." He glanced around to see if anyone might have overheard.

"We could go into the woods."

His inner bear growled, but then he realized she was motioning to the park. It appeared empty, but still, it was right on the edge of town and not nearly private enough for wild, passionate—

"Come on, tell me." She nudged him as they reached the opening in the white picket fence.

A lone lamppost cast a pool of light onto the park entrance and illuminated Elsa's pretty face as she looked up at him. Damn, but he wanted to kiss her.

"Shanna teleported, right?" she asked again.

"Yes."

"I knew it!" She punched the air with her fist.

He lifted his brows. "That makes you happy?"

With a shrug, she smiled. "I like solving puzzles. I could feel it last night, that there was a puzzle." Her smile faded. "Unfortunately, the answers are turning out to be really strange."

He led her into the park. "You . . . you haven't called the police or the FBI, have you?"

"You mean the X-Files?" She gave him a wry look. "No, I promised Tino I wouldn't say anything."

"Good. Thank you."

She stopped suddenly. "There's nothing evil or nefarious going on at the school, is there?" She made a face. "Of course, you wouldn't tell me if there was."

"Relax." He touched her arm. "It's a real school with real teachers. It just has a few students like Tino who wouldn't fit into a normal school. They wouldn't be free to be themselves, and they'd always have to worry about their secrets being discovered. We're trying to give them a normal, happy life."

She studied him, as if trying to decide whether or not to believe him.

"If you like, I could give you a tour and let you meet some of the students."

She bit her lip. "I'll think about it. How many students are there?"

"About twenty-two."

"Are they all special?"

He smiled. "Some have gifts, some don't, but they're all special."

She returned his smile. "You like children, don't you? I guess you can't be too bad after all."

"Gee, thanks."

She turned to walk farther into the park. "So it's your job to keep the kids safe?"

"Yes." He strolled beside her. The narrow path of hardened earth was flanked on each side with full-grown maple trees. Moonlight filtered through the green canopy of leaves, dappling the ground with little dots of light.

She slowed to a stop. "It's pretty here."

"Yes." He turned to face her. "Very pretty."

She blushed.

He tilted his head, studying her. "You seem to be okay with the teleportation issue. It would freak most people out."

"I suppose so." She gazed up at the tree branches. "But I'm not a stranger to weirdness. I spent the first seven years of my life with my great-aunt Ula on an island in Sweden, and she talked to seals and whales every day."

His chest tightened. Her aunt talked to the creatures of the sea? He ran a hand through his hair. It sounded too much like his grandfather's tale about the guardians. But it had to be an odd coincidence.

Elsa slanted him an apologetic look. "Now you're probably thinking my aunt is crazy. But she's really sweet. She took care of me when my mother was . . . indisposed. And then when my mom died, she was there for me."

"I'm sorry." Howard touched her arm. "How old were you when you lost your mother?"

"Three."

He nodded. "I was four when my father died."

She inhaled sharply. "I'm sorry."

"It's all right." He slid his hand up her arm to the short sleeve of her T-shirt. "My mother and grandfather raised me."

"Where?"

His hand reached her shoulder. "The Bear Claw Islands off the Alaskan peninsula. I grew up on the big one, called The Paw—"

She gasped and jumped back.

"What's wrong? Did I make your birthmark burn again?"

"No." She touched her shoulder. "I-it's all right. It's nothing." She strode down the path.

He watched her, frowning. Something had given her a shock, but what?

With another gasp, she halted at the edge of the grove of trees.

"What's wrong?" He moved forward so he could see the clearing ahead. It was full of deer, rabbits, raccoons, and squirrels.

"What the—" She shoved back a tendril of hair that had escaped the plastic claw on the back of her head. "What is the deal with all these animals?"

Howard stayed behind her to mask his scent. "Is this what happened earlier when you were on the road with Tino?"

"Yes." She glanced back at him. "It's . . . kinda weird, isn't it?"

"A bit. The different species don't usually gather together unless they all want to drink from a common watering hole." And they didn't usually approach a human and stare at him. "Do you recall anything like this happening to you before?"

"Not that I can remember, but I've never spent much time in the country. We usually work in cities, and I grew up in the suburbs. Uncle Peder kept his hunting dogs in the backyard, so—" She halted, her face going pale.

"What?"

"I went hunting once with Uncle Peder and his cousin, Tom. Every fall, they would go to his cabin in the woods, and I felt left out, so I asked to go with them. The deer would come right up to the cabin, and then the guys would shoot them. I was so . . . appalled, I never wanted to go back."

"You think the deer were drawn to you?"

"I didn't think so at the time, but now I have to wonder. Uncle Peder called me his good luck charm." She shuddered. "Those poor deer."

He squeezed her shoulders. "It's not your fault. Let me see if I can chase these away." He strode into the clearing and waved an arm. "Shoo!"

The animals caught the scent of were-bear and scattered.

"That was fast." She ventured into the clearing.

"I guess I'm big and scary."

She shook her head and whispered, "Huge and handsome."

That was good news. He smiled and held out a hand to her. "How about we find the falls Shanna talked about?"

She hesitated a moment, then placed her hand in his. "All right."

He led her to the left. "I can hear the water over there."

"With your super hearing?"

He glanced at her. "You don't hear it?"

"No. And I can barely see."

"The clouds are covering the moon right now. But don't worry. I won't let you fall." He pointed to her left. "Big rock there."

She eased closer to him.

After they had walked for a little while, the moon broke free from the clouds and shone down brightly. The grass around them glittered silver with dew. Ahead of them, the creek sparkled.

"It's so pretty," she whispered.

"Yes." It was a beautiful spot, a perfect spot for their first kiss. He inched closer.

"But where is the waterfall?" She released his hand and strode upstream.

Damn. He followed her around the bend. The sound of the falls grew louder. "Be careful."

"Look!" She pointed and glanced back at him, grinning. "I found it."

He smiled back. As far as waterfalls went, it was on the puny side, only about four feet high. But if she liked this, she'd love Alaska.

"There's a bench." She sat and gazed at the falls. "What a lovely spot."

"Yes." This would be even better for their first kiss. He sat on the bench beside her.

"The sound of the water is so relaxing, don't you think?" She tilted her head back. "And look at all the stars. You never see them like this in the city."

"No." He slipped an arm along the back of the bench. "You should see the northern lights in Alaska. Though I guess you might have seen them when you lived in Sweden."

"I don't remember. It's been twenty years since I lived there."

And he'd been banished for twenty years. It was an odd thing to have in common. "You never wanted to go back?"

She sighed. "For years I begged to go back. Unfortunately, my aunts didn't think it was safe for me there."

"Why?"

She shrugged. "If I tell you, it'll just sound bizarre."

"More bizarre than teleportation?"

"That was major bizarro, but it was real. The stuff my aunts believe is nonsense." She rubbed her shoulder, frowning. "Or I thought it was nonsense until . . ."

"Until I made your birthmark burn?"

She gave him a frustrated look. "Why you? What is it about you that's different?"

He winced inwardly.

"One of your secrets, huh?" She crossed her arms and gazed at the sky.

His mind raced as he tried to come up with something he could tell her, something that would reassure her and not frighten her, but he came up with nothing.

"Look! A falling star." She closed her eyes briefly, then glanced at him. "Did you make a wish?"

"I missed it." *I was too busy watching your beautiful face.* "You made a wish?"

She nodded, then gave him a sly smile. "But I won't tell you. I can have secrets, too."

"If you tell me, I could help you make it come true."

Her smile faded as she looked away. "Wishes don't always come true."

He wondered what it was she wanted. And what would he wish for? A kiss? If he was lucky, he could have a thousand kisses in a lifetime. He should wish for something more profound.

He gazed at the sky and thought about his life and those he loved: Carly, his mother, his grandfather. He hadn't protected Carly. He'd failed her, and he'd disappointed his family. He'd made his mother suffer with his long banishment.

"You're deep in thought," Elsa whispered.

"It happens." He smiled. "About once a year."

She snorted. "What were you thinking that had you looking so forlorn?"

"I was thinking I would wish to love without regret."

She turned to face him. "I don't think you can live without at least a few regrets."

"True. But I don't want to make the people I love sad. I would wish that my love would bring them joy."

She nodded with a hint of a smile. "That's an excellent wish."

If only he could bring Elsa joy. "Why did your aunt tell you to avoid me?"

Her eyes widened. "You heard that?"

He nodded. "Is it because I made your birthmark burn?"

She sighed. "I know this will sound ridiculous, but my aunts believe in a family curse."

He stiffened.

"I know." She gave him a wry look. "Silly, isn't it?"

He sat very still so she wouldn't know that his heart was pounding, his muscles clenching. *A curse?* Who the hell believed in curses these days?

His grandfather did. And apparently, Elsa's aunts did, too. "Are you saying I'm somehow involved with your family curse? That's why you were told to avoid me?"

She touched his arm. "Don't worry about it. It's a bunch of nonsense."

That was exactly what he told his grandfather. The curse was nonsense. But it seemed a strange coincidence that Elsa's family would have a curse, too. "You . . . don't believe in the curse?"

"No." She smiled. "If I did, I wouldn't be here alone with you."

He swallowed hard. "Am I supposed to be some kind of threat to you?"

She shrugged. "I'd be scared to death if I was a feral pig."

"Elsa." He dragged a hand through his hair. "I would never hurt you."

She patted his arm. "Don't worry about it. I don't believe in the curse."

He took a deep breath. That was a relief, but still . . . how could both families have a curse? He cleared his throat. "This is going to sound strange, but my family has a curse, too."

Her mouth fell open. "Really?"

"Yes." He gave her a wry look. "See how much we have in common?"

She scoffed. "You're making that up."

"I'm serious. My grandfather has told me the curse story a million times."

"That's so strange." Her eyes narrowed. "What happens if your curse comes true?"

"My family line dies off. And yours?"

She looked away. "I die off."

He flinched. "Bull crap."

She snorted. "My feelings exactly."

He wrapped an arm around her shoulders. "I won't let anything bad happen to you."

"I appreciate that, particularly from a guy who has some superpowers, but it's not necessary. I don't believe in the curse."

"Good. But why you?"

She shrugged. "Apparently it has something to do with my birthmark. Aunt Ula has the mark of a fish on her shoulder. And Aunt Greta has the mark of a bird—"

"Holy crap," he whispered. The Guardians of the Sea and Sky? He jumped to his feet and strode to the edge of the creek. It couldn't be true. Grandfather's story was a load of bull. This was just a coincidence.

How many coincidences did it take to make a reality? Three women in a family with strange birthmarks. Three guardians.

He turned to look at Elsa. Could she possibly be the third guardian? No, it couldn't be. He inhaled deeply to calm himself and caught the scent of many animals, all hiding nearby. He scanned the nearby woods and saw the glint of their eyes. The woodland creatures were staying a distance from him, but they were staring at Elsa.

The Guardian of the Forest.

He shook his head. No, it was nonsense. She couldn't be the descendant of a magical being who had created a race of were-bears and were-wolves over a thousand years ago in Scandinavia. It was a stupid fairy tale.

But were-bears and werewolves existed. And Elsa was from Sweden. The animals were drawn to her. Hell, he was drawn to her. He'd felt an attachment the minute he first saw her.

"Howard?" She stood and walked toward him. "Are you all right?"

"Yeah." He raked a hand through his hair. Could she be a descendant of the woman who had betrayed his kind? He swallowed hard. Was he a descendant of the man who had murdered her?

"Don't let this curse nonsense upset you." She patted his arm. "I don't believe in it."

He pulled her into his arms. "I won't let anything hurt you. I promise."

"Howard." She leaned back to look at him. "Nothing will happen to me. I'll be fine."

He ran his fingers along her jaw, then traced the curve of her ear. "You're so beautiful."

"I—" She winced when he released the plastic claw that held her hair in place. "My hair is a wild mess."

"I know." He ran his hands through her hair, then leaned forward to nuzzle her neck and breathe in her sweet scent. "Wild is good," he whispered against her ear.

She shivered. "Howard."

"It will be all right." He brushed his lips against her cheek. "Elsa."

"My wish was about you," she whispered. "I wished that I could trust you."

"You can." He lowered his mouth to hers.

Chapter Twelve

*E*lsa's mind raced. Shouldn't she stop him? Weren't there a million reasons why she shouldn't kiss him? But all she could think was *handsome Howard.* She tilted her head back, closing her eyes. *Hunky Howard.*

His lips pressed gently against hers, then retreated. *Hesitant Howard.*

She opened her eyes. He was only inches away, his breath caressing her cheek. He watched her with a questioning look as if asking permission to proceed. And in that moment, as she gazed deep into his eyes, a wave of heat swept through her, melting her heart and filling her mind with a realization she suddenly knew to be true.

There was a duality about Howard. He was powerful, but restrained. Strong, but gentle. He could be aggressive, but also shy. Tough, but kind. She suspected his passion could swing from one extreme to the other—fierce to sweet. And God help her, she wanted to taste both.

She placed a hand on his cheek. He must have shaved before dinner, for his skin was soft and smooth.

"I started falling for you months ago when I first saw you on television," he whispered. "But I realize you only met me last night."

"You're waiting for me to catch up?"

A corner of his mouth curled up, and he nodded.

She grazed her finger over the dimple made by his half smile. She'd started falling for him the minute she saw him, too. He'd seemed like the perfect man until he'd activated the curse.

Why should she run away just because he made her birthmark hot? Did that matter, when he could make her hot all over? No other man had ever made her sizzle with desire. Only Howard.

She wrapped her hands around his neck. "I think I'm all caught up."

His eyes flared with heat. "Good." He slid his hands into her hair, cradling her face, as his gaze focused hungrily on her mouth.

She barely had time to draw in a quick breath before he pounced. No more hesitancy or sweetness. This was pure aggression. *Oh, hot Howard.*

He claimed possession, tasted her lips thoroughly, then demanded more, opening her mouth to invade with his tongue. She clung to his shoulders. Never before had she kissed a man taller than her, more powerful than her. A man who could lift her and carry her off like a giant He-Man. It was frightening, but exhilarating. For the first time in her life, she felt dainty and feminine. Sensual and desired.

She swirled her tongue around his, and an answering groan vibrated deep in his throat. She sucked him deeper inside her and he responded, wrapping his arms around her to pull her close. A thrill shot through her, hot and heady. He was big enough to dominate, but she wielded a womanly power that could bring him to his knees. It felt good. Raw and sexy. Powerful and passionate.

He broke the kiss and rested his forehead against her. "Elsa," he breathed. "You're killing me." He planted his large hands on her rump and pulled her against him.

She inhaled sharply. *Huge Howard. Hard-as-a-rock Howard.*

"That's how much I want you." He kissed her brow. "But don't worry. I won't ravish you in the woods like a wild beast."

For a second she wondered if she was disappointed. But then her brain kicked in. She was not the type to have a night of passion with a near stranger. Though to be honest, she'd never been tempted like this before.

He stepped back, releasing her. "Are you all right?"

She nodded. Cool air surrounded her, making her shiver, making her miss Howard's big, warm body.

He leaned over to pick up the plastic claw he'd dropped on the ground. As he wiped it clean on his pant leg, her gaze drifted. *Huge Howard. Hot, heavy, hard Howard.*

She shifted her weight to disguise the fact that she wanted to squirm. *Don't think about it.* She glanced up and discovered him watching her. *Sheesh.* Heat rushed to her face. He'd caught her ogling his crotch.

She turned away. "I don't usually . . . I should get back to my motel room. Alone." She winced inwardly, and her flushed cheeks flamed hotter. *Awkward*.

"Here." He offered her the plastic claw.

"Right." She quickly twisted her hair on the back of her head, then grabbed the claw from his hand and snapped it in place.

"Will you have dinner with me tomorrow night?"

"I—I'm not sure. My aunts might be here by then. I haven't seen Aunt Ula in a long time, so I should spend some time with her."

Howard's eyes widened. "She's coming from Sweden?"

"Yes. And Aunt Greta's driving in from Minneapolis."

"Is there a special occasion I should know about? Like a birthday?"

Or a murder? Elsa waved a dismissive hand. "It's nothing. They're just worried about the silly curse." Worried enough that Ula had left her beloved island and Greta was bringing weapons. But Elsa didn't want to mention that. Howard would think insanity ran in her family.

"Elsa." He stepped closer. "I won't let anything harm you."

Her breath caught at the low, rumbling intensity in his voice. And the fierce passion in his gaze. The more she looked into his deep blue eyes, the more she felt it. A sense of being attached. As if she'd been waiting for him all her life. As if their souls had searched for each other across the mists of time.

His gaze grew more heated, then he looked away. "I'd better walk you back before I forget my promise not to ravish you in the woods."

"Like a wild beast?"

He winced. "Did I say that?"

"Yes." She walked downstream and heard him mutter a curse under his breath before running to catch up with her.

Barely touching her elbow, he escorted her toward the entrance of the park. He was back to being gentle and sweet, she thought with a smile.

And she was falling for him hard.

A few hours later, she kicked at the sheet and blanket that had twisted around her legs from all her tossing and turning.

"Dammit." She sat up in bed. How could she sleep when she kept replaying Howard's kiss in her mind? And imagining what would have happened if she had invited him into her room. *Hot Howard.* He would have burned up her sheets. The smoke alarms would have gone off.

But he hadn't even kissed her at the door. He'd simply squeezed her hand and wished her a good night before walking back to the restaurant parking lot.

"He's a gentleman," she whispered to herself. That was a point in his favor.

Though gentlemen didn't usually kill feral pigs with a knife. She shook her head, refusing to dwell on that.

"He's good with children." There was no disputing that.

She ticked off more good points on her fingers. "He's sweet and protective. Intelligent and thoughtful. Handsome and . . . handsome." Double points for that.

But why this sudden need to list his good points? The answer pricked at her. She was trying hard not to think about his one, major bad point.

He'd made her birthmark burn. And according to his aunts, that made him a threat.

With a groan, she tilted her head back to stare at the ceiling. *There's no curse.* They were simply a man and a woman who were wildly attracted to each other.

Why shouldn't she enjoy it? Why couldn't she fall madly in love with him? She loved the way he made her feel. After a lifetime of feeling oversized and clunky, he made her feel beautiful. Wasn't that a gift she should treasure?

But why had he caused her birthmark to burn? What made him different from every other man she'd ever met? Was it the secret powers he possessed? Super hearing, super vision, super smell. He'd admitted to those. And he was super fast and strong to have killed those pigs.

She rubbed the mark on her shoulder. How strange that it was shaped like an animal paw, and he'd grown up on an island called The Paw.

She shook her head. It had to be a coincidence. Bears were common in Alaska, so a group of islands called The Bear Claw couldn't be considered odd. Bears were common in Scandinavia, too. Even her last name, *Bjornberg*, meant 'Bear Mountain.' Coincidences, nothing more. Her life had become so strange lately that she was looking for strangeness where it didn't exist.

Her cell phone rang, and she jumped. Could it be Howard? *Get a grip.* She'd never given him her number. She scurried to the desk, where she'd plugged in her phone to recharge.

"Hello?"

"Ellie, sweetie," Aunt Greta responded. "How are you? Are you all right?"

"I'm fine. How are you?"

"Tired, but I made it all the way to Buffalo. I just got off the phone with Aunt Ula. She's in Albany. I'll meet her there, then we're hoping to reach you by tomorrow night. Can you reserve a room for us?"

"Yes, of course," Elsa assured her. "Don't push yourself too hard. I'm fine here. Alastair is next door. And Oskar will be arriving tomorrow with some of the crew."

"Good. Stay in your room till you have plenty of guys to protect you."

Elsa groaned. "I have a job to do. I'm not going to cower in my room like a scared rabbit."

"You . . . oh my God, did you go out today?"

"Of course. I have a—"

"Oh no!" Greta's voice rose in panic. "I told you to stay in your room."

"I'm perfectly fine." *And I'm twenty-seven years old.*

"You're not taking this seriously enough!"

"Aunt Greta, please. Calm down."

"This has been going on for centuries! It's not only your grandmother who was murdered but her grandmother, and more ancestors as far back as we can remember."

Elsa gasped.

"And they all had the same birthmark you have."

Elsa's knees gave out, and she collapsed on the bed.

"Ellie? Are you there?"

"Yes," she whispered. She pressed a hand against her racing heart. Her aunt was doing a good job of scaring her now. "They . . . they were all murdered?"

Greta sighed. "We thought you would be safe in America, that you would never run into a berserker here."

"A what?"

"We thought they were all in Norway and Sweden," Greta continued. "Damn. They must have migrated over the centuries."

"Who? What?"

"The berserkers. According to family legend, only a berserker can activate the curse."

Elsa shook her head in confusion. Howard was a berserker? "What?"

"In a way, I suppose it's our own fault," Greta mumbled. "It's part of the curse. We should have never made the berserkers, and now we keep paying for it. Bad Karma, I guess."

"What are you talking about?"

Greta heaved a sigh. "So you didn't stay in your

room like I asked. Please tell me that you at least had the good sense to stay away from the man who activated the curse."

Elsa winced. She'd just made out with him. "Well, I did . . . see him."

"Oh God, no. Didn't I tell you to avoid him?"

"He seemed perfectly normal."

"Berserkers can always *seem* normal. But you never know when they're going to go *berserk*!"

Elsa recalled her aunt's words from the night before. *Did he seem wild or crazy to you?* Was that what she meant by berserk? "He's not like that. He's not wild or crazy."

"Berserkers kill," Greta insisted. "They're killing machines. That's what they were created to do."

A shiver ran down Elsa's spine. How quickly had Howard run off to kill those pigs? "No." She shook her head, refusing to believe he was wild or crazy. He'd only done it to protect the school-children.

"They go berserk and kill everything in sight," Greta continued. "They're like wild beasts."

Elsa's breath caught. *I won't ravish you in the woods like a wild beast.*

"Do you understand the danger now?" Greta asked. "Will you stay away from him?"

Tears crowded her eyes. She didn't want to say yes. She didn't want to believe anything bad about Howard. But she couldn't leave her aunts in a panic. Maybe after they met Howard, they would realize he was all right. They would see how sweet and gentle he was. "I . . . won't see him." For a day or two.

"Good. Now get some rest, and we'll see you to-morrow night." Greta hung up.

Get some rest? Elsa dropped the phone on the desk. Did Greta seriously think she could sleep now?

She paced across the room. *Berserkers?* She checked the lock on the door and paced some more. What the hell was a berserker?

She booted up her laptop and did a search. Berserkers were part of Scandinavian lore. Fierce Norse warriors who went into battle, wearing the pelt of a wolf or a bear. The term *berserk* could refer to a bear shirt. They worked themselves into an animal-like frenzy, killing indiscriminately.

She jumped to her feet and paced across the room. Animal-like frenzy? She halted suddenly, recalling the loud roar she'd heard that afternoon. When Howard was doing battle with the pigs.

Her skin prickled with gooseflesh. Was that why she'd felt like those ladies knew something she didn't know? They knew Howard could roar like an animal?

"No." She sat on the bed. Howard was normal. He didn't go into an animal-like frenzy. He certainly couldn't think he was an animal. That would be crazy.

Wild and crazy. Greta had said the berserkers were like wild beasts, killing everything in sight. Was she right? Was Howard dangerous to be around? But why would Shanna trust him to watch over her son if he wasn't safe?

Was this the duality she'd sensed about him? Powerful, but restrained. Strong, but gentle. Tough, but kind. Human, but animal?

I won't ravish you in the woods like a wild beast.
"No!" She clenched her fists. "I won't believe it."

Hours later, in a fitful sleep, she started to dream. A beautiful man came to her in the night. Large and powerful, he covered her body with his. His big hands roamed over her skin, setting her on fire. She wanted him. She cried out for him. She burned for him.

His hands were magic. Skimming the length of her legs. Fondling her breasts. Stroking her neck. Tightening their grip.

Choking her.

She thrashed against him, but he was too strong. Too powerful.

With a cry, Elsa sat up. She panted in the dark, searching the room. No one was there. It was just a dream.

With trembling hands, she turned on the light, then checked the room more carefully. No one there.

She splashed cold water on her face and looked at herself in the mirror, half expecting to see red marks on her neck. Nothing there.

It was just a dream. No doubt her subconscious was trying to process the new information she'd learned. Or it was trying to scare the hell out of her.

It had to be a psychic thing. Her brain was doing this to protect her. It was warning her what could happen to her in the future. If she wasn't careful.

If she continued to see Howard.

Chapter Thirteen

T he next morning, bright and early, Howard parked his SUV behind Elsa's rental car in front of the gatehouse. He'd gone into town to pick up a few dozen donuts, and he'd planned on surprising Elsa with them for breakfast. When he'd noticed her car was missing from the motel parking lot, he'd surmised that she and Alastair were at the gatehouse.

Shanna was doing her best to help with his courting. Last night, she'd left a detailed list with him to pass on to Elsa and Alastair so he'd have a good excuse to drop by this morning. He grabbed the donuts, along with a brown envelope containing Shanna's list, then strode toward the house.

The front door was slightly ajar, so he nudged it open with his foot. "Hello?"

Alastair peered out an open doorway near the end of the foyer. His eyes narrowed. "Ah, Howard. Come on in."

"I have breakfast." He lifted the box as he crossed the foyer. "And a note from Shanna."

"Excellent."

Howard followed Alastair into what appeared to be the old kitchen. A quick glance around told him the room would need a massive amount of work. It was devoid of all modern appliances and, sadly, also devoid of Elsa.

He set the donut box and envelope on an old scarred table. "Shanna sent a list of things she wanted. She said you'd gone over most of it last night, but she wanted it in writing."

"I understand." Alastair pulled two water bottles from an ice chest on the floor and handed one to Howard. "I'll take a look."

Howard sat carefully in an old rickety chair by the table. It groaned under his weight. While he sipped some water, he strained his hearing to detect where in the house Elsa might be. If she was here, she was being very quiet.

He glanced at Alastair, who was studying the list, frowning. He wasn't behaving in his usual cheerful, charming way.

Alastair nodded. "Yes, this all sounds familiar. They're fairly common requests, except for wanting a second master bedroom suite in the basement. No windows. Sounds a bit gloomy to me." He set the list down on the table. "She mentioned her mother would be living with them, so I assume they plan on stashing the ol' gel in the cellar."

Howard nodded, although he knew Shanna and Roman would be using the basement.

Alastair helped himself to a donut. "Unfortunately, we haven't been able to inspect the cellar yet. The old wooden staircase is half rotted away, and the only other access point is outside, the old coal chute. Oskar will bring a ladder when he comes this afternoon, so we'll have a look then."

"Sounds good." Howard drank more water. "So is Elsa around?"

Alastair shot him an annoyed look. "You'll have to conduct all your business meetings with me or Oskar. Elsa has requested not to see you again."

Howard's mouth dropped open.

Alastair scowled at him. "I don't know what you did last night, but I don't appreciate you scaring the hell out of her. She's a nice—"

"What?"

"She looked dreadful this morning. Black circles under her eyes. She wouldn't say what had upset her, but it was obvious she hadn't slept a wink."

"She—she's upset?"

Alastair gulped down some water. "So what happened? Did you make a pass at her?"

"I—"

"I'm not blind, you know. I could tell you two were attracted to each other, and quite frankly, I was delighted for Ellie. She's a lovely woman and deserves to be happy—"

"I didn't hurt her." Howard gritted his teeth. "I would never hurt her."

"Well." Alastair eyed him suspiciously. "I'll have to take your word on that. But for now, I expect you to honor her wishes and stay away from her."

"Where is she? Is she all right?"

Alastair lifted a brow. "She'll be here later with Oskar and the crew. In other words, she will be surrounded by a group of brawny construction workers who consider her their darling little sister."

Howard's inner bear growled at the implied threat. Did they really believe he was a danger to Elsa?

He rose to his feet. "I would never harm her. And I will honor her wishes. You have my word."

Alastair nodded. "Good." He extended a hand. "No hard feelings, ol' chap. Let's continue to work well together."

Howard shook his hand, then strode from the house.

A few minutes later, he found himself parked in front of the motel in Cranville. He'd been in such a daze that he couldn't remember driving there.

He gazed at her door. Room number five. Even here, he could detect a hint of her lovely scent. What had happened to make her suddenly reject him? Had he moved too fast the night before? Kissed her too hard?

He replayed the scene in his mind, trying to figure out where he'd gone wrong. Yes, he'd kissed her with passion, but she had kissed him back. She hadn't seemed insulted or frightened by him.

Damn. He raked a hand through his hair. What the hell had upset her? Had she experienced a delayed reaction to being teleported? If that was freaking her out, then how would she ever handle the truth about him being a shifter?

He might never get the chance to tell her. She might insist on never seeing him again.

Despair slammed into him, nearly doubling him over. The bear inside him howled in pain. It rammed against his defenses, demanding release. It needed to run, needed to destroy a poor tree with a few ferocious swipes, needed to shred and devour a helpless animal.

"Later," he whispered, sweat beading on his brow as he tightened his control on the beast. Charging around town as a grizzly bear would not help his cause. What he needed now was a new strategy.

He retrieved a pen and small legal pad from his glove compartment so he could write Elsa a note.

WHAT THE HELL HAPPENED? he scrawled, then realized all caps looked like he was yelling at her. He ripped that page off and tried again.

Elsa, I'm sorry I jumped your bones.

To hell with that. He wasn't sorry at all. He tore that page off.

My dearest Elsa:

I heard you didn't sleep well, and I was concerned. What could be upsetting you, sweetheart? Why are you so afraid? I never took you for a COWARD!

He ripped that page off. Dammit, he couldn't let his anger creep in.

"Holy crap," he muttered. There was only one page left on the pad.

He took a deep breath. Fourth down and ten. No pressure here.

Dear Elsa,

I was sorry to miss you this morning. Please call me whenever you get a chance.

He looked it over. Not too bad. He wrote down his cell phone number and signed it simply with his name. It would have to do. He folded it up and wrote her name on it, then took it inside the motel office and asked the sleepy manager to pass it on to her.

With one last glance at her door, he returned to his SUV, then drove back to the school. Instead of going inside, he jogged to the nearby woods, stripped, and let the bear free.

He roared his frustration, ripped his claws through a tree trunk, then ran through the forest. He made a circle around the school, clawing and marking his territory.

She will be mine, the bear growled. *Elsa will be mine.*

The note burned in Elsa's pocket, but she ignored it and walked from the motel office to the local diner. Even though it was almost noon, she ordered breakfast. After a sleepless night, she'd dragged herself to the car at dawn, but thankfully, Alastair had taken mercy on her and given her the morning off. She'd climbed back into bed and dozed away most of the morning.

Now she tapped her fingers on the linoleum table, waiting for her bacon and eggs. She could pass the time by looking at the note the motel manager had given her.

No. She sipped some coffee instead.

She strongly suspected the note was from Howard. Her name was written on the outside with bold, strong strokes, nothing like the fluid handwriting that Alastair used.

Damn, she'd let Howard walk her to her room last night. He knew which room was hers. She shook her head. Howard had acted like a gentleman. He didn't deserve all this suspicion. She was letting those weird berserker legends freak her out.

Howard wasn't behaving like a wild animal. He'd simply left a note for her at the office.

Should she look at it?

She rubbed her brow, not knowing what to think. Her aunt had frightened her with all that berserker nonsense, and then her dream had terrified her. Was she really marked for murder? Was Howard some kind of modern-day berserker who went into an animal-like trance, killing everything in sight?

How had her life slipped so far into the bizarre?

She drank more coffee and looked around the diner. Everything seemed so normal. Small-town America. Down-to-earth people with friendly faces. They were delighted that the *International Home Wreckers* show had come to town. The motel was fully booked for the next four months. She'd booked a room for her aunts and seven more rooms to accommodate Oskar, Madge the camerawoman, her sound and light guys, and the main construction crew. Specialty crews would come and go over the next few months, filling up the rest of the motel.

Madge and her production crew were going to film the "before" footage today. They would return about once a week over the next four months, then film a lot of interviews and "after" footage when the project was finished.

The main construction crew was jokingly called The B Boys, since their names were Bennie, Bradley, Bartello, and Buff. Buff's name was actually Mario, but he liked being called Buff as much as he liked showing off his buff body. All The B Boys had been selected for the show because they were experts on construction with the added bonus of looking fabulous without their shirts. Whenever Madge was around with her camera, she insisted they partially disrobe, claiming a shirtless man in a hard hat was good for ratings.

They were a nice-looking bunch, Elsa thought, but not nearly as huge and handsome as Howard. *Read his note.*

"No!" She realized the waitress was standing there with a coffee pot in hand and a surprised look on her face. "I mean, yes." She slid her nearly empty cup across the table.

The waitress filled it and gave her a wary look. "Your food will be out soon."

"Thank you." Elsa smiled to let the waitress know she was okay.

Read the note, you coward. What could be so bad about a note? It wasn't like Howard could strangle her with a few written words, not like the guy in her dream.

She retrieved the note from her jeans pocket and read it. His cell phone number glared back at her. "No." She stuffed the note in her handbag.

Would it hurt to call him? It wasn't like Howard

could strangle her over the phone, not like the guy in her dream. She winced and shook her head. *Stop thinking about that.*

"Are you all right?" The waitress eyed her suspiciously as she set a platter of eggs, bacon, and toast on the table.

"I'm fine. Thank you." *I'm not going to think about Howard going berserk and killing a bunch of pigs in an animal-like frenzy.* She picked up a slice of bacon and groaned.

Maybe she'd start with the eggs.

Shortly after Elsa's late breakfast, Oskar, The B Boys, and Madge and her crew arrived in two trucks and a van. They quickly settled in their motel rooms while Elsa ordered a dozen hamburger combo meals at the diner. Then, loaded up with take-out food and supplies, they headed off to the gatehouse.

Everyone sat on the floor in the formal parlor to eat their lunch with leftover donuts for dessert while Alastair outlined the plans. Madge and her crew recorded some video, and The B Boys ate without their shirts, just to make her happy. Elsa suspected some of them were making Madge happy when the camera wasn't rolling.

They would start with the basement and work their way up. The bad news: Alastair suspected the basement was only about seven feet high. They might have to dig down another two feet.

The B Boys groaned.

Their first job: set up temporary lighting in the

cellar, clean the place up, and determine if it was structurally sound before they started digging.

It was a horrendous mess. After a few hours, they were all covered in dirt, cobwebs, and coal dust. Elsa had climbed up the ladder to get a bottle of water from the kitchen when her cell phone jangled. She wiped her dirty hands on her jeans, then answered it.

"Ellie!" Aunt Greta exclaimed. "We've just arrived at the motel. Where are you?"

"At work. I'll be there soon." Elsa yelled down at Alastair that she needed to return to town and heard his muffled agreement.

"I'll take you back." Madge climbed up the ladder. "We're done for the day."

Fifteen minutes later, Elsa arrived at the motel. Aunt Greta and Great-aunt Ula bounded from their room, all smiles and open arms.

"Goodness, girl, you're a mess." Greta gave her a quick hug, then stepped back.

Great-aunt Ula grinned at her, then spoke in broken English. "You look very well. We were very afraid for you."

"I'm fine. And you look great, Aunt Ula. I swear you haven't aged a day since I last saw you." And it wasn't flattery. Elsa hoped she would age as well her great-aunt. Ula's hair was silver, but it was thick and shiny and plaited into a long braid. Her glowing complexion had only a few wrinkles, and her green eyes were as sharp as ever.

Ula nodded, smiling. "You grow up very pretty." Her smile faded as she plucked a cobweb from Elsa's hair. "But very dirty."

"I'll jump in the shower." Elsa unlocked her motel room door and ushered the two women inside.

Ten minutes later, she emerged from the bathroom squeaky clean, dressed in new jeans and a T-shirt. While she towel-dried her hair, the aunts sat on her bed, speaking in Swedish.

"We must tell her everything," Ula insisted. "What does she know so far?"

"I told her about the murders," Greta whispered. "And the berserkers."

Ula nodded. "Does she know she's a—"

"A what?" Elsa asked in English. She hadn't understood the last word Ula had said.

"It translates best as guardian," Greta explained in English. "As you know, Aunt Ula can talk to seals, whales, dolphins, fish—all the creatures of the sea."

Ula nodded. "Turtles, too."

Elsa sighed. "Yes, I've heard that." But she'd never believed it.

"I am Guardian of Sea," Ula announced.

And I'm the queen of England. Elsa tossed her damp towel under the vanity.

"That's why she has the fish birthmark," Greta explained.

"*Ja.* Fish." Ula tapped her shoulder.

"And I have the bird birthmark," Greta continued, "so I'm Guardian of the Sky."

"She talks to birds," Ula added.

"What?" Elsa gave her aunt an incredulous look. "You never mentioned that before."

Greta dragged a hand through her short blond hair. As pale as her hair was, the few strands of silver were barely noticeable. "I became your mother, and I was afraid you wouldn't mind me if you thought I was crazy. But remember in junior high when you insisted on walking home from the bus stop on your own?"

Elsa swallowed hard. A hawk had always followed her home.

"And when you went off to college, there was an owl who lived in the rafters outside your room," Greta continued.

"You kept an eye on me with *birds*?" Elsa asked.

Greta nodded. "You wouldn't believe how handy they are. I've never gotten a speeding ticket 'cause they always tell me where the cops are."

"Huh?" Elsa ran a hand through her damp hair.

"That's why I wasn't concerned about driving around with the rifles in the trunk." Greta quickly translated what she'd said to Swedish, and Ula grinned.

"*Ja.* We need guns to keep Elsa safe," Ula said, still smiling.

Elsa groaned. "You can't just walk around shooting everyone who looks at me funny."

Greta waved a dismissive hand. "Don't worry. We'll only shoot the berserker if he comes after you."

Elsa winced. They wanted to shoot Howard?

"Has anything else happened to you recently?" Greta asked. "Other than your birthmark burning?"

"Well . . ." Elsa thought about it. She'd been teleported. She'd been thoroughly kissed by an alleged berserker who seemed much more interested in making love to her than murdering her.

Not your usual run-of-the-mill stuff. "Oh, a bunch of animals keep following me around."

"Ah." Ula exchanged a knowing look with Greta.

"I thought that might happen," Greta said. "That was the reason I always kept you away from the country. Of course, even in the suburbs, there were field mice and squirrels that sought you out, but my hawks and owls took care of them. And Peder's hunting dogs took care of the rabbits."

Elsa sat on the bed. "Are you saying I have always attracted animals?"

"Not all animals." Greta waved a hand. "Just the woodland creatures."

"You are Guardian of Forest," Ula announced.

Elsa's mouth dropped open.

Greta patted her on the arm. "I'm sure it comes as a bit of a shock."

You think? Elsa jumped to her feet. "What . . . this is crazy! We're not some sort of magical beings that talk to animals."

Greta looked offended. "I have nothing to do with animals. I only talk to birds."

Elsa groaned. "That's not normal."

"We're special," Ula said proudly.

Special? It reminded Elsa of how Tino had described himself. "What—what sort of weird things do we do?"

"Mainly, we communicate with different creatures. We're no longer sure how that came to pass." Greta gazed across the room, her eyes unfocused. "Many of the secrets have been lost over the centuries, but I suspect the original guardians were shamans of some kind. We do know that over a thousand years ago, there were three magical sisters: the Guardians of the Sea, Sky, and Forest, and they used their powers to protect a village."

"*Ja*," Ula agreed. "Always three guardians in our family. Always women."

"If an enemy attacked by sea, the Guardian of the Sea called upon the sea creatures to overturn the boats," Greta continued. "And the Guardian of the Sky asked the birds of prey to attack an enemy who came over the mountains."

"But Guardian of Forest—" Aunt Ula shook her head and tsked.

"What?" Elsa crossed her arms. She felt like she'd been caught doing something wrong.

"It wasn't really her fault," Greta insisted. "A group of marauders kept attacking the village. They had too many ships for the sea creatures to stop them all. The villagers begged the Guardian of the Forest to protect them. So she took the twelve best warriors into the woods to live with the wolves and bears, and that's when it happened."

A shiver trickled down Elsa's spine. "What happened?"

"The men became berserkers," Greta said.

Ula shook her head again, making more tsking noises. "Bad. Very bad."

"At first the berserkers were good at defeating the enemy and keeping the village safe," Greta continued. "But then some of them lost control and started killing the villagers."

"Very bad," Ula repeated.

"And then the ultimate betrayal. They turned on their own creator, the Guardian of the Forest." Greta regarded Elsa with a sad look. "One of the berserkers killed her."

Elsa shuddered. "So you think a berserker will . . ." Her heart raced. Howard would fall into an animal-like frenzy and attack her? "I don't believe it! H-he wouldn't do that."

Greta sighed. "I know it's a lot to take in. But don't worry. Ula and I will protect you. And you must do your best to never see the berserker again."

Elsa sat on the bed. "If you could just meet him, you would know that he's harmless."

"No!" Greta stiffened. "We can never trust a berserker."

"But he's not going to behave like an animal!" Elsa cried.

Ula muttered something in Swedish.

Elsa gasped. "What did she say?"

Greta shuddered. "We have no proof, for no one in our family has seen it. Or if they did see it, they didn't live to talk about it. But the family legend claims the berserkers don't just *act* like animals."

Elsa swallowed hard as Aunt Greta's voice softened to a whisper.

"They become animals."

Chapter Fourteen

A beautiful man came to her in the night. Large and powerful, he covered her body with his. His big hands roamed over her skin, setting her on fire. She wanted him. She cried out for him. She burned for him.

His hands were magic. Skimming the length of her legs. Fondling her breasts. Stroking her neck. Tightening their grip.

Choking her.

She thrashed against him, but he was too strong. Too powerful.

His face, half hidden in shadow, twisted in rage. Transformed. He roared like an animal.

Elsa cried out.

"Ellie! What's wrong?" Greta flipped on the bedside lamp between the two double beds.

Elsa squinted at the sudden bright light. She could still hear the animal-like roar echoing in her head. A roar very much like the one she'd heard the day Howard had battled the feral pigs.

Greta scrambled out of bed to grab the loaded shotgun she'd left on the desk.

"No!" Elsa sat up. "It was just a dream."

"Are you sure?" Greta strode to the door with the shotgun.

"Greta, please. You're scaring me with that."

"You're scaring me! You screamed."

"It was a bad dream. That's all."

Greta checked the locks on the door, then peeked between the slats of the closed window blinds. "I don't see anything."

Elsa pressed a hand against her pounding heart. She didn't know which was scarier—her nightmare or the fact that Greta and Ula had insisted they take turns sleeping in her room with a loaded weapon.

"Everything's fine," she assured her aunt. "Let's go back to sleep."

"Are you sure?" Greta set the shotgun back down on the desk. "What was your dream?"

"I don't want to talk about it." *Or think about it.* "Let's go back to sleep." Elsa scooted back under the covers. Aunt Ula had definitely freaked her out with her claim that berserkers actually became animals.

What kind of animals? Elsa had been so shocked by the announcement that she was a so-called guardian that the rest of what she'd heard was all in a daze. Greta had said the Guardian of the Forest took twelve warriors into the forest to live among the wolves and bears . . .

Wolves and bears.

Greta turned the lamp off with a snap, leaving the room shrouded in darkness.

Elsa shuddered and dragged her blanket up to her chin. What was Howard? A wolf or a bear?

Neither. She glared at the ceiling. This was the real world, and Howard was a normal guy. Well, not exactly normal, since he was handsome, huge, and hunky. He could also be hers if she had the courage to claim him.

If she wasn't afraid he'd turn into a beast and kill her.

The next morning, her aunts objected when she tried to catch a ride with Alastair to the gatehouse.

"You have to go with us," Ula insisted in Swedish. "We can't protect you if we're not with you."

Elsa tamped down on her frustration. "I'll be fine. Oskar and the boys will be coming, too, as soon as they're done eating in the diner. There'll be plenty of guys—"

"They don't have weapons like we do," Greta argued. "We're coming."

With an inward groan, Elsa turned to a confused-looking Alastair. "My aunts want to come with me to the gatehouse," she explained in English. "They'll stay outside."

Alastair nodded. "They'll have to. It could be too dangerous inside." He smiled at the older women. "We're delighted you've come to visit Ellie, but we don't want you to get hurt."

Greta smiled back. "Don't worry. My late husband was a home builder, so I know how it is. We'll stay out of your way. And we'll be happy to bring you food. Lots of food."

"Sounds super." Alastair shook hands with them, then jumped into the rental car and drove off.

With the parking lot temporarily empty, the aunts quickly stashed the shotgun and hunting rifle in the trunk of Greta's car.

Elsa sighed. "Nothing's going to happen. You'll be sitting outside all day, bored out of your skulls."

"That reminds me, I should bring my knitting." Greta scurried back into her room.

"Bring my book," Ula called after her in Swedish. She gave Elsa a sheepish smile. "I'm reading a romance book. Very sexy."

Elsa smiled back. "That's good." If the hero was anything like Howard, it would be a very sexy book.

Ula patted her on the back. "Don't worry. We'll keep you safe. If the berserker comes, we'll shoot him."

Elsa winced. So much for romance. "Maybe we should try talking to him first."

Ula scoffed. "Don't be silly."

Greta hurried to the car, carrying a tote bag. "I've brought some water and snacks, too. Let's go."

Fifteen minutes later, they stopped in front of the gatehouse.

"If you get tired of hanging around here, go back to town," Elsa told her aunts as she climbed out of the car. "I'll be okay here."

"We'll be fine, too." Greta shooed her away with her hand. "We'll see you at lunchtime."

Elsa strode into the gatehouse and found Alastair in the kitchen, munching on a donut.

"Oh yum." She reached into the box and grabbed one. So much for her diet. A girl who had nightmares was entitled to some emotional eating.

"Mmm." Alastair nodded, his mouth full.

She looked around the kitchen as she ate, then pointed at the door to the old laundry room. "The note's gone."

"What note?"

"It must have fallen off. I left a warning on the door that the floor inside is rotting away."

"Oh, that. Yes, Oskar mentioned it. He took the broken window out yesterday after you left. I've ordered a new one." Alastair handed her a bottle of water from the ice chest.

"Thanks. And thanks for bringing the donuts." She stuffed the last bite into her mouth.

"I didn't do it. I think Howard must have."

"Huh?" she asked with a full mouth.

"He brought some yesterday. I suppose he brought these."

She swallowed hard. "He was here?"

"I didn't see him." Alastair drank some water. "I guess Shanna gave him a key. He must have dropped these off before we arrived."

Elsa stared at the huge box of two dozen donuts. He'd brought enough for everyone. "That was kind of him."

"Yes." Alastair gave her a curious look. "He seems like a decent chap. I can't help but wonder why you refuse to see him."

She screwed the top off her water bottle. "It's a long story."

"Well, I must say he looked absolutely devastated when I told him."

She winced.

"But he gave me his word that he would honor your wishes."

She nodded. So instead of knocking on her motel room door, he'd left a note for her in the office.

"Has he kept his word?" Alastair asked.

"Yes." *He's a gentleman.* Or was he a beast?

"Well, good." Alastair plucked another donut from the box. "I could get seriously addicted to these. I hope he brings them every morning."

Elsa gulped. What if her aunts caught him making a donut delivery? The poor guy could end up shot just for being nice. Or what if he dropped by to check on their work? As Shanna's representative, it was his job to stay informed.

Loud shouts and footsteps sounded in the foyer as Oskar and The B Boys made their noisy entrance.

"In here!" Alastair shouted.

The guys crowded into the kitchen and attacked the donuts. They were so busy eating that Elsa slipped unnoticed into the formal dining room. She peered out one of the front windows. Greta and Ula had opened the trunk of their car.

"Oh no," she breathed. Were they checking on the weapons, or did they intend to take them out and go hunting?

What if Howard was nearby?

She should warn him. She had his phone number in her handbag. But if she called or texted him, he would have her number. With a wince, she leaned against the wall next to the window.

She didn't want to talk to him. He'd want to know why she was avoiding him, and she didn't know what to say. He'd probably ask her out to dinner, and how could she respond? *By the way, are you intending to kill me?*

She peeked out the window. Greta was loading shells into her shotgun.

"Oh God, no." She had to warn Howard. He'd behaved like a perfect gentleman. He didn't deserve to be shot down in the driveway.

With trembling fingers, she retrieved her cell phone and his note from her handbag. Call or text?

Text. Hearing his voice would make her all quivery inside. She started a message three times and erased it. Finally, she wrote, *Not safe for you at the gatehouse. My aunts are here with weapons.*

She hesitated with her finger above the Send button. Once she pushed it, she couldn't take it back. He would contact her. With a grimace, she pushed Send.

Seconds ticked by with her heart pounding. She glanced out the window. Greta was loading the hunting rifle.

Her phone jangled, and she jumped. *Oh God, it's him.*

She glanced around the room. It was empty. The guys were still in the kitchen. The phone rang again.

Biting her lip, she took the call. "Hello?"

"Elsa?"

She groaned inwardly when his deep, sexy voice shuddered through her. "Yes."

"We need to talk."

"No. My aunts are with me constantly. They're armed."

"I should meet them."

"No! They want to shoot you! They think you're a berserker."

There was a pause, then he replied, "I would never hurt you."

She winced. He hadn't denied being a berserker. "Just stay away from me. Okay?"

"Wait. Why are you refusing to see me?"

"Good-bye, Howard."

"Is it because of the curse?"

"Don't call me." She hung up.

She rested her head against the wall and took deep breaths, waiting for her heart to stop racing.

Her phone dinged, signaling a text. *Ignore it.*

It dinged again. With a groan, she opened his message.

I believe you could be the Guardian of the Forest.

Her heart lurched. He knew about the guardians?

He sent another text. *That's why the animals are following you.*

Tears gathered in her eyes. Why couldn't she just be Elsa? The same Elsa she was a week ago? Amazon Ellie who built beautiful cabinets. Why was she suddenly floundering in a supernatural world where nothing was what it should be? Children could secretly teleport. She and her aunts were secretly guardians. Handsome men were secretly beasts.

She sent him a message. *I believe you are a berserker.*

A message came back. *A descendant.*

He admitted it. Her heart sank, and she wiped a tear from her cheek. Her hand shook as she typed out the next message.

Wolf or bear? Her finger hovered over the Send button. A tear splattered onto the screen.

God help me, this can't be happening to me. She erased the message.

He sent a new text. *I believe our family curses are connected.*

She gasped. Was he admitting his ancestors had murdered hers? She texted back. *Stay away from me! My aunts will kill you.*

The phone rang.

Her heart jumped up her throat, and she turned the phone off. A message appeared in her voice mail.

She dropped the phone into her handbag and pulled out a small pack of tissue to blow her nose. "I won't listen. I don't care what he says."

She stuffed the tissue back into her handbag.

"Dammit." She couldn't stand not knowing. She grabbed the phone and hit voice mail.

"Elsa, I would never hurt you!" Howard's voice sounded strained. "We don't have to live our lives according to some damned curse! It's making us live in fear. All we have to do is reject the fear. We can break the curse. If we love each other."

Love? A tear rolled down her face. Could she trust Howard enough to love him? He'd admitted he was a berserker. Could she risk loving him when he might go into an animal-like frenzy and kill her?

She dropped the phone into her handbag. Was Ula right? Did he actually become an animal?

She glanced out the window. Her aunts were marching up and down the driveway, carrying their weapons, ready to shoot the berserker. Howard.

Wolf or bear?

Chapter Fifteen

*H*oward checked his phone for missed calls or texts. Nothing. A week had passed since his last conversation with Elsa. An agonizingly slow week where each day had dragged by, crushing his hopes that she would contact him.

Had she simply dismissed him from her thoughts? Was he that easy to forget? Or was she keeping a distance in order to protect him from her aunts? She had texted him that warning. Did that mean she cared?

What had the aunts told her? That as a berserker, he was a murderous beast? Since they wanted to shoot him, they had to believe he wanted to attack her. Had they convinced Elsa to be afraid of him?

Dammit, he wanted her to trust him. But how could he prove himself to her if he never saw her? Right now, his strategy was to prove his worthiness by honoring her wishes and staying away from her. But that was frustrating the hell out of him. It seemed lame, even cowardly. The bear in him wanted to barge into her motel room and demand respect. Unfortunately, a move like that

would probably terrify Elsa. And it might earn
him a few bullets in his stubborn hide.

He continued to deliver two dozen donuts to
the gatehouse at dawn each day. And he did a
quick inspection of the house so he could report
to Shanna. In the past week, the construction
crew had dug out the basement floor, lowering it
by two feet. Then they'd laid a vapor barrier and
a concrete floor. They'd reinforced the walls and
rebuilt the staircase to the cellar.

He'd gone to the house for two meetings with
Alastair and Oskar, and one interview with the
camerawoman, Madge. All three times, Elsa and
her aunts were nowhere in sight. Apparently, she
was given a warning to vacate the premises before
he arrived.

Angus, Emma, and all the guys on the mission
in Mexico had returned after successfully rescuing the American hostages. Ian and Robby were
delighted to be back at the school with their pregnant wives. Connor had asked Howard if he and
his wife could borrow his cabin nearby in the Adirondacks. Apparently he and Marielle had fond
memories of the place. Carlos was happy to be
back, helping his wife with their newborn twins.

Howard sighed. It seemed like everyone was in
a happy, loving relationship but him. He pushed
that miserable thought aside and turned his attention to the plan to wreak vengeance on Rhett
Bleddyn.

Harry sent him updates every day from Alaska.
He was printing daily exposés on Rhett in *Northern Lights Sound Bites*, and the mainstream media

was scrambling after his tasty tidbits like a pack of vultures. Rhett was followed everywhere, hounded by the press. Television and newspaper reporters interviewed people who confirmed that Rhett was harassing their towns and trying to force them out of their homes.

As more bad press built up, more disgruntled people came out of hiding. Former employees who'd felt mistreated. Women who claimed Rhett had sexually assaulted them. The snowballs Harry had thrown were quickly becoming an avalanche.

Howard called his friend to congratulate him. "You're doing great, Harry!"

"Thanks." Harry laughed. "I wish you could see Rhett's face these days. He's looking so whipped."

Howard smiled. "It's about time he suffered for all his crimes."

"Yeah. He'll never be able to run for office. And the politicians that used to be in his pocket, they're all trying to distance themselves. I wouldn't be surprised if his minions start to mutiny."

"That would be perfect." Howard couldn't think of a better way to hurt Rhett than making him lose his status as Pack Master. Without all his minions to order around, he'd be rendered virtually powerless.

"I may be hard to reach for the next few days," Harry said. "I'm going up the Yukon River to the site where our fathers had their logging company."

Howard tensed. If his friend's suspicions were correct, their fathers had been murdered. "I don't know if you'll find much. The buildings burned down thirty-four years ago."

"Yeah. But I'm looking for people. Anyone who remembers anything."

"All right. Be careful. I'll talk to you when you get back." Howard hung up.

Was Harry right to suspect foul play? Who would have wanted to kill their fathers? Howard had been four years old when the men had died, too young to know if his father had been plagued with business problems or enemies.

He reached for a donut and, as usual, his thoughts returned to Elsa. Was she eating the donuts he left every morning? Maybe he should try something different, like leaving her flowers. Clearly, his current strategy was yielding zero results. Time to shake things up.

The flower strategy was off to a lousy start. The next morning, after picking up donuts at dawn, he'd discovered the only place in town that sold flowers was the small grocery store, and they didn't open until 7:00 a.m. He'd eaten four bear claws in his SUV waiting for the store to open.

Now, at 7:05, as he was returning to his vehicle with flowers and a card, he spotted Alastair driving down Main Street in the rental car. Elsa and her two aunts followed in another car.

Dammit, he was late! He tossed the flowers onto the passenger seat and turned on the engine. *Wait.* He'd better not catch up with them. If they saw him, they might think he was stalking them. And he couldn't park in the driveway next to them at the gatehouse.

He needed to give them a few minutes. To pass the time, he took a pen from the glove compartment and wrote Elsa a note on the card. Then he slipped it under the ribbon that was tied around the flowers and tissue paper.

He turned onto Main Street and drove slowly out of town so he wouldn't catch up with Elsa. He passed the driveway to the gatehouse, then pulled over and parked at the head of the trail that led to the house. With his arms full, he hurried through the woods. The trail ended at the driveway, but he stopped before that, keeping himself hidden behind some trees. There, on the driveway, he spied two cars in front of the house.

Elsa and her aunts were standing by a car, talking. One aunt looked middle-aged, and the other older with silvery blond hair, but they were clearly related to Elsa. Both were tall and fair, still pretty. As he watched, one of the women opened the car trunk and pulled out a shotgun.

Holy crap. Elsa hadn't been kidding. Her aunts were armed and dangerous.

He circled to the back of the house, keeping himself well hidden, then set his gifts on the steps to unlock the back door with his key.

He cracked the door and peered inside. The foyer was empty. He could hear footsteps toward the front of the house, probably Alastair. He grabbed his gifts and darted across the foyer and into the kitchen.

So far, so good. He set the large box of donuts on the kitchen table, just like he'd been doing every

morning for the past week, then placed the flowers next to it. It was the biggest bouquet they'd had
in the grocery store—pink roses that reminded
him of Elsa's pretty mouth, white daisies as soft
as her skin, and big green fronds that reminded
him of her eyes.

He was halfway to the door when he heard
Elsa's voice. In the foyer.

"Ready for your morning donut?"

"Lord, yes," Alastair answered. "We'd better
grab a few before Oskar and The B Boys arrive."

Elsa chuckled. "I swear they inhale the entire
box in five seconds . . ."

Howard took a quick peek. *Holy crap.* He couldn't
exit the back door without them seeing him.

He surveyed the kitchen. A small window over
the old sink. Too small. Another door on the far
side of the room.

He dashed over to it and peered inside. Jack-
pot. There was a huge opening in the wall where
a big window had been taken out. He could slip
through there and make it back to his SUV without Elsa seeing him.

He hesitated. Was this the cowardly way out?
Why not stay in the kitchen and confront her? But
he'd given his word not to see her. And what if her
aunts came running with their weapons?

No, he'd leave for now. Maybe the flower strategy would work and she would contact him. It
would be better if it was her decision to see him.

He eased inside the small room and shut the
door.

Elsa followed Alastair into the kitchen and smiled when he headed straight for the table. She was getting hooked on the daily donuts, too.

She set her tool belt on the counter, close to the kitchen sink. Today, she would take measurements and plan how to tackle the cabinets. She would need to add more overhead ones. And a big island with more—

"Blimey, look at this."

She turned to see what Alastair was pointing at. Flowers? Her mouth fell open. "For . . . for me?"

Alastair gave her a wry look. "You think Howard has a crush on *me*? Besides, your name is on the card. That's what we call a clue."

"Oh." Her heart swelled in her chest. Howard had given her flowers?

She rushed over to the table. "They're beautiful!"

Flowers from Howard. She touched the card with his bold handwriting, then gently stroked one of the pink roses. She couldn't recall ever getting flowers before. Her last boyfriend had surprised her on Valentine's Day with two tickets to a wrestling match. Somehow, guys never understood that inside her large body there was a woman who craved pretty, girly things as much as any other female.

But Howard understood. And he hadn't forgotten her or given up on her.

"Are you sure you don't want to see him?" Alastair watched her closely. "You have an incredibly sappy look—"

"Hush." She glared at him, then grabbed the flowers and marched toward the kitchen sink, putting her back to him so he couldn't see her read the note. She lay the bouquet down next to her tool belt.

Crack! A loud noise erupted in the room next door, followed by a man's shout.

She jumped.

"What the hell?" Alastair ran toward the laundry room and flung the door open. "Oh my God."

"What?" Elsa bumped up against him, trying to see into the room.

She gasped. There was a huge, gaping hole in the floor. Someone had fallen through? A masculine groan floated up from the cellar. *Howard?*

She rushed forward.

"Careful." Alastair grabbed her arm. "Don't get too close."

She craned her neck, trying to peer into the hole. "Howard, is that you?"

A groan answered, then a muttered, "Holy crap."

Her heart plummeted. Howard could be seriously injured.

"Call an ambulance," Alastair whispered. "I'll go downstairs to check on him." He rushed from the room.

An ambulance? A wave of dizziness swept over Elsa, and she crouched on the floor to keep from falling. Where had she left her handbag and cell phone? In the kitchen? The parlor? Had Howard gotten hurt bringing her flowers?

"Howard?" She crawled toward the hole. It was dark in the cellar, and she could barely make out his form.

"Elsa, don't get close to the edge," he called up to her. "You could fall."

He was worried about her? Her aunts had to be wrong. Howard wasn't a beast, planning to harm her. The poor guy had to be in pain, yet he was more concerned about her safety than his own injuries.

"How badly are you hurt?" she asked.

"Just a few scrapes. No big deal."

She suspected he was making light of it. "What were you doing?"

"I—I was running late this morning. I thought I could leave through the window opening."

A pang of guilt shot through her chest. He had tried to leave the house without her seeing him. He'd gotten injured trying to honor her wishes.

A light suddenly brightened the cellar, and Alastair appeared below, aiming a flashlight at Howard. She gasped at the sight of blood on his arms and chest. He'd fallen at least ten feet right onto hard cement. His clothes had been ripped by the jagged ends of the wooden floor that had cracked and collapsed under his weight.

"Any broken bones?" Alastair knelt beside him. "Did you hit your head?"

"I'm okay."

"We'll let a doctor decide that." Alastair glanced up at Elsa. "Did you call the ambulance?"

"No!" Howard sat up and grabbed his rib cage, wincing. "I don't need that."

"Bloody hell," Alastair hissed. "You should have been backboarded. Now lay still until—"

"No." Howard rose slowly to his feet. "This is no big deal. I'll be fine."

"You're not fine!" Alastair shouted. "You're bleeding."

Howard limped out of Elsa's view. She scooted back, then ran toward the head of the stairs. In a few minutes, she saw him slowly climbing up from the basement.

Her heart squeezed. He looked so beat up. "Can I take you to a doctor?"

He glanced up at her. "I appreciate that, but there's no need."

"I'm so sorry you felt you had to . . . escape out a window. I feel terrible—"

"No, don't feel bad." He reached the top of the stairs and whispered, "I'll be fine. I'm self-healing."

She blinked. "You mean you can—" She leaned close. "It's like a superpower?"

"Something like that." He gave her a wry smile. "Can we meet sometime when I'm not bleeding on the floor?"

She gazed into his eyes, and for the life of her, she couldn't see the wild beast her aunts warned her about. All she could see was a man who was strong enough to retain his sense of humor and polite demeanor even when suffering from pain.

"Howard," Alastair said as he came up the stairs, "at least let me take you to the clinic in town."

"It's not necessary," Howard assured him. "There's a clinic where I work, so I'll be on my way." He gave Elsa a hopeful look. "Will you call me?"

She nodded. "Yes." Her aunts would throw a fit if they found out, but they didn't know Howard like she did.

"Good." He smiled at her. "You must think I'm an awful klutz."

She shook her head, her cheeks warming with a blush. "No." She thought he was the sweetest man she'd ever met.

He glanced toward the front door. "To avoid sustaining further injuries such as gunshot wounds, I'll just make my exit out the back."

She winced. "I understand." As he walked haltingly toward the back door, her heart squeezed.

"Be careful," she called as he eased out the door.

"You're totally smitten," Alastair whispered.

"Hush."

"Not that I blame you. The man nearly killed himself just to bring you flowers."

She shot him an irritated look, then rushed into the kitchen. She spotted Howard through the small window over the sink. He was walking into the woods.

She opened the note he'd left with the flowers. *Give me a chance to prove I'm worthy of you.*

"Oh, Howard," she whispered. She glanced back at the window.

He was going deeper into the woods. Shouldn't he be going toward the road so he could return to the school and the clinic there?

I'm self-healing. Maybe he didn't need a clinic.

She bit her lip, watching him disappear among

the trees. Where was he going? How did he heal himself? Dammit, there was so much she didn't know about him. How could she make an informed decision on whether to trust him, when she didn't have enough information?

She rushed into the foyer.

"Oskar's here," Alastair yelled as he headed for the front door.

"I—I'm going to make sure Howard gets back to his car all right."

Alastair glanced back with a smirk. "Right. Take all the time you need, luv."

"Ah, if you could not mention it to my aunts—"

"Mum's the word." Alastair pretended to zip his mouth.

"Thanks." She slipped out the back door and jogged into the woods in the direction Howard had gone.

After a few minutes, she was surrounded by trees and beginning to wish she'd left a trail of donut crumbs. It would be just her luck to get lost in the woods. The dark, creepy woods.

She snorted to herself. Some Guardian of the Forest she made. All the trees looked alike to her. She glanced back. The house was no longer visible. A deer peeked around a tree, watching her. Then another deer peered around a bush.

"Sheesh," she whispered. "You guys always show up. At least I don't have to worry about being alone in the dark, creepy woods." Though she doubted these two deer could offer her much protection.

The deer ambled closer.

They were bigger than she'd thought. She stepped back. "That's close enough."

They stopped but continued to stare at her.

"What do you want?" Did they expect her to do some sort of guardian thing? What the heck did a guardian do?

She waved a hand in the air. "Carry on, my loyal subjects. Cheerio."

They gazed at her blankly.

Apparently, being a guardian wasn't like being a queen. "Look, I don't mean to disturb your normal routine. I'm just trying to find a man who passed through this way."

The deer sprinted past her, then paused to glance back with an inviting look.

"He went that way?"

They cantered off, and she jogged after them. "I hope you're not taking me to some weird animal ceremony. I never liked venison, okay?" Except in sausage, but she wouldn't tell them that.

She winced. What if they could hear her thoughts?

She followed them for about five minutes, weaving around trees and jumping over moss-covered logs. Then they scampered downhill, moving quickly and nimbly. She slowed down, afraid she would skid on the damp, fallen leaves and hurt herself in the middle of nowhere.

The sound of rushing water grew louder, and the ravine grew steeper and rockier. She picked her way down slowly, grasping the branches of trees to keep her balance.

Finally, she reached the bottom. The trees ended, along with the spongy ground covered with pine needles. A rocky slab extended toward the edge of a creek. The sun shone brightly, and she blinked to adjust her eyes.

The stream serpentined along the bottom of the ravine, tumbling over rocks and meandering around large boulders. Downstream, she spotted Howard, partially hidden behind a pile of rocks. His back was to her, his torso bare. He'd taken off his shirt.

The deer scampered downstream, their hooves clattering on the rocky slab.

He turned toward the sound, and Elsa ducked back behind the tree line. *Chicken. Why don't you let him know you're here?*

She winced. She wasn't sure he wanted her here. After all, if a man wandered off into the woods, didn't that mean he wanted to be alone? If he had to use some sort of superpower to heal himself, he probably wanted to keep it secret.

But if he was serious about having a relationship with her, then he shouldn't keep secrets. She eased quietly downstream, making sure she was hidden behind trees and bushes. Luckily, the deer had decided to scurry back up the hill, and they were making enough noise to cover any noise she made.

Thanks, guys! She called out to them mentally. *Great.* Now she was as crazy as her aunts.

She spotted Howard, standing behind a large boulder that was flat on top. Apparently, he had washed his shirt in the stream, for it was wet, and he was laying it on top of the sunny rock to dry. She tiptoed farther downstream so she could see him from behind.

He was standing where the stream made a sharp turn. A wall of granite had impeded its progress, resulting in a pothole where the water was deep enough for swimming.

She winced at the raw and bloody scrapes along his torso and arms. Poor Howard. He kicked off his shoes, then unbuckled his pants and dropped them.

Her breath caught, and she covered her mouth. With his super hearing, she had to be careful not to make a sound. But it was hard, so hard not to whimper when he hooked his thumbs into the elastic waistband of his blue cotton briefs and slowly eased them over his rump.

Oh God. She squeezed her eyes shut and turned, pressing her back against the large tree that hid her. She was as bad as a Peeping Tom. Ogling the poor guy when he was covered with scrapes and blood.

But shouldn't she see how badly he was injured? She opened her eyes and peered around the tree.

Good Lord. Her heart stilled. He had the most beautiful rump in the world. No, the universe. Poetry should be written and songs dedicated to it.

Her eyes widened as she took in his entire form from the back. Huge, hunky Howard.

He stepped into the pool, walking forward till the water was up to his waist. Then he washed the blood off his arms and chest. Was this part of his healing routine? Whatever it was, it was beautiful to watch.

He scooped up some water with his big hands

and splashed it on his face. Another scoop, and he raked it through his hair. His biceps bulged. The muscles in his back rippled. Her knees threatened to buckle.

She crouched behind the large tree, but a bush obstructed her view. She eased a branch aside. He had turned and was now facing her. *Oh God, lucky break.* He might have seen her if she hadn't knelt in the nick of time.

She closed her eyes, chiding herself. *You should be ashamed of yourself, ogling the poor man when he's injured.*

She opened her eyes and gasped. He was turning gray!

He looked up.

Dammit. She hunkered lower behind the bush. What on earth was going on? A man's skin color didn't just change like that.

She peeked again. Gray! He looked like a Greek god, sculpted out of pewter. His eyes blazed a deep blue.

Her heart raced. This had to be his superpower. This was how he healed himself!

She took another peek and choked. His body was shimmering, growing, changing. Hair sprouted. His face contorted, shimmered, then snapped into sharp focus.

A bear.

Her knees and arms buckled, and she collapsed on the ground. Dazed, she watched him through the branches.

She blinked, and he was still there.

Howard was a bear.

She shook her head. She'd wondered if he could be a wolf or bear, but now, with the proof right in front of her, she still found it hard to believe. But there he was. A huge, freaking bear. Not a cute little panda. A humongous, hulking grizzly bear!

He splashed around in the water, then lumbered out onto the bank and shook himself. Droplets of water shot out in all directions.

Her heart lurched as reality finally slapped her hard across the face. She was about thirty feet away from a grizzly bear!

Panic slammed into her. What could she do? If she ran up the hill, he would see her and chase her down. *He*? Was it a *he*? Was there any of Howard in that huge beast?

Oh God, she should have listened to her aunts! They'd warned her that he was a berserker, that he could turn into a beast, a killing machine.

What did a person do when confronted with a grizzly? Play dead? She pulled her knees up and hugged them, her back pressed to the tree. Her heart raced, thundering in her ears so loudly that she was afraid he would hear.

He would come after her. He would smell her. Hear her. He would come to kill her.

Was this what had happened to her grandmother? Was she mauled to death by a bear?

Elsa heard steps behind her, heavy and lumbering, coming toward her.

Hot tears gathered in her eyes. How could she have been so stupid? Why hadn't she heeded the warnings from her aunts? Would they ever find her body, ever know what had happened to her?

Get a grip. She squeezed her knees to her chest. She would have to play dead. No matter what the bear did to her, she couldn't react. *God, please, let it leave me alone.*

The bush beside her shook, and she heard a snuffling sound behind it.

Don't move. Don't react.

The bear lumbered slowly into view, making a wide circle till it stopped about fifteen feet in front of her.

Her heart raced, and she tensed, bracing herself for impact. It would attack any second now.

It sat.

She waited, but nothing happened. Slowly, she let her gaze wander up its massive body to its head.

It tilted its large head, studying her.

Howard's eyes. She inhaled sharply, then froze, determined not to react. But what grizzly had sharp blue eyes? Intelligent eyes that watched her every move. Was Howard in there?

The bear rose onto all fours, then walked toward her. Her fingers dug into her jeans. *Don't move. Don't react.*

It stopped about six feet from her and sat.

What was it doing? Playing with her before it attacked? Or giving her time to adjust? Adjust to what? Her death or her future?

It stood again and moved closer. She held her breath.

It nudged her foot with its snout, then looked at her. Its blue eyes looked peaceful, almost friendly.

She drew in a shaky breath.

It nudged her knee with its snout, then looked at her again.

"Howard?" she whispered.

It made an odd, groaning sound, then moved closer, its snout only inches away.

This was it. She closed her eyes. It was either going to let her go or maul her to death.

It nudged her right shoulder.

Burning hot flames shot through her birthmark. She gasped in pain, then slumped over as everything went black.

Chapter Sixteen

Holy crap! Howard shifted back to human form.

"Elsa?" He brushed her hair back from her face, his hand still gray from the shifting process.

She was breathing, but unconscious. He didn't know if she'd fainted from shock or pain. Maybe both. His nose still burned from where his snout had touched her birthmark.

With his hands now back to their normal color, he rolled up the short sleeve of her T-shirt. He'd been curious about her mark since their first meeting. The bear had been curious, too, but Howard would have restrained the beast if he'd known the touch was going to hurt her.

Heat radiated from the birthmark, an angry red circle on her shoulder with clawlike extensions. It resembled an animal paw and looked like a large animal had grasped her by the shoulder.

"Elsa, it's all right." No response.

He lifted her in his arms and carried her back to the stream. A few feet into the pool, where it was still shallow, there was a flat rock. He sat on it with her draped across his lap.

"Time to wake up," he murmured, trying not to

think about her lovely rump nestled against his groin.

He dangled his hand in the cool stream, then stroked her cheek with his wet fingers. "Wake up, sweetheart." He dampened his hand again and brushed her hair back from her brow.

She moaned.

Was she still in pain? If he touched her birthmark with his bare hand, would it hurt her again? He looked around for something to use and spotted his cotton briefs nearby on the bank, where he'd dropped them on top of his pants. With his trousers and shirt both torn and bloody, the briefs were the cleanest choice. He grabbed the underwear, dunked it into the cool water, then pressed it against her hot birthmark.

Her eyes fluttered open.

"There you are." He smiled. "You were starting to scare me."

She stared at him, a dazed look on her face.

"You fainted." He sloshed his underwear into the stream again, then pressed it to her birthmark. "I didn't mean to make this burn again. I'm sorry."

A shudder skittered through her, then she frantically looked around.

"It's all right." He gave her a reassuring smile. "You should know by now that I'm not going to hurt you. I'm wild about you."

Her eyes widened, taking on a tinge of panic. "Wild?"

He winced. "Bad word choice. How about smitten? Infatuated?"

"No!" She scrambled out of his arms and

stumbled onto the bank of the stream. "You—" She pointed a trembling finger at him. "You're— you're—" She blinked and looked him over.

"Four letters, starts with a *b*."

"Butt-naked!"

"That, too." He nodded. "Though it's probably a minor issue at the moment."

She dragged a hand through her hair as her gaze darted nervously about. "I didn't imagine it, did I?"

"No."

Her gaze landed on the tree where she'd hidden earlier. With a shaky breath, she pressed a hand to her heart. "I thought I was going to die." Her eyes shimmered with tears. "I thought you were going to kill me."

"Elsa." He started to get up. "Sweethea—"

"*No!*" She jumped, her hands spread out. "Don't move."

He sat back on the rock, half of his rump underwater. With his knees bent and his arms crossed over them, most of his groin was hidden. Which was good at the moment. "There's no need to be afraid of me."

"No need?" She waved her arms. "You're a bear! A huge, freaking grizzly bear!"

"And I didn't hurt you." He winced. "Except for the burn from your birthmark. I didn't expect that to happen. I thought it was a onetime deal." Maybe it was a onetime occurrence for him in each form as human and bear.

She bit her lip, watching him with a look that was part disbelief, part terror.

Dammit, he didn't want her to be afraid of him. Some day they would laugh about this, and the sooner that day arrived, the better. "I knew you were there, Elsa. I could smell your scent. And you moved through the forest like a herd of buffalo—"

"*What?*"

He smiled. That was more like it. He'd take her anger, embarrassment, annoyance—any emotion but fear. "Did you enjoy the show?"

"Watching you turn into a beast?" She shuddered. "Of course not! It was a horror show."

"I was referring to the peep show. When you watched me strip."

She looked away, her cheeks pink. "I—I didn't expect you to do that. I just followed you here out of concern for your health."

His mouth twitched. "That was kind of you."

"It was the least I could do. After all, you were injured bringing me flowers."

"Did you like them?"

"Yes." She gave him a sheepish look. "Okay. It wasn't just concern. I was curious. You said you were self-healing, and I wanted to see how it worked. The last thing I expected was for you to . . ."

"Shift?"

She shuddered. "Is that what you call it?"

"I have to shift in order to heal." He lifted his arms to the side. "See? The scrapes are gone. I had a real bad one here, just above my hip." He leaned to the side to show her.

Her eyes widened, then she looked away. "I believe you."

"And my cracked ribs are completely healed."

She turned back to him with an alarmed expression. "You had cracked ribs?"

"Yes." He ran his hands over his chest and across his abs. "I was in a great deal of pain."

Her gaze followed his hands. "I'm glad you're better now."

He lifted his leg nearest her. "I had some scrapes along my calf, and even here on my thigh."

A glazed look came over her face.

"Of course, you saw all my injuries when you hid behind the tree over there like a Peeping Tom."

She stiffened. "Excuse me?"

"I believe you gasped when I pulled my underwear off."

She gasped. "I did not! I was very careful not to make any noise—" She winced, and her face turned pink.

He grinned.

"You have some nerve!" Her eyes flashed with anger. "Making it sound like I'm some kind of pervert, when you're—you're a *beast*!"

He narrowed his eyes. "Maybe you shouldn't follow men into the woods."

"Maybe you should have warned me!"

"How? For the past week, you refused to talk to me!"

"If you knew I was behind that tree, you should have warned me." She crossed her arms and glared at him. "You scared me to death."

"A warning would have scared you, too." He raked a hand through his hair. "Try to see this from my point of view. I was in a lot of pain, so I needed to shift. I didn't ask you to come along and spy on me, but when I realized you were there, I thought why not shift in front of you? I was going to have to tell you sooner or later, and I thought I could show you how harmless the bear is."

She snorted. "Harmless? Why would I think a grizzly bear is harmless?"

"Because it's *me*! Couldn't you see it was me?"

She bit her lip. "I was too scared to think very well."

"I've been scared since the moment I met you, scared that you would run away from me once you knew the truth." He winced. That was more than he should have admitted. He grabbed his wet briefs and shook them out.

"You cooled down my birthmark with your underwear?"

He gave her a wry look. "They're clean. Reasonably." He'd showered and put them on just over an hour ago. "Do you want to watch again?" He dragged the cotton briefs up his legs.

With a huff, she turned her back to him. "You really are a beast."

"That's true." Smiling again, he stood and pulled his underwear up. He was still semi-aroused from holding her, and the wet material clung to every contour.

"You were so big," she whispered.

"Thank you. I like to think I'm fairly well endowed."

She scoffed, turning to face him. "I meant the bear!" She glanced down at his underwear, then away.

His mouth twitched. He'd known what she was referring to, but it was too much fun teasing her. "I'm actually a Kodiak bear. That's the biggest of the grizzlies."

"Great," she muttered.

He pulled on his trousers. "And in case you're wondering, I'm proportional."

"Huh?" She slanted a suspicious look his way.

"By that I mean—" He carefully zipped his pants up. "I'm big all over."

She snorted and looked away. "As if I'm interested."

"Aren't you?" He leaned against the boulder to pull on his socks. "You followed me here."

She planted her hands on her hips and glared at him. "Fine. I acknowledge your bigness. You have a big chest. And big shoulders."

"Thank you." He tugged on the last sock.

"Big muscles."

"Yes." He stuffed his feet into his shoes.

"An enormously big ego."

He grinned. "That, too." He slipped on his polo shirt. It was ripped in places and still damp.

She lifted her chin. "But I'm not sure you'll do. I hate a man with a big butt."

"I love a woman with a smart mouth." He strode toward her, still smiling.

She stepped back, her eyes widening. "What are you—"

He pulled her into his arms.

She stiffened. "Your shirt's wet."

"Relax." He wrapped his arms around her and

rubbed his chin against her hair. "It's me. Whether I'm human or bear, it's always me."

She groaned. "A man who becomes a bear? It's too strange."

"Stranger than being a Guardian of the Forest?"

"I didn't ask for that."

"I didn't ask to be a were-bear."

She leaned back to look at him. "Is that what you call it?"

He nodded. "Or a shifter. Actually, there are a lot of shifters who didn't come from Scandanavia, so they're not berserkers. I know some panthers and tigers—"

"What?" She pushed away from him. "Are you telling me people turn into those things?"

"There's more to the world than you would normally—"

"I don't want to hear it!" She lifted a hand to stop him. "I'm having supernatural overload. I want a nice, normal world."

"Fine. Then look at it this way. Right now, I'm a man. You're a woman. One hell of a woman." His gaze dropped to her chest, which had been dampened by his wet shirt. Her T-shirt was molded to her breasts, her nipples clearly defined. "And the feelings we're having are completely normal. The attraction. The desire."

She sucked in a deep breath. "I'm not sure I can handle this."

"I want you." He moved closer. "I've always wanted you."

"No," she whispered, but her body betrayed her.

Her nipples puckered, the tips growing tight as beads.

"You want me, too." He cupped her breast, and she stepped back.

"Please. I need more time."

"Elsa." He wrapped his arms around her and pulled her tight. "I'll give you all the time you need, but please don't spend it convincing yourself that I'm dangerous. Or that I'm going to hurt you. How could I hurt you when I'm falling for you?"

"Oh, Howard." She rested her head on his shoulder. "I do want to believe you, but this were-bear stuff is so . . ."

"Amazing?"

"Frightening." She leaned back to study his face. "What if you lose control?"

"I'm always in complete control. Of the bear, that is." He glanced down at his swollen groin. "Other parts seem to have a mind of their own."

She gave him a wry look. "Beast."

"Goldilocks." He kissed her brow. "Will you admit the truth?"

"What truth?"

He leaned close to whisper in her ear, "You liked my butt."

She swatted his shoulder. "Would you get over yourself?"

He chuckled. "I would actually prefer to talk about *your* naked body. If you could give me something to go on." His hand slid over the curve of her rump. "Oh, yeah, this is—"

"Will you stop?" She shoved him away with an

exasperated look. "I'm still in shock, and you keep trying to feel me up?"

"Right." He nodded. "My apologies." He gave her a forlorn look. "I'm a bad little bear."

Her mouth twitched. "Can you ever be serious?"

"I'm serious about you." He smiled. "Seriously."

She gave him a bemused look. "And this is the personality of a grizzly?"

"Think of me as a big, cuddly, honey bear."

She snorted and turned to walk up the hill. "I don't know what to think."

At least she didn't seem afraid of him anymore. He caught up with her. "Can I see you tomorrow?"

"I don't know." She slanted him an annoyed look. "Can you manage to stay human for the entire time?"

"Yes. But it would be fun to act like animals."

"Beast."

"Goldilocks." He took her hand to help her up a steep incline. "So I'll see you tomorrow morning?"

"Maybe." She sighed. "It would have to be secret. My aunts would shoot you on sight."

"I understand."

They reached the top of the hill. The walk back to the house would be easy now, but he didn't let go of her hand. With a smile, he realized she wasn't pulling away. Even though she knew he was a beast.

Chapter Seventeen

A beautiful man came to her in the night. Large and powerful, he covered her body with his. His big hands roamed over her skin, setting her on fire. She wanted him. She cried out for him. She burned for him.

His hands were magic. Skimming the length of her legs. Fondling her breasts. Stroking her neck. Tightening their grip.

Choking her.

She thrashed against him, but he was too strong. Too powerful.

His face, half hidden in shadow, twisted in rage. Transformed. He roared like an animal.

She gazed up at him in horror. In the flicker of firelight, she caught a glimpse of his head.

A bear.

She woke with a strangled cry.

"Elsa?" Great-aunt Ula clicked on the bedside lamp.

She covered her eyes while her vision adjusted to the bright light. "I'm fine."

"Are you sure?" Ula asked in Swedish.

"*Ja*. It was just a bad dream."

"I'll get you some water." Ula headed toward the vanity.

Elsa sat up and leaned against the headboard. A week had passed since she'd last had the nightmare. Seeing Howard turn into a beast must have kicked her subconscious back into action.

"Were you dreaming about berserkers?" Ula asked as she opened a bottle of water.

"Yes." One berserker in particular, although Elsa didn't want to admit that. Why had the dream come back? Was she simply freaked out over Howard's ability to shift into a grizzly? Who wouldn't freak out over that? Or was her subconscious trying to force her to accept a truth she'd been avoiding? That Howard could be dangerous.

He could betray her and kill her. Just like the berserker who killed the original Guardian of the Forest.

She shuddered. How could she be so attracted to Howard, when he was a beast? How could she fall for a real-life berserker who might kill her?

Even her subconscious had succumbed to the attraction. At the beginning of the dream, when the man was making love to her, she writhed beneath his powerful body, hungry for his touch. And in her mind, she knew who he was. *Howard.* Huge, handsome Howard. When his hands cupped her breasts, she arched up to him, begging him to suckle her. When his hands stroked her legs, she opened her thighs for him. She was dying for him. *Hot Howard.*

She'd actually enjoyed the dream until he'd started choking her. *Horror-show Howard.*

"Here." Ula offered her a glass of water.

"Thanks." She took a sip.

"Do you want to talk about it?" Ula asked.

"Not really." She set the glass on the bedside table. "Can you tell me about my grandmother?"

"Of course." Ula perched on the side of her bed. Her face softened with a smile as she remembered. "Birgit was a beautiful woman, much like you. She grew up knowing about the curse, but she never feared it. She loved being the Guardian of the Forest. I tried to keep her with me on the island, where she would be safe, but she never stayed for long. She had a cabin deep in the woods, and she would go there often to be with the animals. They were her dearest friends."

Elsa recalled how she had apparently communicated with the deer earlier that day. "My grandmother could talk to the animals?"

"Yes. As her powers grew, she was able to do even more. One time, I saw her heal a deer with a broken leg simply by touching it."

Elsa's breath caught. Would she actually develop powers like that? "That's amazing."

"Birgit was amazing. The animals would gather around her, wildcats sitting alongside rabbits without harming them. They were at peace with her. They were devoted to her." Ula sighed. "Some of them died trying to save her."

A chill skittered down Elsa's back. "How . . . how did she die?"

"We're not sure. No one was there to witness it, but she was mauled to death by a wild animal. There was a herd of deer scattered around her, also mauled to death. They'd tried to protect her."

Goose bumps prickled Elsa's arms. Mauled to death by a wild animal? It would have to be a big and ferocious animal to take out a herd of deer. Ferocious enough to kill a herd of feral pigs?

She swallowed hard. "You think the animal was a berserker?"

"Yes." Ula nodded. "Birgit had met someone a few weeks earlier who made her birthmark burn. According to family legend, only a berserker can make it burn. And the murder happens soon after that."

"But you don't have actual proof that it's a berserker who commits the murders?"

"Who else could it be?" Ula asked. "The guardian and berserker are forever linked together in a cruel dance that has repeated itself over and over through the centuries. The guardian made the berserkers, dooming those men to roam the earth as beasts. And they, in turn, are doomed to seek out their creator and destroy her."

Elsa grimaced. So she was doomed to die?

She rubbed her brow. Surely they weren't robots preprogrammed for disaster. They had free will. Couldn't they choose a different destiny? What if they loved each other? Wouldn't that break the curse? Howard had suggested that on the voice mail he'd left her.

But Howard was a berserker, a bear. If the bear's instinct was to kill her, could he stop it?

If she continued to see Howard, wasn't that akin to playing Russian roulette? What if he couldn't always control the bear?

A momentary lapse could mean her death.

Howard knew something was wrong when Elsa didn't answer his text message the next morning. He'd asked her to meet him during her break, but she never responded.

He'd half expected this. She had a lot to adjust to, and she'd said she needed time. But time might allow her fear to grow to the point that she rejected him.

He sat at his desk in the security office at Dragon Nest, contemplating his next move. What he needed was a new strategy that would convince her he could be trusted. The bear inside him wanted to haul her off to his nearby cabin and ravish her until she surrendered herself completely.

Howard snorted. The bear tended to think only in physical terms, and while it was true that he was dying to make love to Elsa, her surrender was the last thing he wanted. He wanted her to choose him. He wanted her to love him and come to him of her own free will.

For it wasn't just her body and beautiful face that attracted him. It was her bold spirit, her bright intelligence, her wry sense of humor, her creativity, bravery, generosity, vulnerability—everything that made Elsa who she was. The more he got to know her, the more he craved her.

He wanted to hold her, kiss her, make her moan with pleasure, and watch her shudder with release. He wanted to make her laugh. Wanted to wake her every morning with a kiss. Wanted to cheer her on when she crafted beautiful cabinets and woodwork. He wanted her to succeed. Be happy.

He thought back to the wish he'd made in the park. To love without regret. He wanted his love to bring Elsa joy.

Face it. You're in love with her.

The thought didn't alarm him. Deep in his soul, he'd known he was falling in love with her, and he'd never been tempted to stop it. It felt right. They felt right.

The only problem was the fear generated by his being a berserker. Any woman in her right mind would be afraid to date a man who could turn into a beast. And Elsa had it even worse, for she was descended from a long line of women who were apparently killed by berserkers.

Somehow he had to convince her she was safe with him. That she could trust him. He recalled what she said that night in the park. She'd wished that he could be trusted.

That meant that deep inside, she wanted to trust him, wanted to fall for him. He just needed to tap into that and give her what she truly desired. He wasn't going to give up. He wouldn't even wait.

He would press forward.

Later that afternoon, Elsa was alone, working in the kitchen. The other guys were in the front parlor and dining room, where they were lowering the ceiling by two feet to make room for plumbing and wiring. Madge and her crew had returned from New York City to record their efforts.

Elsa was avoiding the guys today. Yesterday, they had found the flowers and Howard's card on the counter, and now they were having fun teasing her.

She busied herself in the kitchen, removing the cabinet doors. Her plan was to sand and refinish the existing cabinets before building new ones that matched. But first the cabinets needed to be thoroughly cleaned, inside and out.

She was grateful for the hard work. It kept her mind occupied, kept her from thinking about the nightmare with Howard. Or the sexy lovemaking at the beginning of the dream.

She snorted. How foolish could she be? She wanted to think about him fondling her breasts, when his hands eventually grabbed hold of her neck?

Tired of being on her knees with her head inside a cabinet, she straightened and stretched. This was hot, miserable work for July. She pulled off her work gloves, then used some bottled water to wash her hands in the sink and splash some water on her face.

Her cell phone made a dinging noise, signaling a text message.

It was Howard. She groaned. How was she going to tell him she never wanted to see him again? Just the thought brought a pang to her chest. It was going to hurt him. It was already hurting her. And it was too cruel to reject him in a text message. But if she saw him, she didn't know if she could resist him. Huge, handsome Howard.

She read the message.

Look out the window.

She peered out the kitchen window, and her heart swelled. There he was, standing near the woods. How long had he waited there to catch a glimpse of her through the window?

He concentrated on the phone in his hands, and soon her phone dinged again.

I have a picnic basket.

She glanced out the window, and he was lifting a large basket for her to see. A bear with a picnic basket. Her mouth twitched, and she texted back. *Did you get that at Jellystone Park?*

Don't turn me in to Ranger Smith.

She smiled and texted back. *Is it full of donuts?*

Come and see what's inside.

He pocketed his phone, then reached into the basket to pull out a checkered blanket. He stretched it on the ground under the canopy of trees.

Elsa watched as he removed more things from the basket. Horrible Howard. He knew what a curious person she was.

She was also hungry and thirsty. It was after four in the afternoon, and she'd had only a salad for lunch. After long hours of physical labor, the picnic looked terribly tempting. No doubt it was cool and breezy beneath those trees, not hot and stuffy like the kitchen. And he was setting it up close to the house. There were a bunch of guys in the house, and her aunts were stationed on the front driveway. After a week of no action, they spent most of their time in the car now, reading and knitting, but they still had their weapons in the trunk.

It should be safe to meet Howard. For a little while. She wasn't much to look at, with her dirty work clothes, but did it matter, when she was just going to reject him? Another twinge jabbed at her heart.

She grabbed the hairbrush out of her handbag, then quickly brushed her hair and pulled it back into a ponytail.

She took a deep breath. *Enough with the procrastination. Just get the rejection over with. A quick strike would be less painful.*

She marched outside. *Be kind, but firm.*

He glanced back at her and smiled.

Dammit. The man's smile could melt an iceberg. *Stay strong. Determined. Don't waver.* "Is that . . . champagne?"

He filled a second wineglass with white fizzy liquid. "Sparkling white grape juice." He handed her a glass. "I thought this would be best in case you had to operate any machinery."

"Oh." That was thoughtful of him.

"Cheers." He clinked his glass against hers and drank.

Good Lord, she'd never realized how sexy a man's throat could be when his Adam's apple was moving up and down with each swallow. *Don't think about that!* She shook herself and took a sip. The juice was wonderfully chilled. She downed the rest of her glass.

"Good?" He watched her, his mouth curled into the half smile that caused his cheek to dimple.

She nodded, aware of a tingly sensation in her mouth.

"Have a seat." He motioned to the blanket.

"Well, actually . . ." She eyed the plate filled with green grapes, red strawberries, water crackers, and slices of cheese. Another plate held an assortment of Ghirardelli chocolate squares. Would it hurt to share a few bites with him? He'd gone to so much trouble.

"All right." She sat on one edge of the blanket.

He sat on the other side with the plates of food between them. "Let me refill your glass." He leaned closer to pour more juice into her wineglass.

She took a sip. "This was very kind of you."

He popped a grape into his mouth. "The cafeteria lady loaned me the basket. I told her I needed to impress a beautiful woman."

Elsa snorted. "I'm a dirty mess today."

"You're strong and talented at what you do. It's part of what makes you beautiful to me."

She groaned inwardly. Rejecting him was so hard.

"Have some food." He stacked a piece of cheese onto a cracker and bit into it. "How's your day going?"

She nibbled on some cheese. "The guys are teasing me something awful."

"Why?"

"When I followed you yesterday, I left the note on the kitchen counter. You know, the note you wrote . . ."

"Let me prove that I'm worthy of you?"

She nodded, her face growing warm. "Now every time they see me, they bow down and say, 'I'm not worthy'!"

Howard chuckled. "Sorry about that."

She ate another piece of cheese with a cracker and looked about. Three squirrels and a raccoon were watching. A deer was crossing the clearing, headed toward them. "Sheesh, it doesn't take them long to find me."

"Shoo!" Howard waved a hand at them and they scattered.

She huffed. "You don't have to frighten them."

His eyebrows lifted. "Spoken like a true guardian. A week ago, they were freaking you out, and now you're acting protective."

"They don't mean me any harm."

"You can't be sure. I don't think those feral pigs were impressed by your guardianship."

Frowning, she picked a few grapes off the stem. "What do you think? About me being a guardian and all."

"I . . . found it hard to believe at first. My grandfather told me the story a million times when I was growing up, but I always considered it a fairy tale. But now . . ." He sipped some more juice, deep in thought. "It makes sense. Werewolves and werebears exist, so the guardians should exist, too. You made us who we are."

She swallowed hard. Was this why the berserkers killed their guardian? "Do you . . . resent us?"

"For what?"

She winced. "My ancestor turned you into beasts. Doesn't that make you angry?"

"No. Elsa, I'm perfectly happy with who and what I am. I'm super strong, super fast, have superior senses, and I can live for about five hundred years."

Her mouth dropped open. "Are you kidding me?"

"No." He smirked. "How old do you think I am?"

She gasped. "You're hundreds of years old?"

"No! I'm thirty-eight." He dragged a hand through his thick brown hair. "Holy crap. I thought I looked a lot younger."

"Oh. You do." She bit her lip to keep from laughing when he gave her a dubious look. "Sorry. When you said five hundred years, I thought . . ."

"Never mind." He ripped open a foil package of chocolate and stuffed it into his mouth.

"You don't look a day over thirty."

He grunted. "My point is I don't resent being what I am. I like it. And all the were-bears I know like it, too. So you have nothing to fear from them. Or me."

"But we still believe that my grandmother was killed by a berserker. And her grandmother before her."

He grimaced. "I'm really sorry about that. But that happened in Sweden, right? Maybe the berserkers there are a bunch of miserable SOBs. I can tell you for a fact that the were-bears in Alaska are a jolly bunch. We would never harm a woman."

Could that be true? Could the berserkers who left Scandinavia be different? "How did your people end up in Alaska?"

Howard shrugged. "According to my grandfather, they left about a thousand years ago and migrated all the way across Russia."

"How did the line continue? Did they find female were-bears?"

"They didn't have to. The were-bear gene is always dominant, so they were free to marry whomever they pleased."

"And the children were always were-bears?"

Howard nodded. "According to my grandfather, the berserkers did find some were-bears in Alaska. Local shamans who could turn into Kodiak bears. Our line mixed with theirs, and that's why I'm a Kodiak bear."

"Oh." She considered this news. Howard's line of were-bears could be quite different from the berserkers who had remained in Scandinavia. Maybe the curse hadn't followed his people. "But your grandfather still believes you are cursed?"

Howard waved a dismissive hand. "It has no power unless you believe in it."

She nodded. That's what she'd always thought. But the curse had been much easier to dismiss before she'd learned that berserkers were real. "I'm still a bit worried—"

"I know you are. And I've been racking my brain to come up with ways to convince you that I can be trusted." He leaned toward her. "Look me up on the Internet. I used to play for the Chicago Bears."

She blinked. "Football?"

"Yes. I was a defensive—"

"The Chicago *Bears*?" She gave him an incredulous look.

"Yes." His eyes twinkled with humor. "I realize the irony. Anyway, I was a defensive linebacker. I took hits for a living."

"You were a professional football player?"

"Yes. Huge, three-hundred-pound linemen tried to mow me down on a daily basis. Usually, I mowed them down, but believe me, they were trying to hurt me."

"You played professional football?"

His mouth curled into a half smile. "Is there a problem with that?"

"No." *Gosh, no.* She sat back, her cheeks growing warm.

"Well, as I was saying, I was paid to take abuse and annihilate the other team. I sacked a lot of quarterbacks. I realize that sounds . . . aggressive, even violent."

She nodded, restraining an urge to fan herself. When had the afternoon gotten so hot?

"My point is, I was taking hard hits but hitting back even harder. You would think that would anger the beast inside me, right? But with all that violence, I never lost control. I never seriously injured anyone. Even the quarterbacks I sacked were able to jump up and keep on playing."

A vision of him sacking her flitted through her mind. Except when he tackled her, they would land in bed. *Touchdown.*

"If you don't believe me, you can look it up."

Huge, handsome Howard. He probably had women throwing themselves at him.

"Okay?" He gave her a questioning look.

She nodded.

"Then there's my second point. I work for MacKay Security and Investigations, and for the past few years, I've been a bodyguard for the Draganesti family. Currently, I'm stationed at the Dragon Nest

Academy as head of security. They would never trust me to guard their children if I wasn't absolutely in control."

She sighed. He was making good points. And her resolve was slipping fast.

"I would be happy to give you a tour of the school and let you talk to other people. It might alleviate any concerns you have."

She sipped some more juice. "I'll think about it."

"Good." He heaved a sigh of relief. "I don't want to lose you, Elsa."

She didn't want to lose him, either. But wasn't it crazy to date a were-bear? A huge beast of a man? Her gaze drifted over his big, muscular body. Maybe not. She gulped down more juice.

"And then there's my third point." He picked up a chocolate square and ripped open the foil. "You can trust me because I genuinely care about you. I admire you, and I want you to be happy."

She swallowed hard. "I—I appreciate that." She finished her juice and set the glass down. Maybe she should leave before she lost all her resolve. Instead of rejecting Howard, she was tempted to throw herself at him.

"Here, try this." He broke the chocolate square in half, then held one piece up to her lips. "Open."

With her heart racing, she opened her mouth. Just a little, so she could feel his fingers against her lips.

He set the piece on her tongue. "Let it sit there and melt in your mouth." He placed the other piece in his mouth.

She watched his lips brush against his fingers, the same fingers that had been in her mouth. Her gaze lifted to his eyes. They were an intense blue, almost like the blue in burning flames.

"It shouldn't take long," he murmured. "Your mouth was hot."

She was hot all over but still shivered.

He leaned closer, watching her closely. "All melted and gooey?"

She nodded. Heat began to gather between her legs.

He held a huge red strawberry to her lips. "Open."

She did. He pushed the fruit in and she bit down. Juice dribbled down her chin. He caught it with his finger, then brought it to his mouth and licked it off.

She moaned. The strawberry mixed with the melted chocolate in her mouth. So good. And yet so bad. All she could think about was how much she wanted him.

"You like it?" He stuffed the rest of the strawberry into his mouth and chewed slowly, never taking his eyes off her.

Moisture pooled between her legs, and she pulled her knees up, squeezing her thighs together.

"I bet your mouth tastes sweet inside," he whispered.

"Yours, too." He was seducing her, and God help her, she loved it.

He crossed the blanket on all fours, like a beast,

till he reached her feet. He grasped her ankles and tugged, straightening her legs. He knelt in front of her, his legs straddling hers. "Goldilocks."

Her heart pounded. "Beast."

"I'm going to kiss you."

She reached for him. "Yes."

Chapter Eighteen

*H*oward was tempted to drag Elsa deep into the woods and pounce on her, but he restrained himself. Even though this latest strategy was working well, she could still be easily frightened.

So he gently cradled her face and pressed his lips against hers. She wrapped her hands around his neck and leaned into him. An encouraging sign.

"Elsa," he breathed against her luscious mouth. He nibbled on her chocolate-flavored lips, then sucked the bottom one into his mouth.

She moaned, tightening her grip around his neck. Her mouth opened in invitation.

To hell with being gentle. He grasped her head tighter and plundered her mouth. It was hot and sweet. His groin swelled, and he fought the urge to push her down and strip her naked.

He ravished her neck instead, nuzzling and nibbling, reveling in the moans and shivers he incited. She was so responsive, so delicious. Her scent drove him wild. Fresh as a dew-covered meadow at dawn, it was laced with the added scent of her arousal.

No doubt it would shock her that he could smell the moisture whenever it seeped from her core. It made him hard. It made him want to taste her and lick her till she screamed.

With a low growl, he returned to her mouth and gave her a ravishingly thorough kiss. Her body trembled, but she didn't retreat. His brave Elsa kissed him back and suckled on his invading tongue.

He cupped one of her breasts and squeezed. As she moaned, the nipple pebbled beneath his palm. He circled it with his thumb till it tightened into a bead. He pinched it lightly and groaned when he caught the scent of more moisture pooling between her legs.

Take her, the bear urged him.

He broke the kiss and sat back, still straddling her legs. Damn, he wanted her, but he couldn't take her here, so close to the house.

Carry her to the stream and mate with her.

And that's why you're the beast, he scolded the bear. He couldn't afford to frighten her now.

He eased back into a sitting position on the blanket, wincing at the tightness of his pants. "Are you all right?"

She nodded, breathing heavily. "I . . . I underestimated my attraction to you."

He squeezed her hand. "Don't regret it. Please. I want to bring you joy, not regret."

She gave him a sad smile. "That was your wish in the park."

"And you wished you could trust me. In your heart, you want to."

She sighed. "I—I've never felt quite like this before. I mean, I've been attracted to men before, but not . . . like this."

He nodded. "It's intense. Like we're driven." He touched a strand of her hair that had escaped her ponytail. "We're going to be wild together."

Her eyes widened. "I should be going." She scrambled to her feet.

Damn, did he say something to upset her? He rose to his feet. "Can we meet again? Another picnic like this?"

She glanced toward the house. "Maybe. I suppose a few minutes would be all right."

"Good."

She motioned toward the blanket and food. "Thank you. I enjoyed it."

"I thought you did." He recalled all her shivers and moans.

"I meant the food." Her gaze flitted to the swelling in his pants, and her cheeks turned pink. "I—I'll see you tomorrow." She darted toward the house and let herself in.

Howard smiled. His overall strategy was working. Her desire was becoming stronger than her fear.

The following afternoon, she halted her work once again to glance out the kitchen window. Four o'clock and he wasn't there yet. She clicked the electric sander back on and stepped over the long extension cord that connected to an electric generator in the foyer. Between the noise of

the generator and the sander, she was afraid she
would miss his call or text.

Her phone was on vibrate and nestled in a chest
pocket of her denim work shirt. It was another
hot day, and she'd rolled up her sleeves and opted
for cut-off shorts instead of pants. Unfortunately,
now her legs were coated with sanding dust.

The bad dream hadn't haunted her sleep last
night. That had to be a good sign. Maybe her subconscious was accepting the idea that Howard
wasn't a threat. Or maybe it was a sign that she
was being totally fooled.

She winced. Why couldn't she be a normal
person and fall for a normal guy? But after meeting Howard, who would want a normal guy?

At least her aunts seemed to be relaxing a bit.
Today they had announced they would take turns
guarding her at the house. They ate lunch with
her every day at the diner in town, and that's
where they planned to switch shifts, one taking
the morning, and the other, the afternoon.

The phone vibrated against her chest, and she
turned off the sander. It was him! A text: *Setting
up the picnic. Come when you can.*

She stood and glanced out the window. Sure
enough, there he was, in jeans and a navy T-shirt,
stretching the checkered blanket on the ground.

She smiled, her heart racing. *Calm yourself.* She
shouldn't act so excited to see him. Even though
she was. And she shouldn't act like this was the
highlight of her day. Even though it was.

She used bottled water to wash her hands and
face, then brushed out her hair and refastened the

ponytail. She dashed to the back door. Voices filtered from the dining room. Alastair and Oskar were arguing over whether to keep the old-fashioned, candle-lit chandelier as it was or wire it for electricity. The B Boys were carrying in stacks of wood for framing the new lower ceiling.

She slipped out the back door, skipped down the stairs, then forced herself to walk calmly toward Howard.

He turned and smiled.

Her stride froze for a few seconds as her heart flipped over before settling back into place. She smiled back. If she acted nonchalant, he might not notice the effect he had on her.

His cheek dimpled. "Are you all right?"

Damn. The man noticed everything. "So what's on today's menu?"

"Bear food." He knelt to remove some plastic containers from the basket.

"You mean nuts and berries?" She sat on the blanket, kicked off her work boots, and peeled off her socks. With her feet bare, she instantly felt much cooler.

"This is a favorite among were-bears—smoked salmon from Alaska." He sliced off a small piece, placed it on a cracker, and handed it to her.

The smoky taste filled her mouth. "Ooh, that's so good."

He smiled. "I'm glad you like it." He filled a wineglass for her. "Lemonade."

She took a sip. Tart, and not too sweet. "You like eating, don't you?"

He nodded as he poured himself a glass. "I have

heightened senses, not just sight and hearing, but also smell and taste. So I really enjoy food." His gaze drifted over her long, bare legs. "Or whatever I happen to be nibbling on."

She scoffed. "Beast."

"Goldilocks." He tugged on one of her toes. "You're torturing me." His hand slid up to her ankle. "I think this is called bear-baiting. It's against the law, you know."

"Stop that." She swatted his hand away. "I'm all dusty from work."

He gave her a wide-eyed innocent look. "We could wash up in the pool at the stream."

"I'm not skinny-dipping with you."

"Would you do it alone then?" His mouth twitched. "I could watch over you to protect you. I'm a professional security guard, you know."

She snorted. "I have a feeling your protection would be up close and personal."

"That's the best kind."

She shook her head, smiling. "We should use this opportunity to learn more about each other. Important things."

"Okay." He fixed himself a cracker. "So tell me, for future reference, does your bra fasten in the front or the back?"

She threw a cracker at him, and it bounced off his chest to land on the blanket. "Can you ever be serious?"

With a grin, he picked up the cracker and ate it. "Come to the stream with me, and I'll show you how serious I can get."

She didn't doubt it. Howard would be fiercely

passionate. And he was terribly tempting. She drank some lemonade to cool herself down. "Oh." She gestured toward the clearing between them and the house. "My entourage has arrived."

He scanned the collection of small animals. "Holy crap, there's a skunk in the mix. Now I don't dare scare them away."

"Maybe they're hungry." She tossed a few crackers in their direction, and the raccoons were quick to grab them.

Howard winced. "You shouldn't feed wild animals."

"Does that include you?"

He gave her a wry look. "I can be entirely domesticated. You should see me in the kitchen."

She shuddered. "I'm having this strange vision of a grizzly bear wearing an apron."

His mouth curled up as he skimmed a hand up her leg. "I'm having a great vision of you not wearing an apron."

Or anything else, she imagined. She shoved his hand off her thigh. "You seem to have a one-track mind."

"I know. I'm an animal."

She snorted. "Why don't you tell me about yourself? How did you grow up?"

He shrugged. "It's not all that interesting. After my father died, my mom took me back to the Bear Claw Islands, just off the Alaskan Peninsula. We lived at my grandfather's house on the biggest island, called The Paw. There was a small elementary school on the island, but when it was time for middle school, we had to take the ferry to Port Mishenka."

She helped herself to more salmon. "And there were a lot of were-bears there?"

"Not on the mainland. But on the islands, we're all were-bears."

Her eyes widened. "Really?"

"Yes. But not everyone is a Kodiak bear like me. Some are black bears. My best friend, Harry Yutu, shifts into a polar bear."

Her mouth dropped open. "Really?"

"Yeah. He turns solid white. I used to tease him that he disappeared for the entire winter. He'd be right in front of me, and I'd act like I couldn't see him." Howard chuckled. "It drove him crazy."

She shook her head in disbelief. "Your best friend is a polar bear?"

"Yep. Technically, he's bigger than me. But I figure I have him beat on looks." Howard's mouth curled up. "I have a really nice fur coat. Don't you think so?"

She gave him an incredulous look. "I was too terrified to notice."

"I could show it to you again."

"No!"

He grinned. "Then you'll have to take my word for it. I'm a very handsome bear."

Handsome Howard. "You really don't mind being a were-bear?"

"No, I'm happy." He ripped open the square of chocolate, broke it in two, and held a piece up to her mouth.

She opened her mouth and let him set the chocolate on her tongue. He popped the other half in his mouth, then opened a plastic container of fresh pineapple chunks.

"Try this." He placed a chunk in her mouth.

The pineapple juice mingled with the chocolate, filling her mouth with a delicious sweetness. "Mmm." She chewed slowly, enjoying it.

He ate a pineapple chunk, watching her. "Good?"

She nodded and licked her lips.

He moaned, his eyes growing a more intense blue.

There was hunger in his eyes. A fierce desire that made her quiver in response. She pulled her legs in, pressing her thighs together as heat gathered in her core.

His nostrils flared, and he suddenly jumped to his feet. "Come." He grabbed her hands and pulled her up.

"What?" She stumbled after him as he strode deeper into the woods. "Where—"

He pressed her back against a large tree trunk. "I don't want anyone in the house to see us." He lifted her arms over her head, pinning her wrists to the trunk.

She tugged at his grasp. "Let me go."

"I will. After I kiss you."

She huffed. "Beast."

"Goldilocks." He kissed her forehead. "Too hard." He kissed her cheek. "Too soft." He hovered over her lips. "But this is just right."

He molded his lips against hers, tasting, nibbling, ravishing. Meanwhile, his hands moved slowly down her arms, prickling her skin with goose bumps.

She leaned back against the tree, her knees weak, her heart pounding. His mouth was insistent. His hands, seductive. They skimmed over her shoulders, then rested lightly on her chest.

He broke the kiss. She gazed up at him, her breasts heaving beneath his hands. With his eyes gleaming an intense blue, he slowly unbuttoned her shirt. Opened it.

She drew in a long, shaky breath.

With his right hand, he cupped her breast, stroking the cotton bra until her nipple pebbled. His thumb slipped underneath the material and pulled it down, exposing her.

"Beautiful," he whispered.

She shivered, then gasped as he latched his mouth onto her nipple. Oh God, he knew how to use his lips and tongue. Of course he did. He had a heightened sense of taste.

Her knees quivered, and she grabbed onto him to keep from falling. He started on her other breast, suckling the nipple till it was as red and hard as the other.

A movement in the woods caught her attention. She stiffened with a gasp.

Howard looked up, then followed her gaze.

Three large male deer were glaring at him. They lowered their heads to show off their impressive antlers.

"Stay behind me." Howard turned to face them.

"I'm not the one in danger. You are. They think you're attacking me."

He glanced back at her. "You know what they're thinking?"

With a small shock, she realized she did. "Yes. They can sense you're a predator. They're afraid you're mauling me."

"I am." He wrapped an arm around her, pulling her close to his side as he glowered at the stags. "She's my mate. Get lost."

"They're not going to follow orders from you." She quickly adjusted her bra. "And who says I'm your mate?"

"I do."

"I don't recall agreeing to that."

He growled softly, and the deer pawed at the ground with their hooves.

"You're making it worse." She stepped toward the three stags. "It's all right. He's not hurting me."

The deer tilted their heads, still glaring at him.

"They're really protective of you," Howard murmured behind her.

A scene flashed through her mind—her grandmother's mauled body surrounded by a herd of deer that had died trying to protect her.

"Thank you for watching over me," she told the deer. "But I don't need your help right now." An eerie feeling swept over her, and she suddenly knew what to do. She lifted her hands, palms facing the deer. "Go in peace."

The deer slowly ambled away.

"Wow," Howard said softly behind her. "They do what you say."

She swallowed hard. The more time she spent

in the forest, the more she became attuned to this strange power within her. It was growing inside her as surely and steadily as the forest grew. It was changing her, calling her home, making her the guardian.

As she watched the deer disappear into the woods, she was struck by their noble bearing. They were beautiful. And they possessed an instinctual wisdom as ancient as the forest. They knew who she was. And they were loyal.

Did they sense something she was refusing to see? They clearly saw Howard as a threat to her. What if they were right? Shouldn't she respect their instincts with the same respect they gave to her?

She buttoned up her shirt. "I should get back to work now." She hurried back to the picnic blanket just in time to see two raccoons running off with the rest of the smoked salmon.

"Those damned thieves," Howard muttered. "See you tomorrow?"

"Maybe." She stepped toward the house, then paused. "Oh, I almost forgot. I need to see Shanna again. I have a bunch of countertop samples to show her, and I need to know which stain she wants for the cabinets. Stuff like that."

He nodded. "I'll tell her. You want her to come by after sunset?"

"Yes." Elsa wondered briefly why Shanna Draganesti could only come at night, but then she dismissed the thought. She had enough to worry about. After all, she was falling in love with a were-bear who might fulfill a curse and kill her. If she had any sense, she'd heed the warning from the deer. But she didn't have any sense. She wanted to love him. Dear, sweet Howard.

She shoved back a tendril of hair that had escaped her ponytail. "Good-bye."

His eyes narrowed as if he suspected something was wrong. She turned to walk toward the house.

"Elsa," he called after her, and she stopped. Glanced back.

"Whom are you going to believe—a few deer or the man who loves you?"

Her heart lurched. He loved her? Oh God, it was her dream come true. In a normal world, this would be the moment she confessed her love to him and they would run into each other's arms. Music would come out of nowhere, swelling dramatically as they fell into a long, passionate kiss. And they would live happily ever after.

A pang shot through her chest. The world was no longer normal. And she wasn't absolutely sure she could trust him. Even though he loved her. Even though she loved him.

Tears gathered in her eyes, blurring her vision of him. She ran into the house.

Dammit, he was losing her again. Howard paced around his office. A new strategy, that was what he needed. Time to call in the troops.

He sat at his desk and wrote a note to Shanna, explaining that Elsa was having trouble adjusting to his being a were-bear, especially when there was a curse that made it seem like he would kill her. So, when Shanna met with Elsa this evening, could she please put in a good word for him? Convince Elsa he was safe?

Howard glared at the note. He hated having to ask for help. His inner bear took it as a sign of weakness.

"Dammit." He turned to his computer to think about something else for a while. There was an e-mail from Harry, sent late last night.

> *Howard, I found an old were-bear who lives along the Yukon River. He recalls smelling werewolves in the woods the day the fire started. He remembers because his cabin burned down, and he blames it on the werewolves.*
>
> *I did some searching on the company that bought the land from our mothers. It's a front for a company that's a front for another. Finally found out who actually bought the land. Old man Bleddyn, Rhett's father.*

Howard stiffened. He'd always believed the hatred between him and Rhett had started with them during high school. But did the hatred go back even further? Were the two fathers involved in a battle that had ended with his father's murder?

He finished reading Harry's e-mail.

> *I'll see what else I can find out. Take it easy, buddy.*
>
> *Harry*

Another e-mail popped into his inbox from his cousin Jimmy.

Howard,

Grandpa asked me to send you this link. And he says you should come home right away. I'm really sorry, dude.

Howard's chest tightened as he opened the link. It was an online article from a major newspaper in Anchorage.

"Journalist Killed in Car Bombing Incident"

His heart clenched in his chest. His eyes darted around the article, unable to focus. *Morning blast. Apparent murder. Victim identified as Harry Yutu. Memorial service.*

Harry was dead?

Howard jumped to his feet, knocking over his chair.

Harry was dead?

It was obvious who had killed him.

Howard leaned his head back and roared.

Chapter Nineteen

*A*fter the last glow of the sun disappeared over the horizon, Shanna Draganesti came back to life with a powerful jolt to her chest. She sucked in a breath and pressed a hand to her now wildly beating heart. Her vision adjusted to the dark basement bedroom at the Dragon Nest Academy.

Another night. She'd been given another night with her husband and children. A hundred years from now, would she still feel like she was living on borrowed time?

Roman stirred next to her. "Sweetness," he mumbled as he wrapped an arm around her and snuggled close.

She shivered at the coolness of his long, naked body. She could hardly blame him. Her body was cool, too, after lying around dead all day long. They'd both fallen into their death-sleep a few minutes after making love.

She was always terribly hungry when she first awoke, but with her husband gently caressing her breasts, the last thing she wanted to think about was blood. She wanted to thank God for another night and enjoy Roman's sweet and loving touch.

He was pressed against her back, nuzzling her neck and exploring her body. Over the centuries, he'd acquired the strength to delay his first meal for about ten minutes. And he was putting that time to good use. Already, they were growing much warmer. He nudged her bottom with his rapidly swelling groin, and she wiggled, rubbing against him.

With a groan, he squeezed her breast. "I can never get enough of you." His hand slid down her belly.

Anticipation was so sweet. She would be wet before he reached her core. And hot with need.

"Aagh!" Her fangs popped out, and a hunger pain hit her hard in the gut. "Damn!"

Roman patted her on the rump. "Let's feed you first."

She scrambled out of bed and rushed toward the small kitchen area of their suite, where she removed two bottles of synthetic blood from the refrigerator. "I really know how to destroy the mood." She winced. When her fangs were out, her voice sounded lisping and spitty, like Sylvester the cat.

She stuffed the bottles into the microwave and mumbled, "Shouldn't I be able to control my fangs by now?" Sometimes she felt like she was failing Vampire 101.

Roman joined her in the kitchen and set two glasses on the counter. "I think you look adorable with your fangs."

"I can't control them. I get excited, and they pop out."

"I have a similar problem." With a wry smile, he motioned to his erection.

She gave him a clinically assessing look. "That's a rather large problem, but fortunately, I know exactly how to solve it."

"Do you?" He kissed her brow.

"Oh yeah." She was just about to get a handle on the problem when another hunger pain struck. "Aagh." She rubbed her stomach.

"Sorry. I shouldn't have kept you from your meal." He pulled a warm bottle from the microwave and poured the contents into a glass. "Here." He added a straw, then handed it to her.

It was embarrassing to need a straw, but she found it difficult to drink from a glass with extended fangs. At least she was getting used to the taste. Roman claimed that eventually she would enjoy it. She was still waiting for that to happen. After a few sips, the hunger pangs in her belly lessened and her fangs receded.

"Better?" Roman asked as he poured his own glass.

She nodded, still sipping on the straw.

A knock pounded on their door. "Mom! Dad!"

She whirled toward the door, her heart lurching. "Constantine?"

"What's wrong?" Roman called out. He'd already dashed to the dresser, and he was pulling on some underwear at vampire speed.

"See, Grandma?" Constantine whispered, although Shanna could still hear. "I knew they'd be awake."

"Yes," Darlene responded on the other side of

the door. "But you have to give them time to have their breakfast and get dressed."

"I need them now!" Tino insisted.

"I want my mommy," Sofia whimpered.

"We'll be right there!" Shanna hurried to the restroom, then threw on an old T-shirt and pair of sweatpants. Roman had finished dressing and was shoving his feet into shoes while he downed his glass of blood.

He dashed to the door, unlocked it, and flung it open. "What's wrong?" He knelt in front of Tino and Sofia, looking them over. "Are you hurt?"

"They're fine," Darlene assured them. "But they're upset."

"Why?" Shanna's heart squeezed at the sight of Tino's tear-stained cheeks and the forlorn look in her daughter's eyes. "What happened?"

Tino's chin wobbled. "He left. Again."

"Who?" Roman asked.

"Howard." Tino sniffed. "He was so mad. I'm afraid he'll never come back."

"What?" Shanna glanced at her mother for an explanation.

"I'm not sure what happened, but Howard literally roared a few hours ago. Everyone in the building heard it." Darlene winced. "That is, everyone who was awake. We all went to see what was wrong, but he just growled at us. Then he grabbed his car keys and ran out the door."

"It was scary," Sofia whispered, edging close to her mom.

"Sweetie." Shanna lifted her into her arms. "It'll be all right."

Roman picked up his son and headed toward the stairs. "Don't worry, Tino. We'll figure out what happened."

"Phil might know," Darlene said as they climbed the stairs. "He arrived about twenty minutes ago."

"I thought he was at Romatech."

"He was." Darlene paused on the landing. "He said Howard called him from the airport in Albany and asked him to come here and take his place."

"Does that mean Howard won't come back?" Tino asked.

"We can't be sure," Shanna told him.

They reached the ground floor and spotted a small crowd hanging around the entrance to the security office, mostly werewolf and were-panther students, along with a few mortal teachers.

Toni greeted them. "I just got here. I was downstairs with Ian. He'll be here as soon as he gets dressed."

Shanna nodded. "Let's continue with the usual schedule."

While Toni and the teachers herded the students toward the cafeteria, Shanna and her family entered the security office.

Phil was pacing back and forth behind the desk, his face dark with rage.

Something had to be terribly wrong, and Shanna wasn't sure the children should hear it. She passed Sofia to her mother. "I think the children should have their supper now."

Sofia frowned. "We already ate."

"I don't want to leave." Tino wriggled out of his father's arms and climbed into the chair facing the desk.

Phil clenched his fists, clearly trying to control his anger. "I need to join Howard. I can't stay here doing nothing."

"What happened?" Roman asked. "Is there a security problem?"

Phil took a deep breath. "Everything's under control here. And everything's fine at Romatech, too. Austin just got back from Eastern Europe, and he's taken over the security office there. It'll be safe for you to go to work tonight."

"That's good," Roman replied. "So what's going on with Howard?"

Phil leaned over the keyboard to punch some buttons. "When I arrived, I found this window open on the monitor. Take a look." He moved out of the way.

Shanna and Roman skirted the desk so they could read the monitor. As she scanned the online newspaper article, a chill ran down her back.

"Oh my God," she breathed.

Roman muttered a curse.

Tino sat up. "What's wrong?"

She swallowed hard. "Someone . . . passed away." That was putting it as mildly as she could.

"I gather Howard knew this man?" Roman asked.

"Yeah." Phil resumed his pacing, circling the room like an angry caged animal. "I met Harry when I was in Alaska. He was Howard's best friend."

"Oh no." Shanna's heart ached for Howard. "No wonder he was so upset."

"He lost his best friend?" Darlene asked, still holding Sofia.

Shanna nodded. She didn't want to go into the details in front of the children. "You can read about it." She switched places with her mother and took Sofia back into her arms.

"Did he go to Alaska?" Tino asked. "Why didn't he wait for a Vamp to teleport him?"

"It'll be hours before the sun sets in Alaska," Phil explained as he paced. "I'm sure he didn't want to wait. I would appreciate a Vamp taking me there tonight. I'd like to go to the memorial service."

Roman nodded. "We can do that."

Shanna's chest tightened once again. A memorial service. Not a funeral. After a car bombing, there probably wasn't a body left to bury.

"Oh my," Darlene whispered as she read the article. "This is awful. Who would do such a thing?"

Phil drew in a hissing breath. "I know who did it. Harry was a reporter for a tabloid newspaper, and last week, he started exposing the truth about Rhett Bleddyn."

Roman's eyes narrowed. "The werewolf? The one who bit Phineas?"

"Yes," Phil growled. "When Howard called me, he was mad as hell. He knows Rhett's behind the car bombing. And what's more, he suspects the Bleddyns murdered his father. Harry's father, too. Harry was investigating it right before he was blown to pieces."

Shanna winced. This was getting too violent for the children. "Phil—"

"I think Rhett murdered Howard's girlfriend, too," Phil snarled. "I hope he kills that asshole. If he doesn't, I will."

"You want to kill somebody?" Tino asked, his eyes wide.

"Phil." Shanna gave him a pointed look. With emotions running high, it was easy to read minds at the moment. Phil was furious. Roman, angry. Darlene, appalled. Sofia, frightened. And even though Tino was shocked, he was thinking how cool it was to be witnessing all the adult drama. Shanna wished once again that he wouldn't be in such a hurry to grow up.

She patted her daughter on the back. "Don't let this upset you. You know how big and tough Howard is. He'll be okay."

Sofia gave her a hopeful look. "Really?"

"Of course." Shanna forced a smile. "Nothing ever gets Howard down."

"That's right!" Tino nodded. "He beat up a whole bunch of wild pigs with huge tusks!"

"What?" Shanna hadn't heard that story.

"Oh, I forgot." Phil grabbed an envelope off the desk. "Howard left you a note."

Shanna set her daughter on the chair next to Tino, then opened the letter.

"What does it say?" Tino asked.

Shanna quickly scanned the letter. It was calmly written, so Howard must have penned it before finding out about his best friend's murder. He was asking Shanna to meet Elsa tonight to discuss the kitchen. And he needed her help in convincing Elsa that he was a safe and dependable guy. Elsa knew about him being a were-bear, and apparently, she was now afraid to trust him. "I need to go to the gatehouse tonight for a meeting with Elsa."

Tino perked up. "Can I come? I like Elsa!"

Shanna folded the letter. "You saw her television show?"

"No. I met her when—" Tino bit his lip.

Shanna glimpsed some alarming visuals in her son's mind. "Oh my gosh. What have you been up to?"

Tino winced. "Nothing."

"Tino." Roman gave him a stern look.

He squirmed in the chair. "Everything would have been fine if the wild pigs hadn't shown up."

Roman arched a brow. "We'll all go to the gatehouse together, and you will tell us what happened on the way there."

Tino slumped. "Okay."

Roman ushered the children out the door. "Come on. Let's get the van out of the garage." He glanced back at Phil. "Ian should be here soon. He can find someone to teleport you to Alaska. If Howard needs anything, just let us know."

"Yes," Shanna agreed. "Please tell Howard how sad we are for his loss and how much we love him."

"Yeah," Tino shouted from the hallway. "Tell him to come home soon!"

"I will." Phil nodded. "I have a few hours before I can go. I'll be with Vanda till then." He hurried off in search of his Vamp wife.

"I'll be along in just a second," Shanna called out to her husband as he escorted the kids to the front door.

"Can I tag along?" Darlene asked. "I'd like to see what they're doing with the gatehouse."

"Of course," Shanna agreed. "Wait here. I'll be right back." With vampire speed, she zoomed back to the bedroom, threw off the baggy sweat-pants and T-shirt, and put on some tailored pants with a matching top and blazer. She brushed her hair, slipped on some nice sandals, then zoomed back upstairs. "Better?"

"Yes." Her mother looked her over. "You're trying to impress somebody?"

"Sorta." Shanna strolled down the hall with her mother. "Howard asked me to convince Elsa that he's a good guy, and I thought I'd be more believ-able if I looked presentable. I feel so bad for him. This seems like the only thing I can do for him right now."

Darlene nodded. "So he's courting Elsa?"

"He's trying. Poor Howard. He let Elsa know that he's a were-bear, and it's giving her some se-rious doubts."

Darlene winced. "It would be tough to find out your boyfriend is a grizzly bear."

"I know. It reminds me how freaked out I was when I discovered Roman was a vampire. I was so attracted to him, but at the same time, I was afraid he'd attack me."

"Are you feeling any better about your situa-tion?"

Shanna sighed. "I realized something the other

night when I was watching *The Little Mermaid* with the kids. Tino was upset that Ariel had given up her voice and her tail to be with the prince. I said something about there always being a price to pay, and that's when it struck me. If I'm going to live in my husband's world, I have to be willing to pay the price."

Darlene nodded. "So I guess the question is: are you willing?"

Shanna snorted. "I have to be. I don't have any choice in the matter now."

"But I heard there is a choice. Toni told me about a woman named Darcy who was a vampire and turned back to being mortal."

Shanna nodded. "I know about the procedure. Roman did it."

"Have you considered—"

"No. I mean, yes, I thought about it, but no, I won't do it. There's a twenty-five percent chance of death, permanent death, and I'm not taking a chance that my children will lose me completely. At least now, they've only lost me half the time."

Darlene frowned at her. "Do you love them half as much?"

"No, of course not!"

"Then don't say they've lost you."

Shanna swallowed hard. "You're right. I just miss seeing them during the day."

"What if you kept the kids up all night and let them sleep during the day?" Darlene suggested. "You'd have more time with them then."

Shanna shook her head. "I won't subject them to a life of darkness. They're already staying up till midnight. That leaves them waking around noon without us, but Roman and I both agree— they need some sunshine to grow up healthy and happy."

"That's probably true. I'm certainly enjoying my time with them. Caitlyn's babies are a joy, too." She smiled. "Of course I'm not prejudiced in any way."

Shanna slanted a curious look at her mother as they approached the front door. "It still amazes me how quickly you adjusted to it all."

Darlene shrugged. "There's no point in denying reality when it's right there in front of you."

"Yeah, but . . ." Shanna wasn't sure she should mention this. "I don't understand why Dad thought he had to control your mind so you could deal with stress. You handle things really well on your own."

Darlene snorted. "The operative word there is control. Sean is a control freak. He wanted me to handle everything *his* way."

"Does he still call you every night?"

"Like clockwork."

"You . . . still hang up on him?"

Darlene shrugged. "Lately, I've been letting him talk for a little while before I hang up. I get a perverse pleasure out of hearing him wallow in misery."

"Has he ever apologized?" Shanna asked.

"Many times. But then he ruins it by claiming he did it for my own good."

Shanna groaned.

"But for the last week or so, he's been taking all

the blame. He admits he was wrong, and he begs me to forgive him."

"What do you say to him?"

Darlene sighed. "At first, I was so angry, I just wanted to hurt him. But now, I try not to even think about it. Cause if I do, it hurts me something awful. I have eighteen years that I can barely remember. It's like he stole all that time from me and I can never get it back."

"Mom." Shanna hugged her. "I'm so sorry."

"He wants me to turn," Darlene said softly.

"What?" Shanna leaned back, completely caught off guard, which didn't happen often to her.

"Sean wants me to join him as a vampire. He says I could have centuries, and it would make up for the time I lost."

"Oh my gosh," Shanna breathed. It had been shocking enough when Roman had transformed her father in order to save him. But her mother? A vampire?

Darlene smiled sadly at her. "I said no. As silly as it might sound, I actually like my life as it is now. I get to see Tino and Sofia every day. And I spend a lot of time with Caitlyn and her twins. I don't want to give up my days with my grandchildren. I suspect Sean is afraid of spending the next few centuries all alone, but that's his problem, not mine."

"You're sure? There are plenty of mortals around here who can babysit during the day—"

"I'm sure." Darlene patted her on the arm. "I'm very happy now. Besides, I doubt I could last five minutes with Sean without wanting to stake him. I'd never last a few centuries."

Shanna hugged her again. "You are so strong. Dad always underestimated you." She heard the sound of a car braking outside. "They're here. Let's go."

Darlene stepped out onto the front porch and smiled. "Now that's a sight. A vampire husband driving a van filled with children."

Shanna's heart filled with warmth. She was so blessed. She had a wonderful husband, two adorable children, and two parents still alive, or semi-alive in the case of her father. She had a brother and her sister, Caitlyn, and her family. And then there was the big extended family—shifters, Vamps, and mortals like her dear friend, Radinka. She was surrounded by people she loved.

Poor Howard. He'd lost his father, his girlfriend, and his best friend. "I feel so terrible for Howard."

Darlene nodded, her eyes growing misty. "I'll never forget the sound of his roar. So much pain. I thought his heart was breaking."

"We have to help him," Shanna whispered. She took a deep breath to steady her resolve. Somehow, she would convince Elsa Bjornberg that Howard was the perfect man for her. Even if he occasionally turned into a bear.

Chapter Twenty

"*W*hat a lovely family," Aunt Greta whispered to Elsa on the front porch.

"Yes." Elsa smiled as she watched Tino and his little sister scamper around the driveway. The floodlights had been turned on, and the children were pretending they were in a spotlight, with Tino singing and Sofia dancing.

She glanced at the proud parents and grandmother who stood nearby, smiling as they watched. It felt good knowing such a nice family would be living in the house.

Aunt Greta had instantly become friends with the grandmother when Darlene had admired her knitting. Apparently, Darlene also knitted and knew the best local places to buy yarn.

Elsa was more curious about Roman, the scientific genius. He was obviously a doting husband and father, but there was something . . . different about him. She couldn't quite put her finger on it. He'd been very interested in the structural changes in the basement, but like any wise husband, when it came to the kitchen, he'd let his wife make all the decisions.

Elsa turned to lock the door. Alastair and Oskar had left a few minutes earlier to join The B Boys in Cranville for dinner.

"Excuse me." Shanna joined her on the front porch. "Before we go, could I have a word with you in private?"

"Sure." Elsa opened the door. "You want to go inside?"

"Yes, thank you." Shanna stepped inside and strode across the foyer toward the kitchen.

"This will just take a few minutes," Elsa assured her aunt. She knew Greta was eager to return to Cranville to have supper with Great-aunt Ula.

"That's all right," Greta assured her. "I need to find out where I can buy more yarn." She headed toward Darlene.

Elsa followed Shanna into the kitchen and turned on the temporary battery light that she'd installed in there earlier to show off all the samples. "Did you have any more questions about the house?"

"No, I think you're doing a fabulous job." Shanna paced around the kitchen.

She seemed nervous, Elsa thought. Or agitated. "Is something wrong?"

"A few things." Shanna stopped in front of her. "I owe you an apology. Tino told us about the incident with the feral pigs. He should have never come here alone like that. He—he put your life in danger. I'm so sorry—"

"He saved my life," Elsa interrupted. "I'm grateful to him."

"I appreciate how understanding you are, but

he took a terrible risk. He's not supposed to tele-port without our permission. And to teleport you with him—" Shanna winced. "That must have been . . . disconcerting."

"To say the least." Elsa's curiosity got the better of her, and she wondered how much she could get Shanna to reveal. "You warned us to stay away from the school, not because the kids are juvenile delinquents but because they're all special like Tino?"

"Yes." Shanna nodded. "We're trying to give them normal lives and protect them from anyone who would want to study or exploit them. I hope we can trust you to keep our secret."

"Yes, of course. I won't say a word to anyone."

Shanna heaved a sigh of relief. "Thank you. That was our main concern with letting your show renovate this house. We could never forgive ourselves if we endangered the children."

"Are the other kids like Tino?"

"Not all of them, but soon we'll have more hy-brids like Tino and Sofia."

Hybrids? "They run on electricity?"

Shanna chuckled. "I don't know where they get all their energy. Roman thinks they suck it out of the adults. In that way, they're probably very much like normal kids."

"I suppose." It was one of the things Elsa really liked about Tino. His superpowers hadn't gone to his head. He still acted like a normal little boy.

Shanna resumed her pacing. "There's some-thing else I need to talk about. Howard had to go to Alaska. He won't be here for a while."

"Oh." A wave of disappointment swept over Elsa. She would miss him. She caught herself mentally. What was she thinking? She'd decided just that afternoon not to see him again. This should be good news. Now that he was gone, she wouldn't have to go through the pain of rejecting him. But already she missed him. A part of her wanted him back, and that part was growing fast.

Shanna stopped in front of the kitchen sink and stared out the window. "Something awful happened today. I didn't want to talk about it in front of the children."

A chill prickled Elsa's skin. "Something happened to Howard?"

"His best friend . . . died."

Elsa's breath caught. Was this the friend he'd talked so fondly about that afternoon? "You mean Harry?"

Shanna turned to face her. "You know about Harry?"

"Howard told me they were best friends."

Shanna grimaced. "Harry was killed this morning with a car bomb."

Elsa gasped.

"I know. It's horrible."

Elsa pressed a hand against her chest. "Harry was . . . murdered?"

"Yes, the poor man." Shanna sighed. "Howard has lost so many loved ones."

Elsa winced inwardly. Howard had confessed his love to her that afternoon. It would be cruel to reject him now and cause him more pain. But how could she stay with him? She didn't know what to do, but she hated to think about how badly he was hurting. "Why would someone murder his best friend?"

Shanna shook her head. "I don't know all the details, but apparently there's a nasty guy in Alaska who hates Harry and Howard."

And Howard had gone back to Alaska? Elsa's heart raced. Was Howard in danger?

"I'm sorry." Shanna patted her on the shoulder. "I'm afraid I'm screwing this up. I meant to reassure you, but I'm just scaring you."

"I'll be okay. I'm still getting used to all the supernatural stuff." Not only was she adjusting to Howard being a berserker but she could also feel herself transforming into a guardian who communicated with animals.

"You're concerned about Howard being a werebear?" Shanna asked.

"I would say it warrants some concern, don't you think?"

Shanna gave her a sympathetic look. "I'm sure you were shocked at first. But the shifters are very much like humans. There are good ones and bad ones. Howard is definitely one of the good guys. Look at it this way. If you were under attack, wouldn't you want someone like Howard on your side?"

"Well, yes." But could he always control the beast? He was, after all, a descendant of berserkers, who were famous for their lack of control.

"He's been our daytime bodyguard for years," Shanna continued. "He's family. My kids adore him. He's so sweet, gentle, and shy—"

"Shy?"

"Yes. I always thought he was a bit—" Shanna's eyes lit up. "You mean he's not shy around you?"

"Not . . . really." Elsa's cheeks grew warm as she recalled him pinning her to a tree that afternoon, then kissing her and unbuttoning her shirt—she shoved the vision aside before her face could combust in flames.

"Wow." Shanna's eyes widened.

Elsa had a strange feeling that Shanna was imagining a similar scenario.

"This is wonderful!" Shanna clapped her hands together. "I was afraid he would be too bashful. Do you know he was smitten with you for months, but he had all the DVDs of your show hidden under his bed? If I hadn't arranged to bring you here, he could have gone on for years, admiring you in secret and too shy to tell anyone."

"You brought the show here just so Howard could meet me?"

Shanna winced. "We really did need the house renovated. But yes, my main purpose was to fix you up with Howard."

"You thought it was perfectly acceptable to fix me up with a were-bear?"

"Howard's a great guy!"

"He's a grizzly!"

"He's a sweet honey bear," Shanna insisted. "I trust my children with him. We trust the entire school with him. You won't find a more loyal and trustworthy guy than Howard."

Elsa sighed. "He's still a grizzly. It's not that easy to accept."

"I understand how hard it is. I was afraid to fall in love with my husband, too, at first."

Elsa gasped. "Roman is a were-bear?" She'd known there was something different about him.

"No, he's . . . something else. You should meet my sister, Caitlyn. She's married to a were-panther named—"

"What?"

"Carlos. He's a were-panther from Brazil. They have the most adorable twin babies."

"She married a . . . cat?"

"A were-panther," Shanna clarified as if it were a common daily occurrence. "They're extremely happy. And I know you could be just as happy with Howard if you could please give him a chance."

"It's not that simple." As if dating a were-bear was a simple matter. "Howard is what my family calls a berserker, and there's a curse that has been passed down my family for centuries. According to the curse, Howard . . . might . . ." She couldn't bring herself to say the words.

Shanna touched her shoulder. "You're afraid he'll hurt you. That he'll lose control and . . ."

Elsa nodded.

Shanna squeezed her shoulder. "There was a time when I was afraid Roman would lose control and attack me. But I love him, and I've been blessed with a wonderful marriage and two beautiful children. Roman loves me, and he would never hurt me."

Elsa's eyes grew misty with tears. "You think I can trust Howard."

"I know you can. He's a dear, sweet man, who would never hurt you."

Elsa nodded. She'd always felt deep down inside that she could trust him. And in her heart, she wanted to love him. She wanted to grab on to his love and never let go.

"I know it's hard," Shanna whispered. "But with love, sometimes you have to take a leap of faith."

A tear ran down Elsa's cheek. "He said he loves me."

"Then you can believe it. You can trust him."

Elsa nodded. "I'll try." When Howard returned from Alaska, she'd continue to see him. Even though he was a were-bear. Even though it meant she would fall deeper in love with him.

Howard paced across the hotel room as if he could escape reality if he kept moving. Stuck in airports and on planes for the last several hours, he'd thought he would go crazy. His mind had raced, imagining a hundred different scenarios till he'd found one that kept him momentarily sane.

Harry was a smart guy. He would have known about the bomb. And he would have let it explode in order to fake his own death so he could continue the mission in secret. Any minute now, he would contact Howard. They would meet and have a beer like old times, laughing at the way they had fooled Rhett.

Harry hadn't called.

And Howard was the fool. All his damned strategies he'd thought were so clever: they had gotten his best friend killed.

He clenched his fists. The bear inside him wanted to rip the hotel room to shreds. His body shimmered, demanding to shift. For the first time, he understood the power of the berserker blood that flowed through his veins. How easy it would be, how tempting it was, to let himself go berserk and destroy everything in sight.

His hands turned into bear paws with long, lethal claws. What was he doing here? Why stay in Anchorage to attend Harry's memorial service when he should be driving to Rhett's house so he could slaughter every werewolf he could find.

When his cell phone rang, the grating noise jerked him back to his senses. He wasn't a berserker who went on murderous rampages. That was Elsa's greatest fear. He couldn't prove her right. He seized control and forced his hands back into human form.

Meanwhile, the phone had stopped ringing, so he checked the missed call. Dragon Nest Academy. He tossed the phone onto one of the beds and resumed his pacing.

After arriving in Anchorage, he had headed first to the office of *Northern Lights Sound Bites*. Harry's friends there were devastated. They were holding a public memorial service for Harry the next afternoon. Howard suspected it would be a media circus, that the owner of the small tabloid newspaper was using Harry's death to publicize the paper.

A small group was traveling from the Bear Claw Islands to attend the memorial service and collect

the small wooden box containing what they believed to be Harry's ashes. Howard had booked
them rooms at the hotel where he was staying.
And he had called the school to make sure Phil
had arrived to take over his duties.

Ian MacPhie, the Vamp in charge of nighttime
security, had answered, and when he'd started ex-
pressing his sympathy, Howard had hung up. He
didn't deserve sympathy. He deserved a severe
beating for getting Harry involved in his stupid
plan for revenge. He'd wanted to drive Rhett
crazy. He'd driven him to murder.

"Idiot," he called himself. He'd rushed off to
Alaska, as if getting here quickly would somehow
change the facts and make Harry still alive.

His cell phone rang again. Dragon Nest Academy. "What?" he growled into the phone.

"'Tis dark there now, aye?" Ian asked.

"I don't want any damned sympathy!" Howard
heard his voice echo. They'd put him on a speaker
phone. "Dammit, I don't want any company." He
started to push the button to finish the call.

"Howard!" Shanna's voice shouted. "Don't
hang up!"

"Don't you dare come—" He groaned when two
forms materialized. Dougal and Phil.

Then Ian appeared, holding a tote bag and two
duffel bags. "All right, ye can hang up now."

Howard grunted and pocketed his phone. "Go
away. I didn't invite you here."

"I met Harry," Phil growled. "I'm attending the
memorial service."

"I'd like to go, too," Dougal added.

"It's in the afternoon," Howard grumbled.

Dougal sighed. "Verra well." He looked around the hotel room. "Is there a safe place here where I can do my death-sleep?"

Howard snorted. "In the bathtub, but the maid will freak out and call an ambulance."

"Then I'll teleport to yer grandfather's basement," Dougal said. "And take Ian with me."

With a groan, Howard dragged a hand through his hair. "You don't have to stick around."

"Aye, we do," Ian said. "We're part of yer family. Just be grateful the entire school dinna come. They all wanted to." He dropped the duffel bags on the floor. "We packed you some clothes."

"I went through your closet and found a suit," Phil added.

Howard swallowed hard. They were being too damned nice to him, and he didn't deserve it.

Ian opened the tote bag. "I brought some Bleer for Dougal and me."

"I'll take one." Dougal grabbed a bottle.

"And there's a six-pack in here for you and Phil." Ian set the regular beer on a dresser, and Phil opened a can.

"And Shanna packed this for you." Ian passed Howard a box from the bakery in Cranville. "They picked this up after their meeting with Elsa. Shanna reports it went well."

Did that mean Elsa had decided not to reject him? That should have lifted his spirit, but Howard felt strangely numb. He peeked inside the box. Fresh donuts and some cherry streusel. He set the box on the dresser.

"Here." Phil passed him a beer. "What time is the memorial service?"

Howard took a sip. "One."

"We're verra sorry—" Dougal began.

"I don't want to hear it!" Howard slammed his can onto the dresser and paced across the room. "I should have never involved him in my stupid scheme—"

"Bullshit," Phil grumbled.

Howard spun to face him. "I'm telling you it was my fault."

"And I say bullshit," Phil growled.

Howard growled back.

"Och, ye wee beasties," Ian said as he opened a bottle of Bleer. "Take it easy."

"Easy?" Howard shouted. "Harry is dead because of me!"

"Get over yourself," Phil hissed. "Harry was doing exactly what he wanted to do. I was there at the diner when we had lunch. You wanted to keep everything stealthy and secret, right?"

Howard shrugged. "So?"

"It was Harry who insisted on making it public in his paper," Phil insisted. "And you told him to keep it anonymous, but he started putting his name on the reports. He wanted Rhett to know it was him. That was his decision, not yours."

"Aye," Dougal agreed. "Ye canna blame yerself, Howard."

"From what I understand, Harry also had a good reason to hate Rhett," Ian added. "Dinna he lose his father, too?"

Howard raked a hand through his hair. The

guys were clearly trying to relieve him of any blame, but he couldn't let himself off the hook. Harry was the one who had stayed in Alaska, while Howard had run off to a safe place. He'd thought his disappearance would keep his family safe, but he'd only succeeded in making Harry the main target of Rhett's vengeance.

"Harry was investigating your fathers' deaths, right?" Phil asked. "He thought Rhett's father killed them?"

"It looks that way." Howard related what Harry had found out.

"So the feud between yer families has been going on for a long time," Ian concluded.

"I guess." Howard drank some beer. "I was only four when my father died, so I don't know the details. It could have been as simple as Rhett wanting the land that my father and Harry's father owned."

Phil nodded. "For a Pack Master like Bleddyn, more land means a bigger pack, which means greater power."

Howard sat on the end of a bed. "It's a clash of two different cultures. Werewolves always want to grow the pack, whereas were-bears want to be alone. Unfortunately, the wolves usually beat us, because they have greater numbers."

Dougal sat on the other bed next to Phil. "This is more than a clash of cultures. The hatred between you and Rhett is personal."

"Of course I hate him!" Howard jumped up to resume pacing. "He just killed my best friend."

"And your girlfriend," Phil added.

Howard snorted. Nosy bastards.

"Rhett killed yer girlfriend?" Ian sat in the desk chair. "When did that happen?"

Howard paced, remaining quiet.

Phil drank some beer. "Well, it must have happened before he was banished, which means it happened before he went off to college."

"Ah, first love." Dougal sighed. "Puir lass. What was her name? Was she a were-bear like you?"

"She was innocent," Howard grumbled. "An innocent mortal who trusted me. She died because Rhett hates my guts."

"Why does he hate you so much?" Dougal pressed.

Howard sat on the bed and leaned forward, propping his elbows on his knees. How many people would die because of him? First Carly. Now Harry. Was loving him a death sentence? Wasn't that what Elsa feared?

Howard took a deep breath. "It began when I was in high school."

Chapter Twenty-one

"Rhett was the quarterback for a high school team in Anchorage," Howard began. "Since his father was Pack Master of Alaska, Rhett enjoyed the support of hundreds of werewolf minions all over the state. Those who worked in the media turned him into a star. Werewolf boys who played on other football teams let Rhett's team win. Their loyalty to the Pack Master's son was greater than any loyalty to a mortal school. Werewolf teachers gave him perfect grades. He could do no wrong. He was the state's golden boy, destined for greatness."

Phil nodded. "We heard about him in Wyoming. The rumor was he was being groomed to run for governor or senator, and, ultimately, president."

"What went wrong?" Ian asked.

"I did." Howard grabbed his beer and took a drink. "Harry and I were defensive linemen for the football team in Port Mishenka."

Phil snickered. "The Port Mishenka Marmots."

Howard arched a brow at him. "I'm looking for a fight if you want to accommodate me."

"Enough, you two," Dougal muttered. "Back to the story."

Howard drank more beer. "It was our senior year, a pre-season game just for fun. Everyone was expecting the bigger team from Anchorage to slaughter the little team from nowhere. We knew we'd been selected as a scapegoat to make Rhett look good. The media was there, ready to fawn all over him."

Dougal sat forward. "What happened?"

"Harry and I could tell his offensive linemen were all werewolves, willing to die to protect him. And of course, they realized Harry and I were were-bears. We were the only shifters on our team. The rest were mortals, who had no idea why the game was suddenly becoming so violent. Harry would attack as many linemen as possible, keeping them busy so I could barrel my way through. I sacked Rhett ten times."

Phil chuckled. "I wish I could have seen that."

"The werewolves in the media reported I was a vicious psychopath, but the mortal media, who didn't care for the Bleddyns, made me into a hero." Howard sighed. "I started getting more attention than Rhett."

"Rhett's father probably beat the crap out of him for that," Phil muttered.

Howard nodded. "The media was eager to see us pitted against each other again, so they arranged for an all-star game at the end of the season. I was selected to play on one team. Rhett was named quarterback for the other. It was televised all over the state."

"Did ye sack him again?" Ian asked.

"Twelve times. I was named MVP and won a trophy. Scholarship offers came in. I was considered a state hero."

"And that honor was supposed to go to Rhett," Dougal said.

"Right." Howard shrugged. "I didn't think about the consequences at the time. I was too excited about the future. My college expenses would be paid for. I was dating a mortal girl from high school, and I wanted to marry her. Carly was her name."

"Did she know ye're a were-bear?" Dougal asked.

Howard nodded. "She was okay with it. She spent a lot of time with me on Paw Island, and she liked the were-bear community. I was going to propose to her the night of the senior prom. I went to Anchorage to buy an engagement ring. While I was away, there was a full moon, and Rhett and some of his werewolf buddies went after Carly."

"They attacked her?" Ian asked.

"They surrounded her." Howard took a deep breath. "I assume it was Rhett who bit her. They didn't have to do anything more than that. A simple bite, and she was lost to me forever."

"She would become a werewolf instead of a were-bear," Dougal said.

Howard nodded. "When I returned, I didn't see her much. She was ill and missed a lot of school. Her parents thought she'd been bitten by a wild dog, so they took her to get shots. I never realized . . ."

He sighed. If only he had known, he could have prepared her. She could have lived. She'd be a werewolf, but she'd still be alive. "The senior prom took place in the school gym on the next full moon. I was ready to propose, when her body started wavering. She didn't know what was happening. She ran from the school, screaming."

"Puir lass," Ian murmured.

"I followed her outside," Howard continued. "I could tell she was shifting, but I didn't know why. Then I saw Rhett and his buddies, waiting for her. Rhett laughed and said she would be his bitch."

"The bastard," Dougal muttered.

"Poor Carly was so terrified. She shifted and ran up the mountain. Rhett and his buddies shifted and chased after her." Howard scowled. "I knew I had lost her as a bride, but I couldn't let Rhett and his friends take her and abuse her. So I ran up the mountain to stop them."

"The same place where we found you the other night?" Dougal asked.

"Yes. I found her on the cliff, surrounded by snarling werewolves. I told her to stay put, that I would help her. I shifted and started fighting my way through the wolves." Howard rubbed his brow. "Two of Rhett's minions attacked me, and I tossed them off the cliff. The other minions ran away, and Rhett howled with rage. He pushed Carly off the cliff, and when I rushed forward to try to save her, he attacked me. We fought for a little while before I managed to throw him off the cliff."

"And that's why ye thought ye'd killed him?" Ian asked.

Howard nodded. "The three werewolf guys, including Rhett, had turned back to human form, so I thought they were dead. Carly had turned back to human form, too. I shifted back and went to the police to report her murder. Her family thought I had killed her, since I was the last person seen with her. I was arrested that night."

"You dinna tell the police about Rhett and his gang?" Dougal asked.

"Yeah, I said they had chased her off the cliff, but when the police checked the mountain, the werewolf bodies were gone. I figured Rhett's minions had cleaned the place up right after I left."

"But Rhett was still alive, the asshole," Phil muttered.

Howard grunted in agreement. "I was never put on trial, for lack of evidence, but I was banished to keep Rhett's father from declaring war on the were-bears. I was gone for years, so I never knew that Rhett had survived."

"We heard in Wyoming that he was dead," Phil said. "His father must have kept him hidden to make you look guilty."

"And to keep my people afraid of retaliation," Howard added. "Harry was the first were-bear to publicly challenge them in twenty years."

Ian finished off his bottle of Bleer and clunked it down on the desk. "Rhett needs to die."

Howard couldn't agree more. In fact, if his friends hadn't shown up, he might have given in to his berserker instincts and gone after Rhett. "I want him to suffer."

Phil nodded. "From what I can tell, nothing

bothers him more than public humiliation. Harry was humiliating him and became his number-one enemy."

"And I humiliated him in high school," Howard said. "He was too cowardly to go after me. He used Carly as a pawn to hurt me."

"A pawn." Ian stood and fumbled around in his sporran. "That reminds me. Tino wanted you to have this. I doona ken why, but he insisted I give it to you." He handed a wad of napkins to Howard.

Howard unwrapped the napkins and found a chess piece inside. The white knight. *Harry.*

"An odd gift," Phil murmured.

Howard swallowed hard. Tino must have taken the piece from his chess set in the office. The marble was smooth and cool against his fingers. *Harry, what have I done? How could I lose you like this?*

He curled his fist around the piece. "Tino asked me once if it was possible to win the game without losing any pieces."

"Ye said nay?" Dougal asked.

Howard nodded slowly. Like a fool, he'd boasted that a player had to take his losses like a man and press on. His eyes grew moist, and he blinked. Tino was reminding him of his own advice. *I'll press on, Harry. I will avenge you.*

Every tear that was silently shed by Harry's mother felt like a knife thrust into his heart. Howard sat stiffly in a wooden church pew, his clenched hands resting on his knees, while the editor-in-chief of *Northern Lights Sound Bites* stood at the podium, talking about Harry's bravery and persistence when it came to chasing down a story.

Several of Harry's journalist friends had taken turns speaking at the memorial service, and they were all fighting back tears. Howard didn't want to show any weakness, so he tried not to mourn but to focus more on his anger and need for vengeance.

The fact that he'd never met Harry's friends before this service was a painful reminder of the long banishment he'd endured. Twenty years away from home, and it had all been based on a lie, for Rhett had been alive. Even so, the banishment had been easy to endure compared to the guilt he'd felt over Carly's death.

Now he had more guilt. *Harry.* Howard pushed that thought aside. The guilt would cripple him, make him weak, and he needed to stay strong to avenge Harry.

He turned his thoughts back to the enemy, Rhett. Apparently, old man Bleddyn had punished his son, too, for Rhett had been forced to live in secret, his existence known only to other high-ranking werewolves. It wasn't until the old Pack Master had died a year ago that Rhett had emerged into the public eye, making sure the media knew he was powerful and rich. Rhett's history of embezzling from his father's companies had probably been his way to repay his father's cruelty. Like father, like son, Howard thought. The twisted Bleddyn family needed to end.

The pastor said a closing prayer, then mourners lined up to pass by the small wooden box that rested on a table, wreathed with flowers. Howard stood behind his grandfather, his cousins, Jesse and Jimmy, and Phil.

The editor-in-chief, Mr. West, stopped by Harry's mother to convey his condolences, and lights flashed as several journalists snapped photos.

"Bastards," Howard muttered.

Phil turned to look at him. "We could arrange for their cameras to accidentally—" He suddenly stiffened, his eyes wide.

Howard glanced back. "Holy crap!"

The woman in line behind him fussed at him, but he didn't hear. His ears buzzed as red-hot rage engulfed him.

Rhett Bleddyn and two of his minions had just entered the small church.

Phil grabbed Howard's arm, but Howard shook him off and stalked toward Rhett. The werewolf stiffened with surprise, then masked it with a sneer.

"Howard," Phil hissed as he followed him. "Not here. There are too many cameras."

"What's up?" Jimmy asked as he and Jesse joined them.

"Why are those stinky wolves here?" Jesse whispered, then added, "no offense, bro."

"That's Rhett Bleddyn," Phil muttered.

"Whoa," Jimmy breathed.

Howard stopped in front of Rhett and his minions. "Get out. Before I toss you out limb by limb."

Rhett gave him a bland look. "I thought you were permanently banished from Alaska."

"I could only stay banished as long as you stayed dead," Howard said. "It's been a great disappointment all around."

Rhett snorted. "And look who's standing by your side. Phil Jones, the traitor to his own kind. Why am I not surprised?"

"You bastard," Phil growled. "You were going to kill my entire family."

Rhett cast an amused glance toward the journalists who were inching toward them with video cameras. "Go ahead, attack me. I'd love to get that on film."

"Leave," Howard growled.

"I will," Rhett smirked. "I just came to see who showed up. I knew Harry couldn't be the mastermind behind his little smear campaign. He was never all that bright, you know."

Howard seized Rhett by his tie and jerked him forward. Lights flashed as pictures were taken. Rhett's minions jumped on Howard, but Phil dragged one off while Jimmy and Jesse held the second one back.

"You're wrong," Howard hissed in Rhett's face. "We're not smearing you. We're going to destroy you."

"Yeah," Jimmy added. "We already got two of your houses, a-hole."

"And we've got proof you were embezzling—" Jesse started.

"He's a killer!" Rhett yelled to the journalists. "Howard Barr was arrested twenty years ago for killing his girlfriend, and now he's threatening me!"

Howard twisted Rhett's tie till he turned red

in the face. More lights flashed. "You will die for killing Harry."

Gasps echoed around the church.

Howard released Rhett with a push that sent him stumbling back into the doorway. His cousins and Phil shoved the two minions back.

Rhett straightened his tie. "You have no proof. I could sue you for libel."

"Try it," Howard said. "We have proof of your embezzle—"

"You saw how he attacked me!" Rhett shouted at the journalists. He glanced at Jimmy and Jesse, then whispered to Howard, "How many friends are you willing to lose?"

With a growl, Howard stepped forward.

Phil grabbed his arm. "Not now."

Rhett and his minions hurried to his car.

"Wow," Jimmy whispered. "That was cool, man, like really intense."

"Yeah," Jesse added. "It was like a scene out of a movie."

Howard groaned. His cousins didn't realize they'd become Rhett's new targets.

"They're in danger?" Aunt Judy's voice grew louder. "My boys are in danger?"

"Calm down," Uncle James murmured.

"I won't calm down!" Aunt Judy glared at Howard. "You come back from Harry's funeral to tell me my boys could be next?"

"I'll take full responsibility for their safety," Howard assured her.

Six hours had passed since the memorial service, and during that time he'd taken the ferry from Anchorage to Port Mishenka, along with his cousins and grandfather, Phil, and Harry's mother. Then they'd all taken the smaller ferry to Paw Island.

For the entire trip, Harry's mother hadn't said a word. He'd offered to walk her back to her house, but she'd refused.

With the box containing Harry's ashes clutched against her chest, she'd glared at Howard. "He should have never gotten involved with you and your foolish quest for revenge. I told him you were trouble. You're no better than your father! Because of him, I lost my husband. Now I have no husband and no son!"

"Mrs. Yutu, I never meant—"

"Your line is cursed!" she interrupted him. "I regret Harry ever knew you." She marched off, leaving Howard behind.

Regret. The dreaded word echoed in his mind.

"It's the grief talking," Phil whispered. "Don't let it get you down."

Howard snorted. Harry's mother was definitely in pain, but she was correct. Her son would still be alive if he hadn't gotten involved with Howard's plan.

"Walter." He turned to his grandfather. "Will you take Phil home with you? I'll be there in a little while."

"Sure." Walter motioned for Phil to follow him. "You want a beer?"

"Oh." Howard called out to his grandfather. "There'll be two vampires in your basement."

Walter snorted. "Now you tell me. Does your mother know?"

"Yeah, I called her." Howard hadn't wanted his mother to freak out when she went downstairs to do the laundry and found two Vamps in their death-sleep.

Now he was in his cousins' house down the street, trying to break the news to Aunt Judy and Uncle James.

"I thought you were supposed to be some kind of security expert," James said. "How could you let this happen to our boys?"

"No one expected Rhett Bleddyn to come to the memorial service," Howard explained.

"Yeah," Jesse agreed. "I mean, the dude killed Harry. He had some balls showing up there."

"Language," Aunt Judy growled at her son, then turned to Howard. "We should have never let our boys get involved with you."

"We wanted to do it," Jimmy insisted.

"Yeah," Jesse agreed. "We're tired of our people cowering on these little islands, afraid of a few stinky wolves. We need to stand up for ourselves."

"Rhett needs to pay for his crimes," Howard said. "He killed Carly and Harry, and his father killed my father. Uncle James, don't you want the Bleddyns punished for killing your brother?"

"Of course." James gave his sons a worried look. "I was proud to let my boys help you out, but now—"

"It was a mistake from the beginning," Judy grumbled. "Now my boys have to go into hiding? We can't afford to send them away."

"I have it all covered," Howard assured her. "They can go to the private school where I work."

"School?" Jesse grimaced. "Dude, we graduated last spring."

"Yeah, and it's summer," Jimmy added.

"You won't have to take classes," Howard said. "Academic classes, that is. I will expect you to take martial arts and fencing so you can defend yourselves."

"You mean, like swords and karate stuff?" Jesse's eyes lit up.

"Cool," Jimmy said.

"You'll like the school," Howard continued. "There's a swimming pool and bowling alley in the basement, a horse stable close by, and plenty of mountains for hiking. Think of it as a free summer vacation."

"Cool," Jimmy repeated.

"Awesome," Jesse added.

Judy sniffed. "I feel like they're being banished! How long will they have to stay away? Twenty years, like you?"

Howard winced. "No."

"Where is this school?" James asked. "Can we visit?"

"Only if you let one of my vampire friends teleport you," Howard replied. "We have to keep the school's location secret, and booking plane fare could leave a trail." He groaned inwardly. He shouldn't have flown to Anchorage from Albany. But he hadn't been thinking clearly at the time. And he hadn't expected this development.

"Boys, go ahead and pack," James told them, and they hurried off to their bedroom.

Judy watched them go with tears in her eyes. "We should have never let them get involved." She turned to Howard. "What will Rhett do? Will he try to kill them? Will he have his minions attack our island? Are we all in danger because of you?"

"Judy, calm down," James said wearily.

Her eyes flashed with anger. "You should never get between a mama bear and her cubs. I wish they'd never met Howard!" She stormed into her bedroom and slammed the door.

James sighed. "I'll send the boys over to Walter's house when they're done packing."

"Thanks." Howard shook hands with his uncle, then wandered down the street to his grandfather's house. *Regret.* Harry's mother wished her son had never met him. Aunt Judy wished her sons had never met him.

Were all his relationships doomed to end with regret? He knew Elsa was falling for him, but still she kept trying to reject him. Did she regret being attracted to a berserker? Did she regret lying to her aunts, her only family? Did she regret falling in love with a man she couldn't trust? Was it wrong for him to keep pulling her back?

After a few beers with his grandfather and Phil, he felt even worse. Walter was being strangely quiet. He probably regretted that all three of his grandsons were going into hiding.

"If Rhett attacks the island—" Howard began.

"Don't worry about it," Walter grumbled. "If he wants a war with us, he can have one."

Howard sighed. How many people was he endangering? *Regret.*

Jimmy and Jesse arrived with packed duffel bags. After the sun set, Ian and Dougal came upstairs, sipping on bottles of Bleer. Howard explained the situation to them, and they teleported Jimmy and Jesse to Dragon Nest. They would return in a few minutes to take Howard and Phil.

"You have to go again?" Howard's mother watched him sadly.

Regret. "I'll bring the boys back as soon as it's safe."

His mother sighed. "I know you don't mean for others to suffer." She hugged him, then wandered into the kitchen.

"It's not your fault, Howard," Walter grumbled. "It's the damned curse." He sat in his recliner and opened a new can of beer.

What a miserable family, Howard thought. His mother had never recovered from his twenty-year banishment. His grandfather was suffering, too.

And so many more had suffered. Carly had been terrorized and murdered, leaving behind a grieving family. Harry had been killed, and now his mother was in mourning. Jimmy and Jesse would be forced into hiding, leaving behind distraught parents.

No wonder Walter said they were cursed. Even Harry's mother had said his line was cursed. Everyone who loved him lived to regret it. If they lived.

His heart sank. Elsa's instincts to reject him had been right all along. It was the only way she could stay safe. If he tried to hang on to her, it would only cause her regret. She shouldn't have to live with a man she couldn't trust.

If he loved her, he needed to let her go.

Chapter Twenty-two

$\mathcal{T}$he next morning, Howard lumbered into the security office at Dragon Nest Academy. When he'd arrived last night, everyone had greeted him with big smiles as if they could erase his grief just by acting cheerful. His cousins had been welcomed by everyone, and then Toni and Ian had taken them on a tour before leaving them in a dormitory room in the boy's wing. Shanna had told him he could take a few days off, but he'd declined.

Now he stared out the window at the front drive and the grounds that extended to the main road. The sun was up, so Elsa was probably hard at work at the gatehouse. One of her aunts would be out front, guarding her, although it was no longer necessary. She was not in any danger from him. She would be free to live a long and happy life because the local berserker would leave her in peace.

"Hey, Howard! Hey, dude!" Two voices called out behind him.

He turned to find his cousins strolling into the office.

"Nice." Jimmy sprawled in the chair across from his desk.

"Wow, security monitors. Cool!" Jesse perched on the corner of his desk. "But you need more chairs in here, dude."

"That's nothing compared to the real problem around here," Jimmy grumbled.

"What problem?" Howard asked. "Is something wrong with your room?"

"Oh, the room's fine," Jesse answered. "The food's good, too. If you don't mind the stink."

Howard sat in his chair. "The food stinks?"

"Not the food," Jimmy corrected him. "The company. This place is full of werewolves!"

"Yeah!" Jesse gave him an indignant look. "You should have warned us we were going into a wolf den."

"Not all the kids here are werewolves." Howard leaned back in his chair. "There are a few were-panthers."

"Yeah, we met them." Jimmy waved a dismissive hand. "They seem all right."

"The oldest cat girl is really pretty," Jesse said. "But when I was checking her out, the oldest cat boy growled at me."

Howard sighed. "They have names—Teresa and Emiliano."

"Whatever," Jimmy grumbled. "The point is this place is full of stinky male werewolves."

"Have they been rude to you?" Howard asked.

Jesse shrugged. "Not really. We've been ignoring them."

"They're what we call Lost Boys," Howard explained. "They showed leadership capabilities and a potential for going Alpha, which made them a threat to their local Pack Masters. They were banished for life. No home, no family, and nowhere to go."

"Sheesh." Jimmy grimaced.

"That sucks," Jesse mumbled.

Howard nodded. "They're from Montana, Wyoming, and Idaho. They're not like Bleddyn's werewolves in Alaska, who have been raised to hate us. They're more like Phil. You like Phil, right?"

Jesse shrugged. "Yeah, he's okay."

"He's cool," Jimmy agreed.

"So you'll make an effort to get along with the wolf boys?" Howard asked.

The twins nodded.

Jimmy shifted in the chair. "There's still a problem here."

"Yeah," Jesse agreed. "There aren't any girls. I mean, I've seen a few older ladies around here, but I swear they're all knocked up."

Jimmy nodded. "We kinda figured that meant they were taken."

Howard snorted. "Brilliant deduction."

"Is there a town nearby?" Jimmy asked.

Jesse sighed. "It's no use, bro. Even if we found some local girls who were willing to date us, we don't have any money."

Howard groaned inwardly. Was he going to spend the next few months listening to his young cousins' ongoing saga of raging adolescent hormones? He needed to keep them busy. Hard, physical labor would be the best.

An idea struck him and he leaned forward. "Have you guys ever done construction work?"

"Sure," Jimmy replied. "It was about the only work we could find in Port Mishenka."

"There's a house being renovated just down the road. I'll see if they can use a few extra hands." Howard would call Alastair later. If the twins worked there, they could keep him informed on the project. Then he wouldn't have to risk running into Elsa.

"Cool," Jimmy said. "We could earn some money for college."

"The renovation is being done by a television show called *International Home Wreckers*. Maybe you've heard of it?" When his cousins stared at him blankly, Howard continued, "It's on the Home and Garden Renovation Station."

Jesse scratched his head. "Is that like one of those old people stations?"

Howard sighed. "It's a TV show, and if you work there—"

"We could be on TV?" Jesse jumped to his feet.

Jimmy stood. "This is so cool!" He did a high five with his brother.

"The show won't air for another six months or so," Howard warned the boys. "They have to finish the job first." And he'd have to make sure Rhett was no longer a threat.

"Hi!" a young voice called from the doorway.

"Tino." Howard waved him in. "Have you met my cousins?"

Tino approached, studying them carefully. "Are you were-bears, too?"

"Yep," Jimmy replied.

"I bet you're not as big as Howard." Tino

squirmed into the chair. "Nobody is as big as Howard."

Jesse nodded. "You got that right, little dude."

Tino grinned. "I'm glad you're here. My mom says Howard's going to be real sad and he'll need all his friends."

With a groan, Howard rubbed his brow.

"Guess what, little dude?" Jimmy asked, clearly trying to change the subject. "My brother and I are going to do construction work down the road and be on a TV show!"

"It's not set," Howard warned him. "I still have to arrange it with Alastair."

"Oh, then you get to work with Elsa!" Tino exclaimed.

"Elsa?" Jesse asked, his eyes lighting up. "Is she pretty?"

Howard tamped down on a sudden urge to growl.

"She's Howard's dream girl," Tino explained.

"Oh, really?" Jimmy grinned at Howard.

Jesse snickered. "Oh, that Howie, he's a busy boy."

Howard tamped down on a sudden urge to rip a few heads off.

"Howard." Tino looked around the office. "Where are the donuts? I wanted a donut."

"You've got donuts?" Jimmy scanned the room.

"I didn't get any today," Howard grumbled.

"What?" Tino's mouth fell open. "Are you sick?"

"Oh my God, Howie." Jesse feigned a look of horror. "How will you live?"

"Don't you have something to do?" Howard growled. "Move on, so I can get to my job."

"Yeah, yeah, we're going," Jimmy ambled toward the door.

"He wouldn't be such a grouch if he'd eaten some donuts," Jesse added as they left the room.

Tino climbed off the chair. "Did you get my present?"

"Yes." Howard reached into his pants pocket and retrieved the white marble chess piece. He opened his palm to show it to Tino. Harry, the white polar bear, the white knight.

"I'm sorry you lost him," Tino whispered.

"So am I." Howard's hand curled around the piece.

"I hope you'll have donuts tomorrow." Tino shuffled out of the room.

The gatehouse was packed full of people. Elsa had halted her work on the new island in the kitchen, for the wiring and plumbing crews had come in to do their job. Madge and the camera crew were also there, filming. As soon as the pipes and wiring were installed, The B Boys would finish floating the new ceiling on the ground floor.

She was in the utility room, checking where the wall had been removed and plumbing installed for a washing machine, when Alastair strolled in and came to a stop on the newly repaired floor.

"I just hired two more workers." He bounced on the balls of his feet, testing the floor. "Howard says they have experience."

Her heart swelled at the sound of his name. "Howard is back?"

"Yes. The boys are his cousins. Apparently, he brought them back with him from Alaska."

"I see." A twinge of disappointment nicked at her. Howard had contacted Alastair but not her?

"The boys are Jimmy and Jesse Barr. They'll start work in the morning." Alastair sauntered from the room. "I hope Howard starts bringing us donuts again."

Jimmy and Jesse *Barr*? Elsa slapped herself mentally. Why hadn't she realized Howard's last name was such a major clue? But she couldn't recall him ever mentioning his last name. These two cousins were probably were-bears, too. And berserkers.

Great. Now there would be three berserkers close by who could fulfill the curse. She shoved that thought aside. She wasn't going to let the stupid curse dictate her life. It only had power over her if she believed in it and feared it.

Howard felt the same way. So why hadn't he called? Maybe with all the noise in the house, she'd missed his call? She pulled her cell phone from her jeans pocket. No missed calls. No texts. She called his number, but it rang and rang. Was he busy? She left a voice message.

"Howard, I heard you were back. I'm so sorry about Harry. Call me when you get a chance. Bye."

She switched the phone to vibrate so she would feel it when he returned her call.

An hour later, he still hadn't called. Was he really that busy? Or maybe he was too depressed over Harry's death. Should she give him sympathy or give him space?

Another hour passed. An ominous feeling settled in her gut. This wasn't like Howard. He'd always been so determined to pursue her.

After another hour, the ominous feeling threatened to turn into panic. Now that she feared she might lose him, she realized how badly she wanted him.

She called again. It rang and rang.

"Hi, Elsa," he finally answered.

Her heart did its usual somersault at the sound of his deep, sexy voice. "Howard, I was worried about you. Are you all right?"

"Yes." There was a pause. "I've been . . . thinking."

The bad feeling in her gut returned full force. "You're in mourning now. You shouldn't be making any—"

"I don't want you to live in fear of me. It's not fair to you. And I've been putting you in a bad position, forcing you to lie to your aunts."

Her gut twisted. "Howard, don't—"

"I can't let you fall in love with me."

Too late! she wanted to scream.

"Not when I know it will end with regret," he continued quickly. "You tried to reject me several times. Your instincts were correct."

"What do you mean? You were planning to attack me after all?"

"No, of course not. I could never hurt you."

"You're hurting me now!"

There was a pause before he continued. "I'm sorry, Elsa. I'm sure if you think about it, you'll know this is for the best. You can have a full and happy life without any fears that the curse will come true."

"I don't care about the damned curse!"

"It's for the best. I'm really sorry." He hung up.

She stared at the phone. Was this really happening? Had he really dropped her? On the phone? Her heart pounded, thundering in her ears.

This couldn't be happening! The man who had pursued her without fail had suddenly failed on her?

It had to be the grief. With trembling hands, she stuffed the phone back into her pocket. This wasn't like Howard. The Howard she knew was always smiling and joking. But his jolly exterior simply masked how strong and determined he was. He never gave up.

She wandered past the other workers, not even hearing them, till she ended up on the back porch. Her gaze drifted to the spot where she'd had two picnics with Howard. And right there was the spot where he'd told her he loved her.

"This is all wrong," she whispered. It was all backward. From the moment they had met, he'd chased after her while she had wavered. And now that she was thoroughly caught, he was wavering? No, more than wavering. He'd flat out rejected her.

How could he? He'd stood right over there and told her he loved her.

"Dammit." She pulled her phone from her pocket to send him a text message.

What the hell happened? she typed, then erased it. Too angry. The guy was in mourning. She should cut him some slack.

I thought you wanted to jump my bones? No, that made their relationship sound merely physical. It was much deeper than that. Their souls belonged together. She'd felt pulled to him the moment she first saw him. Just like her aunt Ula had said. The two of them, guardian and berserker, were tied together in a dance that was centuries old. It was up to them to give that dance a happy ending instead of a tragic one. Howard had always been up to the challenge. Until now.

How dare he toss their attraction aside? She'd come so far since her arrival here. She'd adjusted to being the Guardian of the Forest. She'd learned to accept him as a were-bear. She'd finally arrived at the point that she was ready to trust him. How dare he reject all the progress she'd made?

She typed another message. *I know you're hurting right now, but don't toss me aside just to ease your pain. I never took you for a COWARD!!*

With a wince, she deleted that. She shouldn't let her anger show. But dammit, she *was* angry!

She tried a fourth time. *Don't give up on me. You proved you are worthy, and I trust you.*

Should she tell him she loved him? No, she'd rather do that in person. She studied the message, then took a deep breath and pushed Send.

She waited, but there was no response. Her mind raced, replaying what he'd said earlier on the phone. He thought she would regret being with him.

No, she would regret living the rest of her life without him.

She had to get him back. Luckily, she had an ally. She sent a long text to Shanna Draganesti. If all went according to plan, Howard would come to the gatehouse tomorrow afternoon.

Howard watched the sun set from his office window. Ian would be here soon to relieve him. And the twins should be back soon from their trip to Cranville. He'd loaned them his car and given them enough money to buy some tools and tool belts at the local hardware store.

He checked the time on his computer. They'd been gone over an hour. The town was a straight shot down the main road. They couldn't be lost. They were probably roaming around the small town, looking for girls. Or spending the rest of his money at the diner.

He'd spent the afternoon compiling his proof of Rhett's embezzlement from his late father's companies. When the report was complete, he e-mailed it to the editor-in-chief at *Northern Lights Sound Bites*. Then he called the editor and asked him to continue the paper's exposé on Rhett Bleddyn.

Mr. West had agreed. He was worried about further retaliation from Rhett, but he thought he could solve it by writing an article himself that stated if anything happened to anyone at his paper, the police should immediately arrest Rhett. Using that as an insurance policy, the editor was eager to wage war on the villain who had killed his ace reporter Harry. Howard promised to send him all the ammunition he had.

He picked up his phone, and for the hundredth time, he read the text Elsa had sent. *Don't give up on me. You proved you are worthy, and I trust you.*

Was he making a big mistake? Was he throwing away the best thing that had ever happened to him? He rubbed his brow. There was no doubt that he loved her. And wanted her. He ached for her.

But how could he live with himself if something happened to her? It had taken him years to get over Carly's death.

"Howard." Shanna rushed in with a glass of synthetic blood in her hand. She had obviously dressed in a hurry, by the looks of her T-shirt and sweatpants. "Tino tells me you stopped eating donuts."

He snorted. "It's not the end of the world."

"This is probably not a good time for you to go through sugar withdrawal."

"I'll be fine." He strode to the door. "You should finish your breakfast."

She took a sip from her glass. "I received a text from . . . Alastair."

Howard stopped, noting the hesitation in her voice. Was she up to something?

She lifted her chin. "He wants you to stop by the gatehouse tomorrow afternoon at two for an interview."

"I'm too busy."

"You have to!" Shanna's eyes widened with alarm. "The camera crew is in town, and they won't be back for another two weeks."

He hesitated.

"You promised you would represent me," she added.

He nodded. "All right. I'll be there." He smelled a trap.

She grinned. "Great!" She downed the rest of her glass, then hurried back down the hall.

He sighed. No doubt Elsa would be at the gatehouse. And she'd insist on talking to him.

Definitely a trap. He should avoid it, even though there was a part of him that desperately wanted to be caught.

Chapter Twenty-three

_T_all, long-legged, broad-shouldered, thick brown hair, and twinkling blue eyes. No doubt about it, Elsa thought, those two boys were Howard's cousins. A pang shot through her chest. She couldn't lose Howard.

It was the next morning, and all the workers had gathered in the parlor at the gatehouse. Aunt Ula was parked outside in the driveway. Aunt Greta would be taking her turn in the afternoon.

Alastair introduced Howard's cousins to everyone. "Thank you for bringing the donuts."

"No problem," one twin said. Elsa thought it might be Jesse, but she wasn't sure which one was which.

"Are you lads up to knocking down a few walls?" Alastair asked.

The boys smiled. "Sure."

Elsa figured they could knock down an entire house if they shifted into were-bears.

"Good. You'll assist The B Boys today," Alastair told them. "They'll be busting down some walls upstairs to enlarge a few rooms. Elsa, I'll give you the floor plans so you can supervise."

"Okay." She noticed the twins were grinning at her. Had Howard mentioned her to them? If so, that was a good sign.

"Oskar, make sure the wiring is completed for the basement and ground floor," Alastair continued. "Did you finish sectioning off the basement?"

"*Ja*," Oskar replied. "We have the walls up for the bedroom suite and storage room."

"Excellent." Alastair strode toward Elsa and handed her the upstairs floor plans. "Let's make some progress before Madge shows up at noon with the camera crew. Jimmy and Jesse, would you mind putting the leftover donuts in the kitchen?"

With that, everyone split up to get to work. The wiring and plumbing crews were concentrating on the basement and ground floor. Elsa headed up the stairs behind The B Boys. The twins hurried off to the kitchen with the last two boxes of donuts.

With one more stair step to go, she felt a tap on her shoulder from behind. An instant burst of red-hot pain shot from the birthmark on her shoulder. She stumbled onto the second floor landing and turned to see Howard's cousins right behind her.

"I'm sorry," one of the twins said, his eyes wide with worry. "I didn't think I tapped you that hard."

"Yeah," the other twin said. "Sometimes we don't know our own strength."

"Howard would probably kill us if we hurt you," the first one added.

"I'm fine," Elsa assured them. "I just lost my balance." So these two boys had the same effect on her birthmark that Howard had. Not surprising, really, since they came from the same berserker family. But she didn't feel immediately drawn to them like she had with Howard.

Another good sign, she thought. It meant she was attracted to Howard not because he was a berserker but because he was Howard. Huge, handsome, hunky Howard.

"We wanted to introduce ourselves," said the one who had tapped her shoulder. "I'm Jimmy."

"And I'm Jesse."

She smiled, hoping Jesse wouldn't realize she was avoiding shaking hands with him. His touch would probably burn as badly as Jimmy's had. "I'm delighted to meet you."

The B Boys gathered around to introduce themselves, then unfolded Elsa's floor plans to study them.

Jimmy slanted a grin at her. "We heard you were Howard's dream girl."

Her heart lifted with a surge of hope. "Did Howard say that?"

"No, it was the little dude," Jesse said. "Howard just growled at us."

"He's not his usual self," Jimmy whispered.

Elsa nodded, her heart settling back into its current condition of pain and despair. "Buff, can you and the others go ahead and get started? We'll join you in just a second." When The B Boys sauntered off with the plans, she turned back to the twins. "I wanted to talk to you in private."

"Awesome." Jesse exchanged an excited look with his brother. "This sounds like a conspiracy."

"Cool," Jimmy whispered, then turned to Elsa. "It's about Howard, right?"

"Yes. He's supposed to come here today at two to videotape an interview."

"Yeah, he mentioned that," Jesse said. "Dudette, he's on to you. He called it a trap."

"The interview is real," Elsa assured them. "Madge will be here filming today."

"And you'll be here to see Howard?" Jimmy asked.

"He probably assumes I'll be here," Elsa continued. "But I won't be. I'm hoping he'll be disappointed enough to realize how much he does want to see me."

"Oh, tricky," Jesse said. "I like it."

Elsa sighed. There was a very big danger that her whole plan could backfire and Howard would be relieved she wasn't here. But if the plan worked, she would be successfully luring Howard back into the role of the pursuer. "Would you mind helping me?"

"What can we do?" Jimmy asked.

"If Howard asks where I am, tell him I'm cooling down at the stream. He knows where that is."

"You're going to reel him in like a fish?" Jimmy grinned. "Cool."

Jesse nodded. "Awesome."

Where the hell was she? Howard had showered and shaved and put on some of his best clothes before walking into Elsa's trap. Dammit, here he was, a willing victim, and she didn't bother to show up?

He hid his frustration behind a forced smile as

he exchanged pleasantries with Madge in front of the camera. In the course of the interview, she'd walked him through the basement, where the plumbing and wiring crews were hard at work. But no Elsa.

Madge had escorted him around the ground floor, even going into the kitchen to inspect Elsa's progress on the cabinets. She wasn't there.

She wasn't upstairs, either. It didn't make sense. She had to be around here somewhere. Her aunt Greta was parked outside in the driveway. He'd spotted her when he'd parked his SUV behind the sporty convertible his cousins had borrowed from Ian.

So where the hell was Elsa?

It didn't matter, he told himself. It was best not to see her again.

There will never be another Elsa, you fool.

The interview ended, and he gave Madge a strained smile as she thanked him.

He hesitated, watching Madge and her crew go down the stairs and out the front door. Should he leave, too? The interview was over.

"Hey, dude." Jesse sauntered toward him with his brother. "You were good."

"Yeah," Jimmy agreed. "Real smooth."

Howard shrugged. "I used to do a lot of interviews when I played football."

"Cool." Jimmy eyed him curiously.

"Awesome." Jesse crossed his arms, watching him.

What did they want? "Are you working hard?" Howard asked.

They nodded.

"You brought everyone donuts like I asked?"

They nodded.

Howard raked a hand through his hair. "It seems a little . . . odd."

"What?" Jimmy asked.

"Elsa's aunt is out front to guard her, but she's not here."

"Hmm." Jesse looked at his brother. "Didn't she tell us she was going somewhere?"

"Yeah." Jimmy scratched his head. "Where was that?"

The twins exchanged an amused look.

Howard gritted his teeth. "Where is she?"

"Well, if you insist." Jesse's mouth twitched. "She said something about cooling off in a stream."

Howard had an instant vision of Elsa splashing around in the pothole where the water was deep.

Jimmy heaved a sigh. "It's a shame you missed her."

"Yeah. I guess you have to get back to work." Jesse patted Howard on the back. "Tough luck, old dude."

Howard clenched his fists. So this was the trap. Elsa alone at the stream. "I'll see you guys later." He marched down the stairs, ignoring the snickers from his cousins.

So they were in on it. Shanna, too. Did everyone think he was that easily manipulated?

He'd show them. He'd go back to work at Dragon Nest. And Elsa could splash around in the damned stream all afternoon, waiting for him.

He reached the bottom of the stairs. It was a

tempting trap, he had to admit, but he wouldn't fall for it. *Cooling down in the stream, my ass.*

Skinny-dipping? He paused by the front door. Was she waiting for him naked? Did she think he was that easy to entice? *Damn.*

He spun on his heel and strode toward the back door. His cousins on the second-floor landing cheered, then laughed when he shot them the finger.

He'd show Elsa not to toy with him.

Elsa paced in front of the stream. Could she do this? She'd never played the seductress before. She knocked down walls. She built cabinets. She wielded hammers. Even sledgehammers. She didn't seduce big, hunky men.

The problem was probably moot. If Howard was serious about rejecting her, he wouldn't come.

On the way to the stream, she'd acquired an entourage of deer, raccoons, foxes, and squirrels. What if Howard did come? She didn't want to put on a show for the woodland creatures.

She lifted her hands. "Go in peace."

They slowly ambled away, except for a squirrel who had found a yummy acorn to munch on.

"Hey there," she called out to the squirrel. "If the were-bear comes this way, could you let me know?"

The squirrel tilted its head, regarding her curiously. She wasn't sure if her request had registered.

With a sigh, she decided to take matters into her

own hands. She twisted her hair up and clipped it
on the back of her head with a plastic claw. Then
she removed her work boots and set them beside
the big boulder that would serve as her dresser.
She removed her socks and tucked them into her
boots.

The small rocks along the creek bed were
smooth and cool against her bare feet. She pulled
off her T-shirt and folded it on top of the boulder.
In preparation for today's attempted seduction,
she'd worn her best underwear—a lacy red bra
and matching red panties.

She unzipped her jeans. A movement nearby
caught her attention. It was the squirrel. It bounced
across the tops of several rocks, then leaped onto
the boulder.

He comes. She heard it clearly in her mind.

Goose bumps skittered down her arms. She
didn't know which freaked her out more—that
she'd understood a squirrel or that Howard had
willingly walked into her trap.

The squirrel bounded away, leaping from one
rock to another before disappearing into the
woods.

Howard was coming.

Was this a mistake? Using the lure of sex to
draw him back? All's fair in love and war, she told
herself. She wanted to show him that she loved
him and trusted him. How better to show her
trust than by making herself totally vulnerable?

She pushed her jeans down. Was he close by
and watching? She folded them and set them on
the boulder. She unhooked her bra. Was that a

quick breath she heard? Her nipples pebbled in response, and she dropped her bra on the stack of clothes. Before she could chicken out, she eased her panties off and placed them on top of the bra.

Some gravel crunched behind her. *Howard.* She rushed into the pool, wincing at how cold the water was. When the water covered her breasts, she turned.

Howard was standing in front of the tree line, glaring at her, his eyes an intense blue.

She swallowed hard. He looked more angry than attracted. "Hi. Would you care to join me for a . . . swim?" Her face flushed with heat. That had sounded so lame. Some seductress she made.

He scowled at her, then pivoted and strode into the woods.

Her mouth dropped open. Her plan had backfired?

A flurry of noises emanated from behind some bushes. Was that Howard? Or something else? She winced, sinking down in the water to her chin. It would just be her luck for a group of hunters to be walking by.

The bushes shook, then a large grizzly bear reared up on its hind legs and roared.

She gasped. Howard? Oh God, she hoped that was Howard.

The bear bounded straight toward her.

"Howard!" She retreated deeper into the water, but it kept coming.

It splashed into the stream.

If this was Howard, why was he scaring her like this? She lunged back till her back pressed against the granite wall where the stream made its curve. The water was over her head now, and she kicked her legs about until she found an underwater rock she could stand on.

The bear rose onto its hind legs and started to shimmer, turning gray before finally snapping back into human form.

Howard frowned at her, his eyes glittering a neon blue. "Don't think you can toy with me, Elsa."

She splashed water at him. "You big bully! First you reject me, breaking my heart, and now you try to frighten me into a heart attack!"

"Are you frightened?" He stepped toward her, the water just above his waist. "I could shift back in a second and maul you. Isn't that what you're afraid of?"

"Screw you!" She splashed water into his face. "I'm not afraid. I'm pissed!"

"So am I!"

"Why? You're the one who rejected me." Hot tears stung her eyes. "I finally get up the nerve to trust you and love you, and you dump me!"

"You what?"

"You dumped me!"

He stepped closer. "You trust me? And love me?"

"I hate you." She crossed her arms over her chest.

"Liar." He lunged toward her, grabbing her around the waist.

She pushed at his shoulders. "How could you reject me?"

"I was crazy." He dragged her back to more shallow water. "I should have known I could never let you go."

"You broke my heart."

"I'll fix it." He pulled her close so her breasts pressed against his bare chest.

She gasped.

"Is that better?" He kissed her cheek, then her temple and brow. "I never stopped loving you. I've been aching for you."

"Oh, Howard." She wrapped her arms around his neck. "I love you, too. I don't want to ever lose you."

"You won't." He planted his mouth on hers, kissing her hungrily.

She couldn't get close enough. She tightened her grip around his neck and wrapped her legs around his torso. He trailed kisses down her neck as his hands skimmed down to her rump.

"Elsa." He lifted her, dragging her up his chest.

She gasped as her core skidded across his skin. Her heels dug into his back so she could press harder against him. He lifted her till he could draw one of her nipples into his mouth. With each tug on her breast, she grew hotter and more desperate.

She squirmed against him. "Howard. Please."

He lowered her and whispered in her ear. "Are you mine, Elsa?"

"Yes."

His hand slipped between her thighs. With her legs wrapped around him, she was fully exposed to his touch. She groaned as his fingers explored her folds.

"Will you shudder and scream for me?" he whispered, his lips against her ear.

She felt moisture building inside. "Yes."

He rubbed against her clitoris, then tugged gently on it. She cried out.

"Will you open for me? Will you let me inside you?"

"Oh yes!" She gasped when his finger slid inside her. Then two fingers. She clenched around him.

"So hot and wet." He kissed her hard as he stroked her.

She broke the kiss, struggling to breathe as tension grew. He stroked harder and faster.

"Howard." She dug her fingers into his shoulders. He was so good. Merciless. She teetered on the edge for a glorious moment, then shattered. Her cry echoed in the woods around them.

She gasped for air as delicious aftershocks racked her body. "Oh, Howard." She hugged him tight.

He nuzzled her neck. "You naughty wench. You seduced me."

With a snort, she swatted his shoulder. "You seduced me, and you know it."

"Me? I've barely gotten started." He lowered her until her core rested on the tip of his erection.

She gasped at the size. And that was just the tip. "Howard. You're such an animal."

He smiled.

She kissed his brow. "I love you."

"I love you, too."

With a grin, she tilted her head back to gaze at the blue sky. The day couldn't be more perfect.

She stiffened.

"What?" He looked around. "Are we being watched by some perverted raccoons?"

She pointed to the top of the granite wall where the stream curved. Along the edge was a row of large birds. Brown hawks and black crows. More than twenty of them.

She unhooked her legs so she could stand in the stream. *Danger.* She heard it echo through the forest. The woodland creatures were warning her. *Danger! Run!*

She stepped back. "We need to get out of here."

"It's okay." Howard reached for her. "They're just birds."

Half of the birds took wing and flew in the direction of the house.

She shook her head. "Those are more than birds. They're spying for the Guardian of the Sky."

"Your aunt?"

Elsa rushed toward her clothes to get dressed. "Hurry. Before she gets here with a shotgun!"

Chapter Twenty-four

"*W*here are you parked?" Elsa asked. They had both dressed quickly and were now hurrying through the woods to the gatehouse.

"In the driveway," Howard replied.

She winced. It would have been better if he'd parked along the main road and taken the short-cut through the woods. He'd done that before in order to keep their picnics secret. "You parked next to my aunt?"

"I have nothing to hide." He glanced around. "We're being followed by deer on both sides."

"I know. They're worried about me. I can hear them."

"They're talking to you? They warned you about the birds?"

"Yes." She jumped over a fallen log. They were still saying *Danger. Run.* She looked back. Howard had stopped and was staring at her. "What's wrong?"

"Two weeks ago you were afraid of the animals. Now, look at you. You're . . . connected to them."

She gave him a wry smile. "Stranger things have happened. I'm in love with a were-bear."

"You're amazing." He stepped closer and took her hand. "I'm sorry I hurt you."

"You were hurting, too. I'm so sorry about Harry."

He nodded. "I was . . . drowning in regret. I didn't want to cause you regret—"

"You won't." She tugged on his hand. "Let's go."

They jogged to the back of the house. The sound of screeching electric saws and pounding hammers emanated from the building.

Good, Elsa thought. The workers would be too busy to notice them sneaking around outside. She led Howard to the right. "Okay. This is the plan. You take the shortcut through the woods. I'll have one of your cousins drive your SUV to the main road to pick you up. Okay? Give me the keys."

"No. I'm not hiding from your aunt." He strode toward the front of the house.

"You have to!" Elsa ran after him. "She has a shotgun!"

"Then don't stand too close to me."

"Are you crazy?"

"Maybe." He gave her a wry look. "Time to meet one of my future in-laws." He rounded the corner and strode toward the driveway.

"What?" She followed him. "Was that some sort of proposal?"

"You're my mate. I'm not letting you go."

She halted with a huff. "That's about the most unromantic—you're supposed to ask, you big—" She gasped when Greta pumped her shotgun.

"Hold it right there!" Her aunt leveled the gun at Howard.

He lifted his hands.

"Greta, stop!" Elsa moved next to him and he shook his head at her, frowning.

"Step away," Greta demanded. "My birds know a predator when they see one. He's the berserker, isn't he?"

"He's not dangerous!" Elsa insisted.

"I can speak for myself," he muttered. "How do you do? I'm Howard Barr."

"Barr?" Greta lowered her weapon, her eyes narrowed. "You're a bear berserker?"

"I'm a descendant. My family's from Alaska, far removed from the ancient Nordic curse. I have no desire to harm your niece."

Greta snorted. "We can never trust a berserker."

"I'm in love with Elsa," Howard continued. "And I would be greatly honored if she would consent to marry me."

Elsa's heart lurched. "Oh." She turned toward him. "Howard."

He gave her a wry look. "Was that romantic enough?"

"Step away from him!" Greta shouted. "You can't trust him."

Elsa gasped as Greta raised the shotgun. "No!" She jumped in front of Howard.

"Elsa!" He grabbed her around the waist to shove her aside.

"No!" She dug her heels into the gravel driveway, skidding as she fought to stay in front of him.

"Dammit." He lifted her up and planted her to the side. "I won't let you get hurt."

She latched onto his arm. "Don't you see, Greta? He's trying to protect me."

Aunt Greta lowered the shotgun. "You poor child. He has you completely fooled."

"He would never hurt me," Elsa insisted. "He's a sweet and wonderful man."

"He's an animal," Greta muttered. She glared at Howard, then jerked her head toward the other cars. "Leave. Before I change my mind and blast a hole in you."

Howard moved slowly toward his SUV. "I realize it will be hard for you to accept me, but—"

"Go!" Greta shouted.

"As you wish. Till we meet again." He nodded at Elsa. "I'll talk to you later."

"Of course." She watched him climb into his SUV and start the engine. "Thank you for not shooting him, Greta. I know you'll like him once you get to know him."

She snorted. "I don't want to know him. I only let him go because you were in the way. I was afraid I'd shoot you."

"Oh, come on." Elsa waved at Howard as he drove slowly past them. "Couldn't you see how nice he was? He was trying to protect me."

"He will betray you." Greta closed her eyes. "I have to kill him before he can kill you."

Elsa gasped. "Don't say that . . ." She looked up as the sky turned suddenly dark. Hundreds of birds were circling overhead. Dozens of black crows gathered along the roof of the gatehouse. It was an army, waiting for their orders.

Her skin prickled with goose bumps. "Greta. Please don't do this."

"You wouldn't let me shoot him." She lifted her hands to the sky. "I have another way."

"No!" Elsa watched, stunned as a thick wave of birds moved across the sky, headed for the main road. "Call them off!"

Greta ignored her, keeping her eyes on her birds.

Elsa glanced around and spotted keys in the nearby convertible. She jumped in and started the engine.

"No!" Greta shouted.

"I'm going to him, so call them off!" Elsa yelled at her, then gunned the engine, spraying gravel as she zoomed down the driveway.

She turned onto the main road, racing after Howard. It didn't take long to catch up with him. He'd slowed to a crawl, his SUV entirely covered with birds. The cawing and shrieking sounds were deafening. Large hawks dive-bombed his vehicle, slamming into the roof as if they wanted to rip their way through. Black crows crashed into the windows and tried to drill through with their beaks.

She leaned on the horn, but the honking blast didn't faze the birds. Howard's SUV came to a complete stop. Maybe he could see her, though she wasn't sure he could see anything with his windows covered.

She parked on the side of the road and searched the interior of the car for anything she could use as a weapon. An empty glass bottle on the floor. She picked it up. Bleer? What was that?

It was better than nothing. She stepped out.

"Shoo! Go away!" She waved the bottle, but the birds didn't budge. She didn't want to throw away her only weapon, so she pulled off a work boot and threw it.

It hit the back of his SUV with a thud, dislodging a dozen birds and wounding a few that plummeted to the road.

She took off her other boot. A dark shadow fell over her, and she glanced up. Birds were circling overhead.

Oh no. She was totally exposed. They spiraled down toward her. She shouted and threw her boot at them.

Hooves clattered onto the road as a herd of deer ran toward her. She frantically waved the bottle overhead and managed to whack some of the attacking birds. The deer surrounded her, and she ducked down, letting them shield her. She winced as the poor animals were pecked and clawed. One of the deer kicked her bottle, and it rolled to the side of the road.

"Elsa!" Howard shouted.

She gasped as she saw him running toward her. His arms were raised to protect his head, but birds were bombing him, tearing at the bare skin on his forearms. "Howard, stay in the car!"

A screech of brakes sounded behind them. Greta had followed them. She climbed out of her car. "Elsa! Come with me."

"Call off your birds!" she yelled back.

"I won't let them hurt you." Greta approached. "Just come with me."

The birds ceased their attack on Elsa and the deer and flew high into the air.

She straightened. The deer sidled up against her, pressing their sides against her. *Thank you for protecting me.* Her heart squeezed at the sight of blood on their backs.

"You poor things." She ran her hand along a deer's back, then gasped when a sudden surge of heat shot down her arm from her birthmark. The heat gathered in her hand till her palm glowed. She skimmed her hand over the deer's wounds, and they healed.

She pivoted, quickly touching all the deer.

"Elsa, hurry!" Greta cried. "Come with me!"

She glanced up. The birds were now flying straight toward Howard. "No!" She ran toward him, the deer following.

"Elsa!" Greta shouted. "Come with me, and I'll stop them!"

Howard grabbed her by the shoulders. "Go with her so you'll be safe."

"I don't—" She hesitated. Was this the best way to make her aunt stop and to keep Howard safe? "Okay." She retreated, moving slowly toward her aunt.

With a great screeching sound, the birds shot away from the SUV and zoomed across the sky.

She glanced back at Howard. "Are you all right?"

He nodded, even though blood dripped down his forearms and trickled from a wound on his forehead.

She watched him trudge toward the SUV and climb wearily inside. He looked so forlorn. Did he think he had lost her?

"Come on!" Greta walked back to her car.

Elsa glanced at Howard's SUV, then her aunt's car.

The deer watched her expectantly. *Go!*

Go where? She asked them.

Go with your heart.

She ran to the SUV and wrenched open the passenger-side door. "Let's go!" She jumped in and closed the door.

Howard's eyes widened. "Are you sure?"

"Yes. Go!"

He stepped on the gas.

She buckled up. "Is she following us?"

He glanced in the rearview mirror. "No. Your buddies are playing defensive linemen."

"Huh?" She twisted to look out the back window. The deer had formed a line across the road.

"You healed them." Howard glanced at her. "I saw it."

She turned her hand over to study her palm. "I didn't know I could do it. It felt so strange."

"You're coming into your power really fast."

She winced at the blood dripping down his forearms. "Maybe I can help you." She touched a wound, but nothing happened. "Oh, I'm sorry." Apparently it only worked on woodland creatures, and Howard was currently human.

"Don't worry about it. I'll heal as soon as I can shift. I would shift now, but the bear is a lousy driver."

"You let him drive?"

"Only on Sundays."

She snorted. Humorous Howard. It was good

to have him back. She pulled some tissues from a dispenser on his console and dabbed at his arm. "I'm sorry about my aunt."

"So am I. She tried to kill me."

"She doesn't know you."

He drove for a while, frowning.

Elsa bit her lip. "Please don't tell me you're having second thoughts again."

He sighed. "I don't want you to have to choose between your family and me. You would regret losing them, and I would be the cause of your regret."

"I won't lose them. And I don't want to lose you."

He pulled to a stop as the main road came to a dead end at a crossroad. "If I turn left here, we could go back to Cranville. I could drop you off at your hotel. And continue to court you."

She nodded. "We could do that."

He shifted in his seat to face her. "If I turn right, I'll take you into the mountains to my cabin."

"You have a cabin?"

"I'll make love to you."

She swallowed hard.

"And you'll be mine. My mate."

Her pulse speeded up. "What does that mean exactly? Do you expect me to become a . . . a bear?"

"Only if you want to." He tapped his fingers on the steering wheel. "I'm not sure you can, since you're the Guardian. I can't predict the future, other than the fact that I will always love you and protect you and cherish you for as long as I live."

Her heart melted. "That's a fact?"

"Yes." His eyes glittered an intense blue. "And it won't change whether you choose left or right. I'll always love you."

She touched his face. Dear, sweet Howard. "Turn right."

Chapter Twenty-five

*H*oward was already growing hard with antici-pation. He would jump her in the bedroom, in the kitchen, in the woods. And that was just today. Tomorrow—he realized he needed to make some calls before they drove out of range. Reception could be sketchy at the cabin. He normally took a sat phone there, but all he had now was his regu-lar cell phone.

He called Jimmy. "You need to pick up Ian's car. It's on the main road."

"How did it get there?" Jimmy asked.

"Long story." Howard glanced at Elsa. He still couldn't believe that she'd endangered herself like that. He'd almost had a heart attack when he saw her standing on the road behind him, trying to chase the birds away. He'd leaped from the SUV to protect her, but the deer had reached her first.

She never ceased to amaze him. She'd fought for him. She'd healed the deer. And she'd chosen to be his mate. That had to be the end of the damned curse. They'd beaten it. And in another fifteen minutes, he would be stripping her naked.

He shifted his weight in the driver's seat. His

pants were becoming uncomfortably tight. "I'm going to my cabin for a few days," he told Jimmy. "Let Ian and Shanna know. They won't mind. They wanted me to take some time off."

"Okay." Jimmy passed the news to his brother and they both snickered. "You're not alone, are you?"

He gritted his teeth. "Tell Alastair that Elsa is taking a few days off, too."

Her eyebrows lifted. "A few days?"

"Talk to you later." He hung up when his cousins started making strange barking noises. "Crazy kids." He dropped his phone on the console.

"I like them," Elsa said. "I gather they turn into bears like you?"

"Yes." His mind raced. Did he have any food at the cabin? Enough to get by, he hoped. He didn't want to stop to buy groceries now. In fourteen minutes, he'd be stripping Elsa naked.

Thank God he'd taken care of business that morning. He had e-mailed the rest of his incriminating evidence to the editor at *Northern Lights Sound Bites*. Mr. West had e-mailed back, claiming that the war on Rhett Bleddyn had begun. The first article on Rhett's embezzlement had been published in the morning edition. The mainstream media was predicting he would be arrested soon.

He's going down, Harry. You will be avenged.

Howard turned onto the gravel road that zigzagged up the mountains. Thirteen minutes to go.

"I sorta bumped into one of your cousins, and it made my birthmark burn," Elsa said. "I guess that happens with any berserker the first time I touch him."

"You don't have to worry about them," he assured her. "They're harmless."

"That's what I figured. They're really cute."

He tamped down on an urge to growl.

Her mouth twitched. "But no one is as handsome and sexy as you."

"Damned straight." His grip tightened on the steering wheel. Another twelve minutes. To hell with that. He stepped on the gas.

In eight minutes, he screeched to a halt behind the cabin. "Let's go." He jumped out and ran up the steps to the back door.

"It's very nice." Elsa approached slowly as she looked around. "Peaceful and rustic. Beautiful trees."

"This is the back." He unlocked the door. "The view is better from the front porch."

"Oh. I'd like to see it." She climbed up the steps to join him.

"Later." He lifted her in his arms and carried her inside.

She grinned. "You're treating me like a bride."

He kicked the door shut and strode through the kitchen area to the front of the cabin.

"Nice open floor plan. Can I have a tour?"

"Later." He turned into the bedroom and deposited her on the bed.

"Howard." She sat up. "You're forgetting. You need to shift to heal those wounds."

"Later." He kicked off his shoes.

"But your arms are bloody."

"Oh." She might consider that a turnoff. He

pulled his polo shirt over his head and used it to wipe the blood.

She winced. "You're smearing it. Is there a bathroom where I can clean your wounds?"

"There's a shower." That would work. He grabbed her hand and led her into the adjoining bathroom.

"Very nice." She looked around as he pulled off his socks. "Lovely tile work." She removed a hand towel from the towel bar.

By the time she had it dampened in the sink, he'd dropped his pants and underwear.

She turned toward him with the wet towel. "Okay, let me see—" Her mouth fell open.

He took advantage of her surprise by unzipping her jeans and pushing them down, taking her panties with them. "Step out of them."

"Huh?" Her eyes were still focused on his erection.

He turned on the water in the shower to give it time to warm up. "We're going to shower, right?"

"I thought I was going to clean your wounds."

"You can. In the shower." He grabbed the wet towel and tossed it onto the counter. Then he pulled her T-shirt over her head and unhooked her bra. "Let's go."

He tested the water with his hand, then stepped into the tiled stall, leaving the door open for her. Quickly he rinsed the blood off his arms and forehead.

"Where do you keep the washcloths?" She peered in at him.

He pulled her inside and closed the door.

"Aagh." The spray hit her in the face.

He moved her against the tile wall, brushed her wet hair out of her face, and kissed her.

With a moan, she wrapped her arms around his neck and kissed him back.

He devoured her mouth as his hands slid up and down her wet, slick body. He palmed a breast and squeezed.

"I want you," he whispered, nibbling on her lips. "I can't wait."

Her breaths panted against his mouth. "I noticed you were ready."

"How are you?" He slipped a hand between her legs and caressed the soft folds.

She shuddered.

He rubbed her clitoris as he nuzzled her ear. "I love it when you get juicy. I can smell it, and it drives me wild."

With a groan, she seeped moisture onto his fingers. "Howard."

He grasped her rump and lifted her. "Put your legs around me."

She did. "Will this work?" She wrapped her arms around his neck. "I've never done it like— ack!"

He drove deep inside her and froze. Holy crap, she was so tight and sweet.

She blinked, staring at him. "I guess it does work."

He adjusted his grip on her rear. "I don't think I'll last very long."

"Completely understandable. After all, it's"—

she whimpered when he dragged himself out to the tip—"our first . . . agh!"

He plunged back in.

"Oh, Howard. You're so—" She gasped when he pushed into her again. "So—"

She gave up speaking altogether as he pumped harder and faster. Her fingers dug into his shoulders, and her heels pressed into his back. With each plunge, he ground her against him.

She tensed and her breath caught. He pulled her hard against him, and she cried out. Her body shuddered, her inner muscles spasmed, and with a shout, he thrust into her, releasing his seed.

Mine. He held her tight. The bear inside him purred like a kitten. *My mate.*

Elsa woke the next morning with the feel of Howard's big body pressed against her back and his fingers gently teasing her nipples. She smiled to herself and closed her eyes. The man was insatiable.

After the shower, he'd taken her to bed, claiming he needed to thoroughly examine his mate. He'd pushed her onto her stomach, and then he'd counted her toes and tasted them. He'd nibbled the entire length of her legs, tickling the backs of her knees. He'd nuzzled her rear and licked a path up her spine. And he'd told her numerous times how beautiful she was.

Then he'd rolled her over to explore the front side. When moisture had pooled between her legs, he'd growled softly.

He'd inserted two fingers inside her, and then he'd licked her juice off them.

Just remembering it made her wet again.

Howard growled softly behind her. "I love your scent." He slid his hand to the curls between her legs.

She loved what he did to her. After sex in bed, they'd gone to the kitchen in search of food, and they'd had sex again on the table. When night had fallen, they'd taken a blanket outside to make love under the stars. That hadn't worked out because too many animals came to see her. So they'd gone back to bed.

She stretched her legs. She was a bit sore. But still getting excited at the thought of another day with him. She rolled onto her back. "Good morning."

"Good morning." His hand slipped between her legs. "You smell so good. I could eat you for breakfast."

More moisture seeped from her.

He threw the covers back and nipped at her thighs till she opened them wide, exposing herself. She clutched the sheets in her fists, dying with anticipation.

With his first lick, she shuddered.

"Relax." He blew on her. "We have all day."

She didn't relax. Within five minutes, she was squirming and panting. He stroked her, tickled her, teased her, suckled her. With a scream, she climaxed.

She climaxed again when he plunged into her. The man was insatiable. And it was contagious.

Thirty minutes later, they were in the shower, soaping each other up.

She rubbed soap over his broad back and shoulders. "We never compared our family curse stories."

He shrugged. "They're the same, aren't they? Three sisters, three guardians. The Guardian of the Forest made the berserkers to protect some village in Norway."

"Wolf and bears." She ran her soapy hands down his arms, then back to his shoulders. "But they lost control and started attacking the villagers."

"And then she betrayed them," he grumbled.

"Excuse me? They betrayed her."

He turned to face her. "She told the villagers where to find the secret berserker lair in the forest. The berserkers were caught by surprise, and a few of them were killed before they could retaliate."

"I never heard that."

"She even betrayed the were-bear she was sleeping with."

"What? She was having an affair with one of them?"

Howard gave her a wry look. "Your family has the PG-rated version?"

She snorted. "Why am I not surprised that your version has sex in it?"

"Ours is better, obviously."

She shook her head. "All I know is that the guardian created the berserkers, and then they betrayed her."

"After she betrayed them."

"I think what they did was worse. They actually killed her."

He shrugged. "She was a traitor."

She narrowed her eyes. "Are you saying she deserved it?"

He raked a hand through his wet hair. "Am I getting myself in trouble?"

Her mouth twitched. "No. We need to stop taking it so personally. I'd like to think we've beaten the curse."

"I agree." He leaned into the spray to rinse off.

"So there are other shifters that aren't berserkers? Like panthers?"

"Yes. And I've met some tigers and dolphins."

"Dolphins?" She pressed a hand to her chest. "Wow. I wonder if my great-aunt Ula knows any of them."

"You'll have to ask." He squirted liquid soap onto his hands and massaged her back.

She moaned. "That feels so good."

His hands slipped around to fondle her breasts.

"So is Shanna a shifter, too?"

His hands stilled.

She turned to face him. "What's wrong?"

"I'm their guard. They trust me to keep their secrets."

She bit her lip. It didn't seem right for him to keep secrets from her. "What about Tino? Shanna said he was a hybrid."

Howard nodded. "Half human. The human half came from Shanna."

"Oh. So she's a normal human?"

"Not anymore." He nudged Elsa under the water nozzle to rinse off.

"Then what is she?" Elsa turned the water off and grabbed a towel. "She can teleport. She only comes out at night. She shifts into some kind of night creature?"

With a wince, Howard dried himself off.

"Doesn't Shanna expect us to be together? If I'm going to live in your world, I should know what's going on."

Frowning, Howard wrapped the towel around his waist. "You have a point."

"So tell me." She pulled on a terry-cloth robe and belted it. "What exactly is Tino?"

"Half human, half"—Howard took a deep breath—"vampire."

Elsa blinked. "What?"

"Vampire. Tino's father, Roman, is a vampire. Shanna is, too, but she wasn't when Tino was born. Vampire women can't carry a baby to term, because they're dead half the time. They could use a surrogate, I suppose—"

"What?" Elsa shook her head. "Shanna can't be a vampire. They're not real."

Howard shrugged. "Berserkers and guardians are real. Why not vampires?"

"Because they're . . . dead."

"Undead," he corrected her.

"Like that makes any sense." Elsa recalled how pointy Shanna's teeth were. "Shanna's really a vampire?"

"Yes. She was mortal when she fell in love with Roman, and they had two children. But then she

accidentally touched an angel of death and was
about to die, so Roman had to change—"

"An angel of death?" Elsa asked.

"Yes. Marielle. She's married to a vampire
named Connor. She's not really an angel anymore."

"Right." Elsa dragged a hand through her wet
hair. Vampires? Angels of death? Maybe she
shouldn't have asked. "How do they eat? Do they
go around biting people?"

"No. They drink synthetic blood from Romatech Industries. That's Roman's company. He invented synthetic blood."

She grimaced. "So they drink blood every
night."

Howard nodded. "They get tired of the same
meal every day, so Roman invented Vampire
Fusion Cuisine. Stuff like Bleer, that's half blood
and half beer."

She recalled the empty Bleer bottle in the convertible. Vampire food. "This is too weird."

"Come on." Howard escorted her to the kitchen.
"You'll feel better with some food inside you."

She poured two glasses of orange juice they had
made the night before from some frozen concen-
trate they'd found in the freezer.

Howard rummaged in the pantry. "Here's some
granola bars. And some graham crackers."

"Is there any jelly or peanut butter?" She finished her juice and bit into a cracker. It was plain
food, but at least it was food. She shuddered at the
thought of having to live on bottled blood.

"A-ha!" Howard's eyes lit up as he removed a

plastic container from the pantry. It was shaped like a bear and held honey.

She snorted. "You would like honey."

He glanced at the bear, then at her, then back at the bear. "Mmm."

She backed up. "You wouldn't dare."

He stepped toward her, his mouth curling up into a smile.

She made a face. "But it would be so sticky."

"I'll lick you clean. Promise."

With a squeal, she ran into the bedroom.

"Oh, sweetheart," he called as he ran after her.

An hour later, she had to admit he'd kept his promise. She was licked clean.

That night, they were dressed in bathrobes and eating some warmed-up canned soup at the kitchen table when a form wavered near the fireplace, then solidified.

Elsa gasped.

Howard stood. "Is something wrong?"

The stranger set a bakery box on the coffee table. "Shanna sends these with her regards." He nodded at Elsa. "Delighted to meet you, lass. I'm Ian MacPhie."

Elsa sidled close to Howard. "He-he's a . . . ?"

"Vampire," Howard finished.

"In a kilt?"

Howard smiled. "There are a few of them like that."

"Aye." Ian walked toward them. "I dinna want to disturb you, but our phone calls werena getting through. Phil told me a Mr. West from Anchorage was e-mailing the school all day, trying to contact you. I thought ye should know."

"Okay." Howard nodded. "We'll drive back in the morning."

"Verra well." Ian shook hands with Howard and inclined his head to Elsa. "If I might say so, lass, ye've found an excellent man here with Howard."

"Thank you." She couldn't believe she was talking to a vampire. In a kilt.

"Good evening." He vanished.

"Wow." Elsa sat down at the table.

Howard brought the pastry box over. "There's a note on top from Shanna. It says Best Wishes."

Elsa nodded. They would need that, for tomorrow they would be returning to the real world. "Who is Mr. West?"

"Harry's boss at the paper where he worked, *Northern Lights Sound Bites.* He's helping me wage war on the bastard who killed Harry."

"You know who killed him?"

Howard nodded. "A nasty werewolf named Rhett Bleddyn. He's hated me for years."

Her skin chilled. "Why?"

Howard shrugged and removed a donut from the box. "It's a long story. Harry believed Rhett's father killed our fathers. He was gathering information when Rhett killed him." He bit into the donut. "But we'll avenge Harry. I'm going to destroy Rhett."

She swallowed hard. This new world of vampires and shifters was a bit violent. She shook herself. The real world was violent, too.

"You want a donut?" Howard pushed the box toward her. "They're fresh."

She gazed at the note from Shanna. *Best wishes.* With a sinking feeling, she suspected none of her wishes could come true.

She wished her aunts didn't want to kill Howard. She wished the nasty werewolf didn't hate Howard. She wished he wouldn't wage war with the werewolf. There had already been too many casualties—the fathers and Harry.

Who would be next?

Chapter Twenty-six

"Do you want me to come in and talk to your aunts?" Howard asked.

"Oh gosh, no." Elsa covered her mouth as she yawned. She was too tired to start her morning with a shootout in the motel parking lot. "Just drop me off."

"I could stop by the gatehouse this afternoon," he offered.

"I don't think I'll go to work today." She gave him a wry smile. "I didn't sleep much the last two nights."

"I know. You're insatiable."

"Me?" She swatted his shoulder.

He grinned. "I'll see you soon." He leaned over to kiss her.

"Bye." She climbed out of his SUV and hurried across the motel parking lot. Aunt Greta's car was parked nearby, so hopefully her aunts were in their room. She didn't have her key, since she'd left her handbag in the gatehouse two days ago.

She knocked on her aunts' door. "Aunt Greta! Ula!"

The door swung open.

"Oh my God! You're still alive!" Greta pulled her into a tight embrace.

"Thank God!" Ula exclaimed in Swedish and hugged her, too.

"I'm fine," Elsa assured them.

Tears streamed down Greta's face. "I thought I'd never see you again. I thought I'd failed you."

"No, no." Elsa forgot all the anger she'd harbored over her aunt's vicious bird attack. Obviously, Greta had thought she was fighting for Elsa's life. "I was perfectly safe. Howard's a wonderful man."

Ula shook her head, tears glimmering in her eyes. "When Greta told me you'd run off with the berserker, I thought we had lost you."

"Howard would never harm me."

Greta wiped her face. "I went to the police, but they said there was nothing they could do because you went willingly with him."

Ula hugged her again. "My poor child. I was so afraid for you."

Elsa patted her on the back. "Everything's fine."

"He didn't hurt you?" Greta looked her over.

"Of course not. He loves me."

Ula frowned. "The berserker who killed the first guardian loved her, too. Then he betrayed her."

Elsa winced. So the ill-fated lovers appeared in her aunts' version, too.

"He's luring you in," Greta told her. "Making you believe in him before he betrays you."

"Howard's not like that."

Greta gave her a sympathetic look. "I'm afraid he is. While you were gone, we met a reporter from

Alaska who's staying here in town. He showed us . . . well, I'll let you see it for yourself."

Greta grabbed the key to Elsa's room off the dresser. "This way." She headed next door and unlocked Elsa's room.

Elsa was relieved to see her handbag on the bed. "You brought my purse back from the gatehouse. Thank you."

Ula perched on the second bed while Greta sat at the desk and booted up Elsa's laptop.

Elsa flopped onto her bed and closed her eyes. It was a good thing she'd run off with Howard. Her aunts would see that he could be trusted, since she'd returned unharmed.

"Here it is," Greta said. "The newspaper article the reporter told us about. It's the *Port Mishenka Post*."

Port Mishenka? Wasn't that where Howard had gone to school? Elsa yawned. "What does it say?"

"It's a report on a girl who was murdered twenty years ago," Greta said as she vacated the desk chair. "You should read it."

With a moan, Elsa moved into the chair. A young high school girl, Carly Evans, had been discovered at the base of a mountain cliff overlooking the town of Port Mishenka. The last person to see her alive was her boyfriend, Howard Barr.

Elsa's breath caught. Howard had lost his high school girlfriend? She read more, her skin chilling with goose bumps. Howard had been arrested for suspicion of murder.

The next two paragraphs contained quotes from Carly's parents. They both believed Howard had killed their daughter. "You've seen how violent he is on the football field," Mr. Evans declared. "He's a dangerous psychopath. He went crazy and murdered our daughter!"

Elsa sat back, her heart racing. This couldn't be true. The parents were just desperate for someone to blame. She finished the article. Howard had been released for lack of evidence, but the people of Port Mishenka were convinced of his guilt.

"He's a berserker," Greta said, shaking her head. "It's like a sickness. He'll seem okay, but then he'll go berserk."

"You must never see him again," Ula said.

Elsa exited the newspaper article. "There has to be a mistake."

"I know it's hard to believe." Greta regarded her sadly. "I bookmarked the report if you need to look at it again."

Elsa shook her head. "I don't want to see it." She collapsed on the bed and covered her face. *I don't want to think about it.*

"You're tired." Greta pulled the curtains shut. "Get some rest. Ula will watch over you."

"*Ja.*" Ula turned off all the lights. "You'll feel better after some sleep."

Elsa slipped under the bedspread. She wouldn't believe it. There had to be an explanation. Howard would never harm a woman. He would never betray her. He loved her. And she had so many sweet memories of him making love to her.

A beautiful man came to her in the night. Large and powerful, he covered her body with his. His big hands roamed over her skin, setting her on fire. She wanted him. She cried out for him. She burned for him.

His hands were magic. Skimming the length of her legs. Fondling her breasts. Stroking her neck. Tightening their grip.

Choking her.

She thrashed against him, but he was too strong. Too powerful.

His face, half hidden in shadow, twisted in rage. Transformed. He roared like an animal.

She gazed up at him in horror. In the flicker of firelight, she caught a glimpse of his head.

A bear.

She slapped at him. Clawed at his face. No, not her lover!

Words slipped from her mouth, then echoed in her mind.

"I curse you and your kind for all time!"

Elsa sat up with a gasp.

"Are you all right?" Ula opened the curtains to let in the afternoon light. "Did you have the bad dream again?"

Elsa whispered the words that were repeating in her head. She didn't know the language, but somehow she knew what it meant. *I curse you and your kind for all time!*

"What?" Ula stepped closer. "What did you say?"

She repeated the line. "I said it in my dream."

"Oh my." Ula perched on the second bed. "That is an ancient Norse language."

Elsa leaned back against the headboard. "How do I know ancient Norse?"

Ula's eyes narrowed. "It must be an ancient dream. A memory passed down through the generations."

Elsa gasped. All this time, she'd assumed the dream was a warning predicting her future. But it was the opposite. A warning from her past. She was remembering the murder of her ancestor, the first Guardian of the Forest.

And she was remembering the murderer. Howard's ancestor, one of the first were-bears to roam the earth. The guardian's lover.

She closed her eyes. *Howard's not a murderer. He's a sweet, gentle man.*

Then what had happened to his first girlfriend in Alaska?

Howard went straight to the security office at Dragon Nest to check his messages. He'd barely started on his e-mail when his cousins cracked open the door and peeked in.

"He's back," Jimmy whispered loudly to his brother.

"Without his girlfriend?" Jesse asked.

Jimmy snickered. "I guess she wore him out."

"Can I help you?" Howard asked drily.

"Just checking on you." Jimmy sauntered inside.

"Yeah. We wanted to make sure you were still alive." Jesse exchanged a glance with his twin. "We heard that Viagra stuff can kill you."

Jimmy snorted and slapped his thigh.

Howard groaned inwardly. "I'm not taking Viagra."

"Maybe you should." Jimmy grinned. "You are kinda old."

"Yeah," Jesse agreed. "I mean, you only lasted two days, dude."

"Don't you guys need to go to work?" Howard asked.

"Oh, yeah." Jimmy sprawled in the chair. "We're going."

"Some time today?" Howard muttered.

"Guess what?" Jesse perched on the corner of his desk. "After you ran off to your love nest, I got interviewed for the TV show."

"Me, too!" Jimmy added. "Madge said we were cute."

"Congratulations." Howard figured the interview wouldn't air for another six months. If everything went according to plan, Rhett would already be destroyed and no longer a threat to his young cousins.

"Our friends back home are so jealous," Jesse said.

Howard sat up. "You told your friends? Did you forget why you're here? You're in hiding. You can't tell anyone where you are."

"Chillax, dude," Jimmy told him. "We don't know where we are. We were teleported here, remember?"

"It's no big deal," Jesse said. "We just talk to our friends on Facebook."

"And Twitter," Jimmy added. "We posted some photos yesterday."

Howard winced. "Did you mention the name of the show?"

"Well, sure," Jesse said. "They have to know which show to watch."

Howard groaned. "Anyone with minimal investigative skills could find out where the show is currently being filmed."

Jimmy scratched his head. "You mean we goofed?"

"Delete those posts immediately," Howard ordered. "How long have they been up?"

Jesse shrugged. "We started posting and tweeting the first day on the job."

Damn. Howard dragged a hand through his hair. "I should make you quit. It might not be safe for you at the gatehouse."

"Dude!" Jimmy jumped to his feet. "Nothing's going to happen to us."

"Yeah," Jesse agreed. "The place is full of guys with saws and nail guns. Nobody's going to mess with us."

Howard took a deep breath. "Fine. But be careful. If any strangers come around looking for you or asking questions, call me immediately."

"Aye, aye, Captain." Jesse saluted.

"Do you really think Rhett and his minions would come all this way to get back at us?" Jimmy asked.

"We're trying to destroy him," Howard replied. "This is war, and he'll fight back. Remember what he did to Harry."

The twins grew pale.

"We'll be careful." Jimmy headed for the door.

"Tomorrow's Sunday," Jesse said. "No one works on Sunday. We'll stay here."

Howard watched them go, wondering if he was being too lenient. If things worsened, he might make them quit on Monday. Hell, even the school might be at risk now. He'd ask Angus for more guards.

He turned back to his computer to finish checking e-mails. Mr. West had sent several messages the day before, and one included a link he wanted Howard to see.

It was an article written by a mainstream paper that employed a lot of werewolf reporters who protected Rhett and the Lycan community.

The headline read "Madman Attacks Bleddyn." Beneath it, there was a large photo in color, shot at Harry's memorial service, showing Howard gripping Rhett by the tie.

Howard winced. Apparently he was the madman. The article reported that Rhett Bleddyn had gone to a memorial service to pay his respects when a madman had attacked him. The madman was identified as Howard Barr, formerly arrested for murder.

He snorted. So Rhett was fighting back, using his reporters to make Howard sound like the enemy.

He exited the article and read the latest e-mail from Mr. West. Stockholders in Rhett's company were throwing fits, demanding that he be investigated for embezzlement. The police had not been able to find him. Rhett had gone into hiding.

Howard nodded. Alaska was an easy place to

hide in. Especially for a werewolf with hundreds of minions sworn to protect him.

A new e-mail appeared from Mr. West. A link to an article published this morning. "Rhett Bleddyn Missing." The report stated that Rhett had been missing for two days, and authorities wanted to question Howard Barr, who had attacked Rhett at a memorial service.

"Holy crap," Howard muttered. Was Rhett going to pretend to be dead again, and make everyone believe Howard had killed him?

He called his grandfather. Walter might have heard some news through the shifter grapevine, news that never appeared in papers.

"How are the boys?" Walter asked. "Your aunt Judy is hounding me every day. She wants to know how they're doing."

"The twins are fine," Howard replied. "Have you heard anything about Rhett?"

Walter snorted. "You did it. You broke the bastard. I heard his minions rebelled and kicked him out as their Pack Master."

A surge of victory swept through Howard. "We destroyed him!"

Walter chuckled. "Yeah. There's been some celebrating on this island, I can tell you. We don't have to worry any more about Rhett ordering his minions to attack us."

Howard smiled. "That's good."

"Yep. Of course, your aunt Judy is insisting the boys come home now. I tried to tell her they're safe with you, but she didn't listen. You know how she is."

"Yes." Howard hesitated. "About the curse; I thought you should know that the story is true."

"Of course it's true," Walter huffed. "You think I've been lying to you all these years?"

"I met the Guardian of the Forest."

"Hot damn! Are you serious?"

"I'm in love with her."

"What?" Walter sounded shocked. "When did this happen?"

"The last few weeks."

"Damn, boy. You work fast."

Howard grinned. "I just wanted you to know that I intend to marry her. That should put an end to the curse, don't you think?"

"Well . . ." Walter paused. "I'd be kinda worried about the curse repeating itself."

"I'm not going to hurt her."

"I don't mean that. The first guardian betrayed us."

"Elsa would never betray me," Howard insisted. "She loves me."

"Well . . ." Walter hesitated again. "I think you'd better be careful. You still have an enemy out there. You know Rhett has to be furious."

"I know."

"He's lost most of his minions and his power," Walter continued. "He's going to blame you for that."

Howard swallowed hard. He'd been so busy avenging Harry's death that he hadn't thought about the consequences. Now Rhett would be seeking vengeance. "I heard he's disappeared."

Walter sighed. "It's worse than that. Rumor has it that Rhett has left the state. Watch your back, son."

Elsa was finishing supper with her aunts at the diner when her cell phone dinged, signaling a text.

"Is that him?" Greta grumbled.

"He's a good guy," Elsa insisted, although she knew her aunts didn't believe her. She read the message.

> LET ME KNOW IF ANY STRANGERS COME TO TOWN, ASKING QUESTIONS ABOUT ME OR MY COUSINS. DON'T LET ANYONE KNOW YOU'RE IN-VOLVED WITH ME. IT WILL MAKE YOU A TARGET.

What? She read the message again. A target for what? A target like Harry? She gulped and dropped her phone into her handbag.

"Are you all right?" Ula sat across the table, finishing a piece of apple pie. "You look a little pale."

"I just hope she isn't pregnant," Greta muttered.

Elsa stiffened. She certainly wasn't pale now. Her cheeks burned as she wondered about the possibility. She was on the pill, but she'd gone to the cabin without them, so she'd missed a day.

Baby were-bears? Her hand pressed instinctively on her stomach.

"Well, hello there." A man stopped by their table and smiled at Greta. "We meet again."

"Mr. Pelton." Greta smiled at him, then leaned close to Elsa. "This is the reporter I told you about. From Alaska."

"And you must be Miss Bjornberg, the niece Greta was telling me about." Mr. Pelton gave her a sympathetic look. "I'm sorry to be the bearer of sad news, but I'm afraid Howard Barr is a dangerous person to associate with."

"We've been telling her that," Greta said.

Elsa winced. "He's done nothing wrong."

"I see." The reporter removed a pen and pad of paper from his briefcase. "Then perhaps you can tell me where I can reach him? I'd like to interview him and get his side of the story. That seems only fair, don't you think?"

Howard's text ran through Elsa's mind. "I don't know where he lives."

"What?" Greta gave her an incredulous look.

Elsa lifted her chin. "We meet at my place of work."

The reporter checked his notes. "And that would be the gatehouse down the road that's being renovated?"

Elsa's heart raced. What was this reporter up to?

"Yes, that's it," Greta answered.

Elsa nudged her aunt with her foot.

Greta leaned close and whispered, "He's trying to help you."

With a frown, Mr. Pelton dropped his pad of paper into his portfolio and removed a few pages of paper. "I can see you need further convincing." He set the papers on the table. "This one is a copy of yesterday's paper, and this one is from this morning's paper."

Elsa saw the big headline "Madman Attacks Bleddyn" and the photo of Howard seizing a man by the tie. The man had to be Rhett Bleddyn, the nasty werewolf who hated Howard. She studied the photo. Rhett had shoulder-length black hair and dark eyes. His mouth was twisted into a smirk. The article made it look like he was innocent and Howard was a crazed criminal.

The second paper said that Rhett had gone missing and authorities suspected Howard. She recalled his words in the cabin. *I'm going to destroy Rhett.*

"So you still can't tell me where Howard Barr is?" the reporter asked.

Elsa swallowed hard. "No."

Her aunts shook their heads at her.

Mr. Pelton scowled at her. "A detective from the Anchorage Police Department is arriving tomorrow morning to investigate Mr. Barr. I suggest you cooperate with him."

A chill ran down Elsa's back.

"Oh, she will," Greta assured the reporter.

"Here's my card if you change your mind." Mr. Pelton passed a business card to Elsa.

When she took it, her hand brushed against his. An instant burst of heat exploded from her birthmark. With a gasp, she dropped the card on the table.

The reporter narrowed his eyes.

With a forced smile, she grabbed the card. "Sorry. I guess I shouldn't have eaten the chili cheese fries."

He nodded. "Good evening." He strode toward the exit.

A berserker. Elsa watched him leave. She'd bet anything he wasn't a bear like Howard and his cousins. No, Mr. Pelton was probably a werewolf. Like Rhett Bleddyn.

She glanced down at Rhett's photo in the paper. The article had clearly been biased in his favor. Was the paper owned by werewolves? Was Mr. Pelton working for Rhett Bleddyn?

She waited until she was alone in her hotel room before she texted Howard.

A REPORTER FROM ALASKA, MR. PELTON, IS LOOKING FOR YOU. AND A POLICE DETECTIVE FROM ANCHORAGE WILL ARRIVE TOMORROW MORNING. MR. PELTON IS A BERSERKER.

A text came back from Howard.

STAY AWAY FROM THEM. THEY PROBABLY WORK FOR RHETT.

She showered and sat up in bed, reading the articles once again. Apparently, the photo was taken at Harry's memorial service. And since Rhett was the one who had killed Harry, she couldn't blame Howard for attacking him. The article also mentioned how Howard had been arrested for killing a girl twenty years earlier.

She tossed the paper onto the bedside table. What was the truth behind that? She really wanted to know, but how could she text Howard and ask him if he'd killed his high school sweetheart? As hard as she tried, she couldn't come up with a nice way to ask him about it.

The next time she saw him, she'd show him the papers. Then he could explain.

With that settled in her mind, she turned off the bedside light. Aunt Ula was already asleep in the second bed. Aunt Greta had the room next door. She was probably polishing her guns.

Elsa snuggled under the covers and rubbed her birthmark. She would need to shake hands with the detective from Anchorage. If her suspicions were correct, he would make her mark burn.

She tossed and turned most of the night, not fully falling asleep until the wee hours of the morning.

A beautiful man came to her in the night. Large and powerful, he covered her body with his. His big hands roamed over her skin, setting her on fire. She wanted him. She cried out for him. She burned for him.

His hands were magic. Skimming the length of her legs. Fondling her breasts. Stroking her neck. Tightening their grip.

Choking her.

She thrashed against him, but he was too strong. Too powerful.

His face, half hidden in shadow, twisted in rage. Transformed. He roared like an animal.

She gazed up at him in horror. In the flicker of firelight, she caught a glimpse of his head.

A bear.

She slapped at him. Clawed at his face. No, not her lover!

Words slipped from her mouth, then echoed in her mind.

"I curse you and your kind for all time!"

She shoved at his shoulders, and his fur came loose in her hands. The bearskin fell off him, revealing her attacker in the firelight. Not her lover.

The berserker who hated her lover.

The wolf.

Elsa sat up with a gasp.

"Are you all right?" Ula turned on the light.

"It wasn't a bear who killed the guardian!" Elsa jumped out of bed. "It was a wolf!"

"A wolf?"

"Yes." Elsa paced about the room. "I think it's always been wolves. The guardian was in love with a bear berserker, and the wolves hated him for it. They killed her, making her think her lover had done it so she would curse the bears for all time."

"Then you think your Howard is innocent?" Ula asked.

"Yes! I think Mr. Pelton is a wolf berserker. He made my birthmark burn."

Ula stood up. "We must tell Greta." She rushed to the bathroom and got dressed while Elsa texted Howard.

YOU'RE IN DANGER! THE WOLVES ARE COMING FOR YOU.

When Ula left the bathroom, Elsa dashed inside. Five minutes later, they were dressed and ready to go. She rushed outside with Ula and banged on Greta's door.

Greta cracked it open. "It's awfully early. You should go away."

"I know who killed the original guardian," Elsa told her. "It wasn't a bear. It was a wolf!"

Greta's face turned pale. She mouthed the word, *Go!* Then suddenly she was pulled back. Mr. Pelton pressed a knife to her neck.

The door opened wider, held by a strange man who aimed a pistol at Elsa. Her heart lurched. Beside her, Ula gasped.

"You are correct, Miss Bjornberg." A man rose from the bed.

She recognized him from the photo. Rhett Bleddyn.

"It won't be a bear who kills you. It'll be a wolf." His mouth curled with a smirk. "Me."

Chapter Twenty-seven

"Come inside, Miss Bjornberg," Rhett said. "Rocky is a police officer and an excellent shot."

Rocky had aimed his pistol at Greta. "Come in, or I'll shoot her."

Elsa and Ula entered slowly.

Rocky handed his pistol to Rhett, then he closed the door and grabbed some handcuffs from the dresser.

"Leave their hands in front," Rhett ordered. "I want Miss Bjornberg to be able to use her phone."

Rocky snapped cuffs on Ula, then Elsa. She gritted her teeth when his touch set her birthmark on fire. He was definitely a berserker. He dropped her handbag on the floor next to Rhett.

"I'm sorry, Ellie," Greta whispered.

"Quiet." Mr. Pelton jerked her back, then sneered at Elsa. "Your aunt made the mistake of thinking I cared about your safety."

Rocky snapped cuffs on Greta.

Rhett scowled at her. "She hasn't been helpful at all. We asked her to call you here an hour ago and she refused. Even after we slapped her around."

Elsa winced. Poor Greta.

"Go to hell," Greta hissed.

"See how unfriendly she is. I certainly hope you will be more cooperative." Rhett aimed the pistol at Aunt Ula. "You care about your aunts, don't you?"

Elsa lifted her chin. "Let them go, and I'll cooperate."

Rhett chuckled. "Feisty, aren't you? I hope you put up more of a fight than Howard's first girlfriend. She was such a coward."

Elsa swallowed hard. "You killed his girlfriend?"

"The stupid bitch fell off a cliff. Well, I might have pushed her a little, but she shouldn't have run up there in the first place." He snorted with disgust. "We only meant to have some fun with her. She ruined everything."

He passed the pistol back to the police officer. "Here, Rocky. Shoot the old one if Miss Bjornberg gives us any trouble."

"Right, Boss." Rocky aimed the pistol at Ula.

Ula closed her eyes and murmured a prayer.

"Pelton, call our drivers. We'll take both SUVs."

"Yes, sir." Pelton murmured into a cell phone.

Drivers? Elsa groaned inwardly. How many wolves were there? If there were two SUVs, that meant two drivers. A total of five werewolves.

Rhett grabbed Elsa's handbag off the floor and removed her phone. "I want you to call Howard and tell him to meet you at the gatehouse." He pressed the phone into her cuffed hands. "Make the call or watch your aunts die."

Elsa nodded, ignoring the burn from her birthmark. She had to protect her aunts. With trembling fingers, she pushed Howard's number. Rhett stepped closer to listen in.

"Elsa, how are you?"

She took a deep breath. "Hey, Howard. How about meeting me at the gatehouse? We could have a picnic."

"Now? It's early."

"My aunts want to meet you. They're really sorry for misjudging you."

"They—they're all right with me now?"

Elsa glanced at Greta. "Yes, they know you're the good guy now."

Greta nodded, and Rhett snorted.

"So you'll come?" Elsa asked. "Right away?"

"Give me about ten minutes. I have to pack us some food."

"Okay!" Elsa said brightly. "See you soon, Howie! Kisses!" She hung up.

Rhett ripped the phone from her hands. "Okay, guys, let's go bear hunting."

Howie? Kisses? Howard stared at his phone. Even after two days of lovemaking at the cabin, Elsa had never called him Howie. And somehow, saying "Kisses" for good-bye seemed totally out of character for her.

He checked her last text, sent ten minutes earlier.

YOU'RE IN DANGER! THE WOLVES ARE COMING FOR YOU.

He smelled a trap.

And Elsa was luring him into it. He shook his head. She wouldn't betray him. She was being coerced. The detective from Anchorage and that reporter, Mr. Pelton, must have taken her and her aunts prisoner.

And they wanted him at the gatehouse.

A final showdown. And that meant one thing. Rhett Bleddyn had come for revenge.

Howard set the heavy picnic basket on the front porch at the gatehouse. Under a layer of cheese and crackers, there was a loaded pistol and an assortment of knives. He had another knife strapped to his leg under his jeans, and a pistol with silver bullets in a shoulder holster under his jacket.

He'd parked his SUV in the driveway after dropping off Phil, Carlos, and his cousins on the main road. They were going to hike in and position themselves for a surprise attack. As an Alpha wolf, Phil could shift at will. Carlos could shift into a were-panther whenever he wanted, and as were-bears, his cousins could, too. The Vamps would be sorry they missed the action, but they were all dead at the moment.

Howard tensed when he saw two black SUVs approaching. Rhett always traveled with a pack. The windows were dark, so Howard wasn't sure how many men were with Rhett. He probably had Elsa and her aunts with him. Threatening Elsa was the easiest way to make Howard submit. And threatening the aunts would keep Elsa in line.

Howard stepped into the driveway, lifting a hand in greeting as the two vehicles came to a stop. It might look like a friendly gesture, but he wanted to get as close to the SUV as possible.

When the drivers opened their doors, he lunged forward, slamming the door shut on the first driver. The man stumbled as Howard reopened the door. He grabbed the driver and tossed him into the woods. His cousins dragged him off to tie him up. Meanwhile, Phil and Carlos hauled the second driver away. Two down. And none of them had even needed to shift.

"Stop!" Rhett jumped out on the passenger side, pulling Elsa with him. He held a knife to her throat. "Attack any more of my men, and we start killing the women."

Two more men exited the SUVs, dragging Elsa's aunts with them. The women were all hand-cuffed. One of the men snapped an additional pair of cuffs on Aunt Ula, fastening her to the rear door handle of the first SUV.

Howard made eye contact with Elsa, trying to assure her that everything would be all right. She glanced up at the sky, then back at him. A quick look up and he realized what Elsa was trying to tell him. A line of birds was forming along the roof of the gatehouse. Greta was using her powers. No doubt Elsa would use hers, too.

"Rocky," Rhett called to the guy who had cuffed Aunt Ula. "Check Howard for weapons."

Rocky approached slowly, halting momentarily when Howard glared at him.

"Cooperate," Rhett growled. "Or I'll have Pelton slit Greta's throat."

The other guy, Pelton, pressed the tip of his knife against Greta's neck till a bead of blood formed.

"Fine." Howard lifted his hands.

Rocky removed Howard's pistol and the knife strapped on his leg.

"It's me you want," Howard said. "Let the women go."

Rhett snorted. "No way. I want to watch you suffer while I torture them."

"Only a coward picks on women. You hate me, Rhett?" Howard opened his arms wide. "Come and get me. A duel. One on one."

Rhett growled.

"I'm unarmed. It's your chance to tear into me. Isn't that what you've always wanted?"

"You bastard," Rhett hissed. "You've plagued me all my life! I should rip you to shreds."

"Try it." Howard motioned with his fingers. "Come on, you coward."

Rhett scoffed. "You think I'll fall for that? You're just trying to get me to release your girlfriend. You're scared to death I'll kill her, aren't you? You nearly died when I killed Carly, the pain was so bad."

Howard clenched his fists.

"I watched the car blow up, you know," Rhett sneered. "Saw your friend Harry explode into flames."

Howard gritted his teeth. The bear inside him growled, urging him to attack.

"Harry was right, you know. Your fathers were murdered. They refused to sell their land to my father, so he killed them."

The bear inside him raged, demanding to go berserk.

"Go ahead, try to attack me," Rhett goaded him. "I'll slit her throat before you can reach me."

"Let her go." Howard spotted a group of deer in the woods along the driveway. Large stags with antlers. They lowered their heads, ready to attack.

"Maybe I should bite her like I did Carly." Rhett bared his teeth and hissed in Elsa's ear. "And when she shifts into a wolf, I'll make her my bitch."

Elsa's eyes flashed with anger.

"Let her go!" Howard removed his jacket and tossed it to the ground. "It's me you hate. Fight me."

"I will. After you suffer." Rhett's head shifted into a wolf's head, and he opened his jaw to bite Elsa.

Behind him, the deer lunged.

Rhett cried out as antlers pierced his back. His knife plummeted to the driveway, and Elsa pulled away, running toward Aunt Ula.

A flock of birds flew straight at Pelton, and he screamed, releasing Greta.

The deer reared up, slashing at Rhett with their hooves. With a growl, he shifted and the wounds in his back healed. He charged after Elsa, but before he could reach her, Howard shifted and pounced on him.

They rolled on the driveway, bear and wolf, Rhett twisting and snapping his jaws. He landed a few bites, causing Howard pain but not any concern. As a were-bear, he was immune to the Lycan virus. He slashed his claws across Rhett's torso, then another slash across his neck. Rhett tried to wriggle away, but Howard pinned him down.

"Stop!" Pelton yelled.

Howard glanced to the side and froze. Pelton, his face covered with blood, had managed to knock Greta out, thus putting an end to the bird attack. He and Rocky held Elsa and Ula with knives pressed to their throats.

A sharp pain pierced Howard's arm as Rhett clamped his jaws onto him, ripping into his flesh with his teeth. Howard lunged back and Rhett scrambled away, retaking his human form.

Phil and Carlos attacked Pelton and Rocky from behind, and Howard, still in bear form, dashed toward the women.

"Watch out!" Elsa cried.

Howard stumbled to his knees as Rhett leaped onto his back and plunged a knife into his ribs. With a roar of pain and anger, he flung Rhett onto the ground. Rhett waved his knife about wildly, cutting Howard wherever he could.

With a swipe of his claw, Howard disarmed Rhett, then slashed him across the chest. The bastard had to die. He slashed again. Die for killing Harry. Another slash. Die for killing Carly.

Howard kept swiping and clawing till he succumbed to dizziness and fell onto his side. He was losing too much blood from the knife wound and all the cuts and bites. If he didn't shift before losing consciousness, he could bleed to death.

He changed back to human form and slowly sat

up. Rhett was dead. He looked around to make sure Elsa was all right. She was standing next to her aunts. Carlos was in panther form and sitting next to Rocky's dead body. Phil had shifted and taken care of Pelton. The birds had flown away, but the deer remained gathered on the side of the road, watching Elsa.

The twins, still in human form, rummaged through the shredded remains of Rocky's clothes till they found the keys to the handcuffs.

"You're free." Jimmy unlocked the cuffs on the women. "Go in peace."

Jesse retrieved some extra sets of clothing from Howard's SUV.

Howard dressed, noting his wounds had healed, though he still felt a little sore. The blood would remain till he could wash up.

Elsa stepped toward him. "Are you all right?"

"Don't." Greta pulled her back. "He's still a berserker. You saw how vicious he was."

"He was protecting us," Elsa insisted. "He would never hurt us."

Howard's heart swelled. She still trusted him. Even though he'd been forced to kill in front of her.

She ran toward him. "Thank you, Howard."

He took her hand in his. "Guardian of the Forest. I will protect you for as long as I live."

She smiled, her eyes glimmering with tears. "Berserker, I will love you for as long as I live." She touched his face. "With no regret."

Epilogue

$\mathcal{F}$ive days later on Friday night, Elsa drove Greta and Ula to Dragon Nest Academy for the small party Shanna had planned.

"Oh my!" Greta peered out the window as they parked in front. "What a huge mansion!"

"It's a school for special children," Elsa explained.

"You mean berserkers?" Ula asked as she gawked at the impressive building.

"There are all kinds of children and adults here," Elsa said. "As far as I can tell, they're like one big happy family."

Howard exited the front door and came down the stairs to welcome them. He looked dashing in a suit and tie. Ula kissed his cheek, and he grinned.

Greta shook his hand. "So you're the head of security here?"

"Yes, ma'am. I'll be happy to take you on a tour later. But for now, we need to go to the party. It's already started." He took an aunt on each arm and led them along the front of the building.

Elsa walked alongside them, amused at how much he was buttering up her aunts.

He glanced at her and winked. "The party's in the gymnasium. That's the biggest room we have around here."

"I thought it was going to be a small affair," Elsa said.

He snorted. "When these guys party, everybody shows up."

"And some of them are vampires?" Greta asked.

"Yes, ma'am. But they're very friendly."

Elsa bit her lip to keep from grinning. She and Howard had decided it was best to let her aunts know what kind of world she was marrying into. The women had taken it in stride, probably because they weren't exactly normal themselves.

She gasped when they entered the gym. A crowd of people bustled about, talking and laughing. Colorful balloons floated along the high ceiling. She did a double take. Yes, that was Tino, floating in the air, laughing and batting the balloons around.

A buffet table ran the length of one wall. Round tables were set up, leaving an open area in the middle for dancing, and a stage had been erected at the end of the room. A band was warming up.

"We're going to have live music?" Elsa raised her voice to be heard over the noise.

Howard nodded. "Those are the High Voltage Vamps. They play at all the parties."

A wave of exclamations swept across the gym as everyone realized the guests of honor had arrived. They lined up to meet Elsa and her aunts.

Howard introduced one couple after another. Phil and Vanda. Austin and Darcy. Emma and Angus. The line went on and on.

"I'll never remember all these people," Elsa whispered to Howard.

"You will in time."

"Welcome!" Shanna's mother, Darlene, ran toward them and hugged Elsa. "I'm so excited for you. A wedding!" She turned to Greta and Ula. "Aren't you excited?"

Ula nodded. "*Ja*. Howard is a good catch."

Greta smiled. "I'm just relieved Elsa is safe now."

Darlene nodded. "And you don't have to guard her every day. Why, we could go shopping!"

"For yarn?" Greta's eyes lit up.

"Of course." Darlene grabbed Greta, and the two walked off to discuss knitting patterns.

"Hi!" Tino bounced up to them, a cookie in his hand.

Elsa hugged him. "I saw you on the ceiling."

He laughed and looked at Aunt Ula. "You want to know where the cookies are?" He took her hand and led her toward the buffet.

More couples came to meet Elsa. Toni and Ian. Robby and Olivia. Phineas and Brynley. Connor and Marielle.

Elsa leaned close to Howard. "All those women are expecting?"

"Yes." He gave her a sly look. "Just let me know when you're ready."

She snorted. As if she needed a pair of bear cubs. But if they turned out as cute as Jimmy and Jesse, that wouldn't be bad. Not bad at all. She glanced at Howard, who was watching her with a twinkle in his blue eyes. "I could be persuaded."

He grinned. "I can be very persuasive."

She swatted his shoulder.

More people came by. She was shocked to meet the president's daughter, and even more shocked that Abigail was married to a vampire.

Finally, Elsa was able to sit at a table with her aunts. Darlene joined them with her grandchildren, Tino and Sofia. Howard brought them all plates loaded with food.

"This food is so good!" Greta exclaimed as she bit into a crab cake. "We're really getting tired of that diner in town."

"You should live here!" Darlene exclaimed. "I'm sure we can find a room for you."

Greta pressed a hand to her chest. "You don't mind?"

"Of course not." Darlene waved a dismissive hand. "Elsa, you should live here, too."

"Yeah," Howard agreed. "I've got a room for her."

Elsa snorted, and the ladies laughed.

"We'd better get her married fast," Ula said.

"You could have the wedding here," Darlene suggested.

Greta smiled. "That sounds wonderful."

"I will stay until the wedding," Ula said. "But then I must get back to my island." She turned to Elsa and Howard. "You must come see me often."

"We'd love to." Elsa squeezed her great-aunt's hand.

A waiter came by and gave all the adults at their table a glass of champagne. Sofia and Tino were given grape juice.

Elsa noticed that even the Undead were receiving champagne flutes. "What are the vampires drinking?"

"It's called Bubbly Blood," Howard explained. "Half blood, half champagne, for those special vampire occasions." He grinned. "And this is one of them."

"May I have your attention?" Roman spoke into the microphone on the dais, and the room grew quiet. "Thank you for coming. Tonight we welcome some new members to our family—Elsa, Greta, and Ula." He lifted his glass. "Welcome."

Everyone cheered and drank.

Elsa looked around with tears in her eyes. All her life, she'd hardly had any family, and now she would have a huge one.

"Congratulations to Howard and his lovely fiancée, Elsa," Roman continued, and everyone drank.

"I have a toast." A young male vampire stood. "Here's to Howard and Elsa for defeating that rotten SOB, Rhett!"

Everyone cheered and drank some more.

"That's Phineas," Howard explained. "Rhett bit him, and now he's part werewolf."

"Oh, how sad," Elsa murmured.

Howard smiled. "Not really. He's married to a werewolf girl, so it all worked out."

Shanna joined her husband on the dais, and he handed her the microphone. "I wanted to say a few words. As some of you know, I had a little trouble adjusting to being Undead. But after seeing Howard and Elsa struggle to be together, it reconfirmed in my heart how blessed we all are to have found each other. I couldn't be happier."

The crowd cheered for her, and Shanna's face glistened with pink-tinted tears. Her husband kissed her cheek.

"I have some good news, too," Shanna continued. "It nearly broke my heart to put our house for sale, but guess what? We're selling it to Austin and Darcy!"

Everyone clapped. Austin and Darcy grinned and waved at Shanna.

"Austin will be the new head of security at Romatech," Shanna explained. "And Darcy is working at the Digital Vampire Network in Brooklyn. They're moving into the house next week with their little boy and another baby on the way. And yes, Tino, they have invited you over to play."

"Yay!" Tino levitated in the air, and everyone laughed.

Shanna smiled at Howard and Elsa. "You have to admit, I made a great matchmaker."

Elsa leaned close to Howard and whispered, "Did you really have DVDs of me hidden under your bed?"

He nodded.

"And were you intending to admire me in secret forever?"

He smiled and took her hand. "I had already contacted your station to see where you would be working next. I just didn't realize it would be down the road."

She squeezed his hand. "I'm so glad you were going to hunt me down."

"And finally, let me congratulate the happy couple." Shanna lifted her glass to Howard and

Elsa. "May you have a long and happy life to-gether."

Everyone drank one last toast. Elsa joined them, although her heart sank. This was the only problem she could see in their future. Howard would live for hundreds of years, and she wouldn't.

"*Ja*, a long and happy life." Ula looked at her and smiled.

"That's true," Greta said. "Now that you're no longer in danger, you can live as long as the other guardians."

Elsa blinked. "What do you mean?"

Greta sipped some champagne. "Your mother was my younger sister, but I never told you that she was thirty years younger than me."

Ula waved a hand. "You are still very young, Greta."

Elsa turned to her great-aunt. "How old are you?"

"Four hundred and eighty-two. Or three?" Ula shrugged. "I lose count."

Elsa's mouth fell open.

Howard leaned toward her aunts. "Are you telling me Elsa could live for hundreds of years?"

Greta nodded. "It's part of being a guardian."

"Oh my gosh." Elsa pressed a hand to her chest. "You never told me that."

Ula shrugged. "We weren't sure you would live very long. Not with the curse."

"But the curse is gone now," Greta added. "You can have a long and happy life."

Elsa looked at Howard. "We can be together for centuries."

His mouth twitched. "I guess I'd better treat you right."

"I guess so."

He leaned close. "How about a tour? I could show you my room."

She snorted. "You're an animal."

"I'm wild about you."

She glanced around the gym. Everyone was busy partying. "Let's go."